THE WITCH'S TOWER

TWISTED EVER AFTER: BOOK 1

TAMARA GRANTHAM

THE WITCH'S TOWER
Copyright ©2018 Tamara Grantham
All rights reserved.
Printed in the United States of America
First Edition: March 2019

CLEAN TEEN PUBLISHING
WWW.CLEANTEENPUBLISHING.COM

Summary: Gothel's choice is simple: either stand guard over Princess Rapunzel—or die. But just because a choice is easy doesn't mean it's pleasant. Protecting Rapunzel means watching her lay trapped in a tower, bedridden by hair that is so long and heavy it's driving her insane. Gothel's life has become one of imprisonment and solitude, too—until a prince and his handsome squire appear at the tower....

ISBN: 978-1-63422-334-8 (paperback)
ISBN: 978-1-63422-335-5 (e-book)
Cover Design by: Marya Heidel
Typography by: Courtney Knight
Editing by: Kelly Risser

COVER ART
© stuart/fotolia
© mash3r/fotolia
© lavrentyeva/fotolia
© tatoman/fotolia

Young Adult Fiction / Fairy Tales and Folklore / Adaptations
Young Adult Fiction / Fairy Tales and Folklore / General
Young Adult Fiction / Fantasy / Wizards and Witches
Young Adult Fiction / Legends, Myths, Fables / General

For more information about our content disclosure, please utilize the QR code above with your smart phone or visit us at www.CleanTeenPublishing.com

The world is full of magic things, patiently waiting for our senses to grow sharper.

-W. B. Yeats

ONE

BLOOD. MY BLOOD.

Rapunzel was getting bolder. A gust of rain-scented wind rushed through the clearing as I pulled a scrap of rolled linen from my cloak. I wrapped it around my wrist where she'd clawed my skin. Droplets soaked through, staining the fabric.

Sighing, I straightened to stare at the moonlit tower looming over me. I didn't know what to do with Rapunzel. She was growing more unstable. It didn't help that my mother had placed a curse on her. How could Rapunzel's mind be right when she was forced to lie in bed all day, a prisoner to her hair that was so heavy, it prevented her from moving?

The clouds thickened, covering the sky, making the tower seem to disappear. I lit my lantern. The flame burned bright inside the glass as I started down the trail through the forest. As I walked, twigs snapped under my boots. The sounds of chirping crickets, and the occasional hoot from an owl, filled the air.

The scent of rain lingered on the wind. I hoped it held off until I made it to the village. The trail sloped downward, and I followed it over a narrow footbridge spanning

1

a stream. As I crossed, my footfalls echoing over wooden planks, I reminded myself why I was traveling through these cursed woods. We needed supplies. Going into the village was the only way to get them, although leaving the tower was risky. If the high sorcerer found me gone, he'd hang me for sure, but what choice did I have? The flour was growing rancid, I would eat dirt before I touched another wild beet, and I was certain the dirt would taste better. It would help if I had skills in gardening, but I'd always had rotten luck when it came to growing things.

A breeze rushed through the woods, stirring the turquoise blue strands of my hair. I tucked it beneath my cowl, hoping to keep it hidden. It made me easily identifiable, and if anyone saw its strange color, they'd start asking questions.

I hated questions. I hated answering them even more.

The trees grew thicker along my path, making it hard to see anything.

A noise caught my attention.

Hoof beats came from up ahead. I ducked behind a briar bush as two forms emerged from the trail. Dousing my lantern's flame, I stared at the shapes of two men on horseback approaching me.

I held my breath, my own heartbeats sounding too loud.

"Halt!" one of the men called. "I see you there."

"Come out," the other man shouted.

Under the light of their lanterns, the gleam of their swords' pommels shone, peeking from their scabbards strapped to their backs. Would they use their weapons?

Breathing deeply, I attempted to keep my cool. They had no reason to harm me. I kept that in mind as I stood and stepped away from the bush.

"What are you doing out here?" one of the men asked.

"I'm on my way to Willow Wood village."

"At this time of night?"

"Yes."

"Why?"

"That's my business, if you don't mind."

"Very well, then. What's your name?"

Should I lie? If I did and they found out, what then? Better to play it safe. Hopefully, they'd never heard of me.

"I'm called Gothel," I answered.

His eyes lit up. "Gothel. What luck! You are just the witch we seek."

Drat.

Both men dismounted. Holding their horses' reins, they approached me. The man nearest me wore armor that gleamed in his lantern's light. He also wore a cloak and cowl that partially hid his face, though from the light stubble sheathing his jaw, and his full lips, I got the impression he wasn't much older than me. The man behind him was taller, and he stayed in the shadows. I couldn't distinguish any of his features.

"We are seeking the princess in the tower. Do you know where it is?"

Double drat. Now I had no choice but to lie.

"I'm afraid I don't."

"Really? That is odd. We were told a witch named Gothel could show us the way."

"It must've been someone else. Now, if you'll please excuse me."

I attempted to brush past them when the tall man caught my arm. I gasped as he gripped me.

"Release me," I said.

"Gothel, listen," the first man said. "We really must find that tower. We've been riding for weeks trying to find it. Please, the war must end, and the only way for the fighting to stop is for the high sorcerer's daughter to be united with a prince of our kingdom. We left the war in search of the princess in the tower—the woman rumored to be the high sorcerer's only offspring—the last princess left alive in the land."

He seemed to know a lot, which piqued my curiosity. "Who are you?"

The man threw back his hood, revealing a silver crown atop his crop of unruly blond hair. His eyes were dark blue under the firelight, and the shape of his nose and jawline made him look as if he came from nobility.

"My name is Prince Merek Duc'Line."

"You're the king's son?"

He nodded.

My stomach knotted. A prince? Could he be the one? If he was, then I should've fought him off. I should've kept him as far away from the tower as possible. There was a foretelling that a prince of noble blood would free the princess and kill the witch.

Kill *me*.

But after five years of being trapped inside a tower, I no longer feared soothsaying. Those tales were usually rubbish anyway. If he could save Rapunzel, shouldn't I let him try?

"The tower is down that path," I said. "But there's a spell in these woods to keep it hidden, which is why you couldn't find it."

"Can you remove the spell?"

"Perhaps."

"Will you do it for us? Please?"

He sounded sincere, but I still wasn't sure if I should help him. If the high sorcerer found out, he'd have my head. But if there was a chance the prince could undo the curse, wouldn't it be worth it to tell him?

"I can show you the way, but once you reach the tower, you must speak the spell to get inside. Call the princess's name two times, then command her to let down her hair."

His eyebrows rose. "Her hair?"

I nodded.

"Very well, and what is the princess's name?"

I hesitated. What if he wasn't the one? Then again, he was the king's son. If anyone was worthy, it would be him. I hoped.

"Her name is Rapunzel."

"Thank you," he said, heaving a relieved sigh. The tall man with the hood held my arm a moment longer than necessary, then released me. I rubbed my arm. He'd most likely left a bruise.

Filthy knave.

"Be careful," I said as the men mounted their horses. "There's a spell on the princess. If you are not worthy, if your heart is not noble, or if you have ill intentions, you will be under her enchantment."

"I do not fear enchantments," the prince said. "I've vanquished many enemies in the war, fought dragons, slaughtered giants, and delivered justice to my enemies. Magic doesn't scare me."

He sounded overconfident, but maybe if he were as brave as he said, he would be the one to break the curse. I opened my pack and removed a vial of crushed primrose petals. After uncorking the glass, I emptied its contents on my open palm, then with a whisper of magic, I gently blew the petals across the path.

A blue glow appeared, snaking along the trail and through the forest, leading the way to Rapunzel's tower.

"Follow the magic to the tower," I said. "And do not forget my warning."

"No need to remind me," he shouted, then kicked his horse. The two men galloped away. As I watched them go, their lantern's light quickly disappearing in the thick foliage, I regretted my decision to help the prince. Someone so self-assured could never beat the spell, but one could always hope.

"May the goddess protect your souls," I said, my words a quiet whisper that got lost in the wind.

Two

"HOW MUCH DO YOU WANT for the herbs?" the old lady asked, the afternoon sunlight beating down on her weathered skin.

"Five pence, if you please," I answered.

"Nay." She spat. "I'll give you three. Not a pence more."

Sighing, I held on to the satchel. It had been a slow day. At this rate, it would take me until nightfall to earn enough money for our supplies.

"Four," I said, "and I'll throw in an extra sprig of lavender."

"Is it fresh lavender?"

"Yes. I gathered it myself."

"Ah, very well then. Four it is." She fumbled with her coin purse and pulled out four copper coins, then pressed them into my hand as I gave her the satchel and the lavender.

Around us, carts rolled past, their wheels creaking, and voices of the street vendors carried through the narrow lanes. I wiped beads of sweat from my forehead as the woman ambled away.

Checking my coin purse, I counted my money. Seventy-five shekels. I could buy a cask of flour and a few apples, enough to last a week, but that wouldn't do. I'd need more than that if we wanted to survive through winter. This wasn't going how I'd planned.

I walked down the lane, hoping a different spot would attract some new customers. My stomach rumbled as I walked, and I realized I hadn't eaten anything all day. I blamed my coin purse.

A shadow loomed over me, and I stopped, staring up into the dark eyes of a man with deep bronze skin.

"Gothel?" he asked.

I eyed him. "You know me?"

"Yes, we met last night. Don't you remember?"

"Last night?" I studied him. Was he an Outlander? No one in Willow Wood had such dark skin, but I wasn't sure I'd ever seen an Outlander here. I wasn't even sure there were any left. I thought they'd all been killed.

"Were you the man with the prince?" I asked.

He nodded.

"You hurt my arm!"

"Did I?"

"Yes! You almost bruised me."

"I'm sorry. It wasn't my intention. I was only trying to protect the prince."

"Against me?"

"I had no idea who you were. Plus, it was dark. You could've been anyone."

"Fine. What do you want?"

"I need your help. You must return with me to the tower immediately."

"Why?"

"Because something happened to the prince."

My heart sank. The prince had failed. I wished I

was surprised, but I was beginning to believe that a noble-hearted prince didn't exist.

"I'm sorry," I said.

"Yes, I told him he needed to stop and think before he climbed into the tower, but he never listens to me. I'm only his squire, anyway. And now something has happened to him and I need your help."

"Sir, I'm sorry, but I can't help you."

"No, you have to. Don't you see? It's the prince. If something happens to him, I lose my head. I'm supposed to be his protector. And I'm not a Sir, by the way. I'm merely a squire. My name is Raj Talmund."

"Raj?"

He nodded. With a name like that, he had to be an Outlander.

"Raj, I'm very sorry, but there's nothing I can do. I warned the prince not to enter the tower unless he had a noble heart. If he never returned from the tower, then he must've fallen under the spell. If that happened, then there's nothing I can do to help him."

"Nothing at all?"

"I'm sorry, no."

His face fell. "Then what am I to do?"

"The spell most likely put him to sleep. If that's the case, then he'll wake in a week or two. I would suggest bringing his body back to the king and explaining what happened. It was the high sorcerer who locked his own daughter inside that cursed tower. If the king wants to be angry with someone, it should be with the sorcerer. Now, if you will please excuse me, I've got a million herbs to sell before I can buy my supplies and leave this village."

I brushed past him. He grabbed my arm. Again. In

the very same spot where he'd grabbed me last night. This was a habit I was hoping he'd break.

"Release me," I said, hoping he heard the steel in my voice.

"There has to be a way. I can't wait a week or two. Please, if you're to earn money, then let me help. I've more than enough to buy all your supplies. Let me buy your evening meal. There's a tavern down the way that serves the best honeyed baguettes you've ever tasted."

"I know of the baguettes. I've lived near Willow Wood for a few years, you know. Word gets around. And I'm shocked that you want to buy my supplies *and* my meal? How desperate are you?"

"I will do whatever it takes to restore the prince. There must be something you can do for him."

I pondered his offer. If it meant I got my supplies and a meal, wouldn't I be a fool to pass up such an opportunity—especially with the lure of honeyed baguettes involved? But it wouldn't be right, and I knew it.

"I wish I could take you up on your offer, but I'm afraid it wouldn't be fair. I wish you would understand that I'm powerless to help the prince. I can't take your money."

He flexed his jaw as he glanced at the sun sinking toward the horizon.

"You live in that tower?" he asked.

I nodded.

"The high sorcerer put you there?"

"Yes. I'm bound to the tower and the princess. I can only leave if an emergency arises, such as when we're starving—and we are."

"Then let me buy your evening meal and your supplies. It's not right what the high sorcerer does to people. If I can help you in any way, then I feel I must do this, especially if you're starving as you say."

I grumbled under my breath, wishing I'd never brought up the state of my empty stomach.

"Fine," I relented, "but only if you let go of my arm."

"Oh." He released it quickly, as if he'd forgotten he was still holding it. I wasn't sure if he realized what a strong grip he had.

"Come, let me escort you to the tavern."

"You have no need to escort me. I know the way."

"Nonsense. I'm a knight in training. It's my duty to escort you." He held out his arm, and I looked at it. No one had ever paid me any attention since I'd come to Willow Wood, and certainly hadn't thought to lend me their arm. I had half a mind to refuse him, as I knew he was only trying to get my help, but I wasn't a complete imbecile. If it meant I got a free meal, I wouldn't turn him down.

I took his arm, and he led me through the village. We walked past the fountain shaped as a Pegasus, the sounds of trickling water following us. Horses and carts passed us by, their wheels squeaking over the cobbled lanes. We stopped when we reached a tall building with a thatched roof and red shutters that reflected the evening sunlight.

As we entered, the heavenly scent of baked bread washed over me, bringing back memories from my childhood, when I'd been a scrawny kid running through the castle halls, scrounging up morsels of bread to take home to Mother.

"Shall we sit here?" Raj asked, motioning to a table near an open window where a breeze rushed through.

"Yes, that's fine."

I took a seat across from him. He smiled at me, revealing dimples in his cheeks I hadn't noticed before. I'd never seen such a genuine smile, his white teeth contrasting his smooth, bronzed skin. His dark, exotic eyes were attractive, yet held a calculated intelligence. My heart gave a slight flutter, confusing me. Surely, I couldn't be attracted to him. He'd hurt me!

I straightened the napkin on my lap and dodged his bewitching smile. The last thing I needed was to be distracted by a squire—the king's son's squire—no less. What would High Sorcerer Varlocke say to that?

I'd be flayed.

A woman placed a basket of baguettes and a tumbler of honey on the table, then ambled away. I wanted to keep my composure. Looking desperate at a time like this wouldn't be prudent, but my hunger won out, and I grabbed a piece of bread, drowned it in honey, and took a bite.

My taste buds danced at the flavors of soft bread and sweet honey. Why did starvation make food taste so heavenly?

Raj cleared his throat as he watched me eat.

"Tell me," he said. "How is it you came to live in the tower?"

"It was because of a fight between my mother and the high sorcerer. It was a stupid argument. Long story. You probably don't want to hear it."

"We have time."

Did we? I glanced out the window. Assuming I could buy all my supplies tonight, and assuming I was able to get a cart to carry them in, I would be able to make it back to the tower tonight and be there before morning. I supposed I had nothing better to do than sit around and talk about my harrowing past. At least it made a good story.

"All right," I said, "but it's a depressing tale. Are you sure you want to hear it?"

"Yes."

"Very well. Before I was born, my mother lived in a cottage near the castle. Her name was Aethel. She grew things in her garden, and she was very skilled at it. In fact, her radishes were said to be magical—they could make a person invincible."

"Really?"

"Yes. Unfortunately, the then King Varlocke found out about her radishes. He started stealing them from her. After that, he did something he hadn't been able to do before, he started vanquishing all the outlying villages around him, and then the other kingdoms. It's how he became high sorcerer."

"With magical radishes?"

I nodded.

He rested his fisted hands on the table. When he looked away from me, I saw the pain in his eyes. "Most of my people were killed by the high sorcerer, including many of my family. My little sister." He breathed deeply to keep his composure. "He sacked our nation and wiped out our kingdom. He destroyed my home."

I nodded. It was a painful subject, but no one had experienced High Sorcerer Varlocke's wrath as badly as the Outlanders.

"My mother discovered what the king was doing," I said. "She was infuriated, but there was nothing she could do to harm him—the magical radishes made sure of that—so she did something petty and stupid, something I'm ashamed of, and something I pay the price for every

13

day. She cursed his only offspring, his daughter Rapunzel. She made it so that her hair would grow unnaturally long, weighing so heavy it left her bedridden. My mother created the curse so that only a prince with a noble heart would have the ability to break it.

"The high sorcerer killed my mother after she cursed his daughter, but it didn't stop his rage. He cast a spell to kill all the princesses in the land, making sure everyone felt his suffering, and then he locked his only daughter in a tower, and demanded I be her protector as punishment for my mother's crimes."

"It's true, then? You really are Witch Aethel's daughter?"

I nodded as he attempted to look under my hood's cowl. "And you have…?"

"Blue hair? Yes."

I pushed my cowl back for a moment. His eyes widened. It wasn't only the color that made it stand out, but the magic that came with it. Sparks danced through the strands, reflected in the greenish-blue color of my eyes. I quickly replaced my head covering before anyone else noticed.

A serving girl arrived with two steaming bowls and placed them in front of us.

"Onion stew," she said, then turned away. I grabbed my spoon and took a small bite. The saltiness of the broth mingled with the sharp, rich flavor of the onion. I ate guiltily, thinking of Rapunzel stuck in the tower with nothing but moldy bread and those awful wild beets. I would return soon. She would be eating like a queen by tomorrow morning.

"You said only a prince with a noble heart could break

14

Rapunzel's curse?" Raj asked.

"Yes."

"So, it is possible to break the curse?"

We were back to the curse again. Somehow, I knew he wouldn't let it go.

"No, it's not possible. I told you that already."

"But you said—"

"I said a prince with a noble heart could break the curse, but there are none."

He worked his jaw back and forth, and I couldn't help but notice the way his muscles played along his strong jawline. Mesmerizing, in a way.

I stopped myself. I couldn't seriously be attracted to this man, could I? No. I refused to entertain such thoughts.

Turning back to my stew, I ate in silence.

"If we were to find a prince—"

"No."

He sighed in exasperation. "There's got to be something. I can't bring Prince Merek's sleeping body back to his father without freeing the princess, and I can't leave him inside that tower the way he is. He was barely breathing as it was."

"Wait," I said, my spoon halfway to my mouth. "How do you know he was barely breathing?"

"It was dark for one thing, and that hair! By the gods, I've never seen anything like it. He fell unconscious as soon as he saw that poor girl, and when I left, I could tell he was still breathing, but—"

"Back up. You *saw* Rapunzel? You *went inside* the tower?"

"Yes, how else would I have known what happened to him?"

"I didn't realize you *went inside* the tower."

"Well, I couldn't have done my job of protecting the prince if I'd stayed outside, could I?"

"How?" I sputtered. "It's not possible for anyone to enter the tower but me and the high sorcerer without falling under the spell…"

"I got lucky, I suppose."

I eyed him. I wasn't entirely sure he was telling the truth. He was desperate to save the prince. What if he was trying to trick me?

"Raj." I said his name slowly. "I want you to be very sure you're recalling last night to the best of your ability. Are you certain you went inside the tower?"

"Of course! I have no reason to lie to you."

"Actually, you do."

"Are you accusing me of lying?"

"I'm accusing you of remembering incorrectly."

He sat back, crossing his arms, making his muscles bulge, which I tried hard not to notice, but failed. "Then let me prove it to you. Take me back to the tower, and I'll show you how I entered without falling under Rapunzel's curse."

"I'll think about it," I said, taking another bite. "It's probably because you're not a prince. The spell must only work if someone with noble blood tries to free her. Since you're not, it didn't affect you."

"Does this mean you'll take me back to the tower?"

"Fine," I relented. "But first, I finish my stew."

THREE

MOONLIGHT ILLUMINATED THE TOWER AS Raj and I crossed into the meadow. The handcart's wheels squeaked as I pulled it to a stop at the base of the tower. Raj had been true to his word and purchased all the supplies we needed for winter. I couldn't complain—I was grateful he'd done it. I only hoped he didn't expect a miracle in return.

Now I had the chore of transporting everything into the tower. Luckily, I'd brought my largest knapsack. As I loaded vessels of lentils, bags of flour, and a few jars of syrup into my bag, Raj stood over me.

"You're bringing all that up there?" he asked.

"It's better than leaving it down here."

"You really live up there all the time?"

"Yes, I only ever come out to gather edibles, or when we're desperate for supplies."

"But how do you get water?"

"We have a well inside the tower. Can you help me?" I tossed him an empty burlap sack. If he was so insistent on being here, he might as well help me.

"It seems like a lonely existence."

I eyed him. Lonely? What did he know of loneliness?

I didn't feel like admitting to this stranger how desperately lonely the past five years had been, how I lay awake at night wishing I had someone to talk to, feeling as if the silence would drive me to insanity. No, he didn't need to know any of that.

"It's not that bad. Rapunzel isn't one for talking, but we have a cat. His name is Jester. He keeps me company most of the time."

"A cat?"

"Yes. He's mostly feral. But he's friendly enough, and he comes and goes as he pleases. He's even learned to climb the vines to get in and out of the tower. He's quite clever." I adjusted the pack's straps on my shoulders. "Now, let's get up there before Rapunzel…" I stopped myself. "Let's get up there."

With the pack strapped to my back, I turned to the tower. Wind rushed past, battering my hair against my cheeks, as I prepared to speak the spell.

"*Rapunzel, Rapunzel, let down your hair!*" My words carried on the wind, echoing through the forest.

I waited, nervousness making my hands grow clammy as I held to the pack's straps, but why did I feel so uneasy? Was it because Raj was with me?

I turned to him. He stood with haunting dark eyes as he watched a coil of ropy, matted hair drop from the tower's only window high above us. I stepped to the length of hair and grabbed it, holding my breath against the scent of unwashed scalp. I never got used to that smell.

"Should I follow you?" Raj asked.

"Yes. But let me enter first." Gripping the hair tightly, I started the climb. I made my way toward the window at the top of the tower. Halfway up, my muscles burned, and I focused on breathing to make it the rest of the way. This part was always the hardest, and the sack of supplies weighing me down wasn't helping. Why did Varlocke have to put his daughter into such an impossibly tall tower?

When I reached the window, I grabbed the ledge. The worn stones felt smooth under my palms as I climbed over, then landed inside. As I straightened, I pulled off the pack and left it on the floor, then focused on the room. Moonlight illuminated the bare stones walls, the well sitting at the room's center, the wooden chairs, roughly-hewn tables, huge bookcases cluttered with dusty spell journals and vials, and the bed where Rapunzel lay.

I stepped over the matted coils of hair. Pieces of rat and bird bones lay trapped in the knotted strands, seeming to glow white against the dark hair. The sound of gnawing stopped me.

She wasn't.

"Rapunzel," I said quietly. "What are you doing?"

The gnawing continued. I approached her on quiet feet, afraid of what I might find. Behind me, Raj scrambled inside the room.

Please don't let it be the prince.

When I reached her side, her pale, skeleton-white skin glowed in the moonlight. She held a rat.

I exhaled, grateful it was only a rodent and not something—*someone*—else. A crust of bread and a handful of wild beets sat on the bedside table, but they were untouched.

Raj's footsteps echoed, and I turned to face him. His tall, lean frame looked so out of place. Only the high sorcerer ever visited, and to have an Outlander squire inside my home unnerved me.

"Is she eating something?" he asked. "What is that?"

"Sorry. It's the cat's fault. He catches them and leaves them on her lap. He thinks he's giving her a prize or something. Rapunzel does that with them sometimes— with the rats—eats them, I mean." I stumbled over my words, feeling immeasurably mortified that Raj had to see it. But it could've been worse.

I approached her. She looked up, as if only seeing me now, and she hissed. With her red-rimmed eyes, it looked as if she hadn't been sleeping, and her collarbones seemed to be protruding more than I remembered. Her white gown hung off her meatless frame, but at least it was the clean one I'd left for her. She'd managed to change clothes—at least there was that.

"Where is the prince?" Raj asked.

"I don't know." I scanned the room. With the large piles of hair covering the floor, he could've been hidden, but we should've seen some clue he was here—his feet or a hand poking out. Something. "You're certain he came up here?"

"Yes, positive."

I studied the tower more thoroughly but didn't see anything that resembled the prince. Odd. Where was he?

"Rapunzel," I said, turning to her, "we're looking for a prince. Have you seen him?"

She shook her head, clutching the rat, her fingers digging into the carcass.

"Please," Raj said. "I need to find him. His father is the king. He'll be very sad if he loses his only son. Can't you tell us where he is?"

Rapunzel focused on the man, but she remained silent. Outside, the sky lightened. Pink streaked through the gray as dawn approached. As the sun rose, sunlight streamed into the room, giving light to the dark places. Something thudded inside the well, and Raj followed me as I maneuvered around the coiled hair toward the raised ring of stones surrounding the deep drop that went straight through the bottom of the tower.

"Is there something in the well?" Raj asked.

"Some*one* probably."

I pried open the lid. Sitting atop the wide-mouthed bucket was the prince, who stared up at us with a vacant expression. Hair coiled around him as blue bands of magic wrapped his wrists and ankles. I grabbed his tunic with both hands and attempted to lug him out. He was heavier than he looked.

"How'd he get in there?" Raj asked.

"Rapunzel. She tried to throw him down, I assume."

"She can do that?"

"With her hair, yes. She's clever when she's motivated."

"He was looking at me!" Rapunzel yelled. Well, at least she was finally speaking.

"She can talk?" Raj asked.

"Yes, when she feels like it. Can you help me?"

Raj grabbed the prince's feet and helped me lift him out of the well. We placed the prince atop a coil of hair. He lay motionless, his wide eyes frozen with fear. The prince's sallow skin and sunken, gaunt cheeks made him almost unrecognizable.

The spell washed over me, brushing my skin with its intensity. Reaching out, I searched my mother's magic, trying to determine the damage her spell was doing to him. I'd been under the impression the spell would put him to sleep and nothing more. He would wake in a few weeks and all would be as it was. But seeing him now made me wonder if there was darker magic at work.

I took his wrist in my hand, feeling for his life's blood. Only a weak thrumming pulsed beneath his skin. The enchantment's poisonous taint made me shudder.

With sickening horror, I realized the magic was poisoning him. He was dying.

Swallowing my fear, I stood away from the prince to distance myself from the overwhelming magic.

"What's the matter?" Raj asked.

I wasn't sure how to tell him, but he had to know. "I'm sorry, but the curse is worse than I thought. Your friend will be dead in two weeks. Three, maybe."

"What?" he asked, shocked. "Can't we do anything for him?"

"There's only one thing that can be done. We would have to take away the spell that made him this way. We'd have to cut Rapunzel's hair."

From her bed, Rapunzel barked a shrill laugh. "Ha! Can't be done!"

"It could be done," I corrected, "if one had the golden shears."

"What are the golden shears?" Raj asked.

"A magical talisman. They're guarded by infinitely powerful beings."

"Who guards them?"

"My aunts Gwynna and Neleia. They live in the Ice Mountains."

"Then we'll travel to the Ice Mountains and get the shears."

"It won't be easy—if it's even possible. We'd have to

pass through Spirit Woods and the Outerlands—and that's assuming my aunts would willingly give up the shears in the first place. I'm certain they won't, not without some sort of trade."

"Then we'll trade."

"For what?"

"Whatever they want."

"Impossible," I said. "You need to know who my aunts are. They're witches, and they're not friendly. In fact, if we were to approach them without a trade that interests them, they'd have no problem killing us."

"But you're their niece."

"They don't care."

He crossed his arms, his brows knitted, as if deep in thought. "We'll have to figure out something. Prince Merek came here to rescue the princess. He was trying to end the war. Don't you see? If he marries Rapunzel, the high sorcerer's throne passes to him. No one will recognize Varlocke as high sorcerer once his daughter weds. There are men dying on the battlefield as we speak. This war has been going on for years, and more people die the longer the high sorcerer fights. King Duc'Line sent me and his son here to claim the high sorcerer's daughter, so that the prince could marry her and end the war. We have to undo the spell. If we don't, more people die, and not only soldiers, but anyone who crosses the high sorcerer. Women and children, entire families. Surely you must know how evil the high sorcerer is."

"Yes," I said quietly. "I know." All too well.

"Then you must help me."

Inhaling deeply, I knew what Raj said was true. The high sorcerer needed to be stopped. He'd already wiped out the entire Outlander nation, and he'd been battling for years to do the same to King Duc'Line's kingdom.

"There is one way," I said.

"Yes, what is it?"

"The radish," I said.

His eyebrows rose. "Radish?"

"Yes. Remember, I grew up in Varlocke's castle before he declared himself high sorcerer. That castle still exists, but before my mother died, she not only cursed Varlocke's daughter, but his castle also. It was taken over by a magical radish that she cursed to grow thorn-covered vines. They took over the entire castle, forcing him to move away. The radish has unusual qualities. It's what gave the high sorcerer invincibility, and my aunts knew it. They always begged my mom for a piece of the radish, but she knew how dangerous it was, and refused to give it to them."

"If we were to find the radish, it might be possible to take a piece of it and trade it for the shears?"

"If we survive making it to the castle, and then through the Outerlands and Ice Mountains, then I would say yes." I could hardly believe I was contemplating this. Who would take care of Rapunzel while I was gone? And I couldn't very well leave the prince with her for such a long time, or he'd end up like the rats.

"We'll leave today," Raj said, as if it was settled. "You may use the prince's mare, as he won't be able to travel. The horses are stabled in the village. If we leave today, we can make it to the village, gather the horses, and ride hard. I've traveled the road to the village near Spirit Woods many times, and I know the best inns. We should have no problem getting there—"

"Raj," I interrupted. "I can't."

24

"What? Why not?"

"Because I can't leave Rapunzel."

He glanced at the girl on the bed, who stared at him with a distant gaze.

"She can't be left alone for long periods of time. Plus, if High Sorcerer Varlocke found out, he'd hunt me down. It's not possible for me to come."

"Can't someone else keep watch over her? You don't understand—this quest doesn't happen without you."

"I wish I could, but I can't leave the tower. Not only would Rapunzel suffer, but I would be executed."

"But if you don't, then you both remain here forever, the prince dies, and the high sorcerer destroys what's left of our lands."

I stepped away from him. I wasn't expecting the rush of emotions. Could I just leave? Wouldn't it be best for Rapunzel if I tried to break the spell? She was digressing faster than I wanted to admit. If the spell wasn't broken, what would be left of her?

"I suppose I could use a spell to put her to sleep, but we'll still have the problem of the high sorcerer. Once he finds out I've left the tower, he'll send a squadron after me."

"What if he doesn't find out?"

"He will. Sometimes he sends squadrons to check on me. Other times he uses a spell to appear inside the tower at random times, just to make sure I'm here. He'll know soon enough that I've left."

"Then we'll outrun them, or we'll hide, or we'll fight them if we must. I've had my fair share of experience with the high sorcerer's squadrons."

"You've fought them?"

"Yes, many times."

"How?"

"With my sword, of course."

I scrutinized him. Most who challenged the high sorcerer's elite squadrons didn't live to tell about it. "Are you being truthful?"

"I am. I give you my oath that I will protect you. You've no need to fear squadrons, Spirit Woods, Ice Mountains, or anything else of the sort. If you agree to help me find the shears and free Rapunzel and the prince, I will protect you with my last breath. That I swear."

I stared at him, shocked at his admission. No one had ever sworn to protect me, and though I'd only just met him, somehow, I knew he meant it.

"Very well," I said. "I will help you find the shears, but under one condition. I want Rapunzel to choose whether she'll marry the prince. She doesn't need to be forced into a marriage, or it might very well break her. I know you might not understand, but I won't go on this quest unless you agree to it."

"Then I agree. I wouldn't want the marriage forced on her either."

"Are you saying that to appease me?"

"No. I'm saying it because I agree. It's not my wish to force a marriage on Rapunzel."

"But… you're an Outlander…"

"What's that got to do with it?"

"Don't your people arrange marriages?"

"We do."

"And still you believe Rapunzel should choose?"

"Yes. Arranged marriages are an outdated notion anyway."

Well, since we'd gotten that out of the way. "Fine. If that's the case, I suppose I should pack up before we leave, but first, I'll have to make a sleeping potion for Rapunzel."

I eyed the princess, who laid propped on the pillows, staring out into space, as if she'd been oblivious that Raj and I were discussing her future marriage. Had she understood a word we'd said? How long had she'd gone without sleep?

"Rapunzel," I said, "I'm going to make you a potion. It will make you sleep."

Rapunzel frowned at me, her eyes narrowed.

"You need the rest anyway. You haven't slept in a week."

"I don't want to sleep!"

"But you need to," I said. "I have to go away for a little while, and I won't be able to take care of you. It's for the best."

"No, no, no," she screamed, pounding the mattress with her fists.

I went to her, careful not to trip on the hair, and sat beside her. Gently, I patted her shoulder. At my touch, she stopped screaming, and looked at me.

"*No, no, no,*" she whispered, her eyes filling with tears.

I hugged her. Something inside me broke as I held her close, feeling her frail frame through her nightgown. She hadn't always lived a life of isolation and insanity. If I went on this quest, I would be doing more than stopping a war. I would be returning a life to a friend.

"Be brave, Rapunzel. When you wake up, I'll have the golden shears, and then we'll cut your hair, and you'll be free to move around again. How would you like to sit on the river bank with our feet buried in the sand like we used to do?"

She only shook her head as she sobbed into my shoulder.

Raj approached us. He moved a clump of hair off the bed and took a seat near Rapunzel's feet. She glanced at him, then buried her head on my shoulder again.

"Don't be afraid," he said, his voice calm, soothing, yet strong—the kind of voice that made you feel safe. "If we succeed, you'll have your life back again. Would you like that?"

She only stared at him, then nodded once.

"Will you let me put you to sleep?" I asked.

She closed her eyes tight, tears making her lashes wet. She nodded.

Nerves pinched my insides. I wasn't sure if I was doing the right thing. Was I being too hasty by agreeing to go on this quest with Raj—a stranger? I could easily be killed, and then what would happen to Rapunzel? She'd be stuck sleeping for the rest of her life.

But I'd told Rapunzel to be brave. Perhaps I should take my own advice.

"I'm going to prepare the potion," I said. "It will take some time."

I stood and made my way to the massive bookshelf cluttered with journals, jars, and potions. Most of them had belonged to my mother. She'd collected every possible spellcasting item on the planet.

I searched the leather-bound journals lining the stacks until I found the one I needed. Pulling out my mother's chronicle of spells, I carried the thin book to the table and placed it on the wooden top. After opening it, I leafed through the inked pages. The smell of the well-worn paper brought back memories of my mother, who'd written on these pages as I'd stood clutching her skirts, listening to the scratching of the quilled pen.

When I found the spell I needed, I perused the ingredients. Water from a Nymph's pool, dried thyme and rosemary, ground bones from a viper, dragon eye, the gallbladder of a horned mountain frog, oil of lilac, and a drop of the potion maker's blood. A scrawled note stood out at the bottom of the page, but the ink had blurred, and reading it was impossible. Despite that, the ingredients were common enough, and I was fairly certain I had them all. Scanning the shelves, I searched for the items. Glass jars clinked as I rifled through them, then placed the bottles and jars on the table.

Grabbing my mortar and pestle, I began adding the dried herbs.

Raj sat on Rapunzel's bed, telling her a story of the Outerlands, which included a starving dog, a skinny boy—which I assumed was himself—and a leg of lamb. Rapunzel actually laughed as he got to the punchline, surprising me. I hadn't heard her genuinely laugh in ages.

I crushed dried thyme and rosemary, then poured it into a beaker filled with ground bones. After adding a pinch of lilac, I grabbed the jar of dragon eyes.

Behind me, Raj unsheathed his sword and let Rapunzel hold it. Her eyes lit up as she touched the blade.

"Careful," I called over my shoulder.

"She won't stab me," Raj called. "Will you, Rapunzel?"

"It's a real sword?" she asked

"Very real. I've vanquished many foes with it."

"You killed people?"

"Only the ones who tried to kill me first."

"Killing is bad," she said.

"Yes. It's very bad." His voice held a hint of sadness, almost undetectable, but I heard it. How many people had died in his life? It dawned on me that it must have been a lot—there weren't many Outlanders left in the world. How had he managed to survive? I was curious to know how he'd left his lands to become the prince's squire, but those were questions I didn't feel comfortable asking.

I didn't feel comfortable with a lot of things around him. He made me feel self-conscious, and made my stomach feel flighty. It wasn't a bad feeling—I rather liked it—but how would I feel questing with him—sleeping, eating, and changing clothes. Bathing.

Bother. This was going to be a difficult quest.

Turning back to my potions, I concentrated on adding the last ingredient—my blood. I pricked my finger with a needle, squeezed it, then allowed a drop of blood to drip into the concoction.

The liquid fizzed as my blood interacted with it, causing a cloud of blue magic to emanate from the potion. Lavender, iron, and less pleasant smells wafted from the bowl. I would have worried about the taste, but this was Rapunzel drinking it. Couldn't be worse than eating rats. I grabbed a wooden tumbler from the cabinet and poured the potion inside.

Carefully, I lifted the tumbler and walked toward the bed. When I reached her side, she took it from me, sniffed it, and wrinkled her nose.

"You're sure that won't kill her?" Raj asked.

"Positive." I hoped.

She took a small sip.

"Bleh," she whispered, then drained it. She sat looking at me and Raj, her eyes wide and dark. I was reminded of the girl she used to be, intelligent and beautiful, so much potential.

"When I wake," she whispered, "I will be fixed? My mind…" She blinked slowly. "My mind will be well?"

"Yes." I took the tumbler from her, then squeezed her hand. "You will be well. Once you wake up, you'll be yourself again."

Magic gathered around her as the spell worked through her veins. Her eyes closed.

"You promise?" she asked, her voice barely audible.

"I promise," I said, praying it wasn't a lie.

FOUR

RAPUNZEL SLEPT, THE MAGIC CREATING a bluish glow around her body. With her face relaxed, she looked at peace. I hadn't seen her that way in ages.

"Will she be okay?" Raj asked.

"She should be. The spell will keep her from starving. Technically, she could sleep for a hundred years and be okay."

"Let's hope she doesn't have to."

Raj looked from Rapunzel to the prince, who still lay atop a coil of hair. "What about him?"

I stood and crossed to the prince. "This spell is different from the sleeping potion. He'll last two weeks—three weeks tops."

My cat, Jester, jumped down from the top of the bookshelf, startling me. The cat had a habit of scaring me. He meowed as Raj and I stood over the prince. His sleek black coat resembled a panther. Yellow eyes peered up at us. He yawned, then walked to the prince, sniffed him, and sat on his chest.

"Will you watch over Rapunzel and the prince while we're gone?"

Raj shot me a confused glance. "You're asking the cat

to guard them?"

"Jester is very protective." I knelt and scratched the cat's ears, hoping the animal got the hint.

"You won't do anything stupid, right?" My whispered voice hissed through my teeth. Jester was an idiot. If they survived, it would be a miracle, but Raj didn't need to know that.

Purring, Jester nudged my hand, and I felt obligated to pet him. Maybe he'd understood me; maybe he would watch over the prince and Rapunzel like I'd asked. Sure, he was only a cat, but I'd feel better knowing someone— even an animal—was with her.

"I think it best if we leave now," Raj said. "It will take a week at least to travel to the Ice Mountains, and a week more to return, and that's assuming we don't get into any trouble. We need to make good time if we want the prince to still be alive when we return."

"I agree. Let me gather a few things first. Would you mind waiting for me at the bottom of the tower?"

"Outside?"

"Yes, I'd like to pack my things in private if you don't mind."

"Of course." He grabbed up the coils of hair, then walked to the window where he tossed them out. As he climbed over the ledge and disappeared, a mixture of anxiety and excitement made my heart beat too quickly. I would finally be leaving the tower, but at what cost?

I turned away from the window and grabbed my large knapsack, considering what I should pack. Going on expeditions to the Ice Mountains—or anywhere outside the village—was a new experience for me, but I knew I needed to be smart. I grabbed a few loaves of bread, some dried fruit, my water canteen, some extra riding gowns, and leather breeches to wear underneath.

My mother's spell journal still sat on the table, and I grabbed it as well. Where we were going, I knew I would need it. I also searched through the vials of herbs and potions, looking at the labels written in my mother's perfect calligraphy. None of their contents would be powerful enough to defeat my aunts, but they would be the greatest defense I possessed. If we were forced to fight my aunts, we would lose. We would die horrifically, but I tried not to ponder it.

Before leaving, I stood at the wall of bookshelves, then knelt, looking for a wooden box. I found it on the bottom shelf. The wood grain felt smooth in my hands as I opened the lid and removed my mother's knife. As I studied the carved bone handle, and sharpened steel blade, the danger of this quest came into focus. I would need this weapon for the creatures of Spirit Woods—for bandits and mutated animals—but that wasn't the reason I'd searched it out.

Traveling alone with a man I barely knew was a risky, stupid move—one I only did out of desperation. If Raj attempted anything, I would be ready. I stuck the knife in my boot, then stood.

As I walked to the window, I took one last look at the room. It wasn't much of a home, and I'd always felt like a prisoner here, but leaving meant danger. When the high sorcerer found me gone, he would send his squadrons to hunt me down. But I couldn't afford to turn back now. I had to do this for Rapunzel. She didn't deserve this fate.

I climbed out of the tower. Humid air thick with fog chilled my skin as I held tightly to the hair, climbing down until I reached the ground. I stepped away from the tower. Raj stood beside me, and we watched as the hair was magically drawn back inside through the only window. As I looked up at the tower, I whispered a silent prayer for Rapunzel.

May the goddess keep you safe.

Turning away from the tower, we trudged through the field toward the forest. Wet grass squished beneath my boots. I knew I was doing the right thing. But leaving her behind felt as if I were leaving a part of myself. She'd been in my life for so long. Sure, she'd been insane most of the time we'd lived in the tower. Caring for her was part of my daily routine. It had become ingrained in me. I had to admit, leaving her wasn't as easy as I'd hoped.

By the time we made it to Willow Wood, the sun cast long shadows that stretched away from the inns and taverns. Raj didn't talk much. We'd made a few comments to each other about the weather, how autumn seemed to be coming more quickly this year, the rainfall, but we avoided speaking about anything of substance.

When we reached the stables and gathered the horses, it was growing dark. The stables smelled of hay and horses, two scents which brought back memories of the stables in Varlocke's castle. Raj hung his lantern on a nail, and we set to work saddling the horses.

"If we ride all night, we can make it to Grimlore Village which is near Spirit Woods." He placed a blanket on his black stallion. The horse was a majestic Arabian, with long legs and a lean, sleek body. I patted the horse's velvety nose as I pondered Raj's suggestion.

"You think it's safe to ride through the night?" I asked.

"We'll be safe enough. I'm more worried about traveling through Spirit Woods, which is why we'll travel tonight, then rest a few hours so we can journey through the forest during the day."

Raj led me to the prince's horse—a tall, bay mare who stood over me munching a mouthful of hay. She shook her head, jangling the metal buckles on her bridle.

"Don't let her fool you. She may look imposing, but she's a gentle giant for sure. You should have no problems with her."

"What's her name?"

"Sable."

"Sable," I repeated, running my hands over her coat, which was beginning to thicken with the weather growing cooler. "What's your horse called?"

"Tranquility," Raj answered, "though she's anything but tranquil. Merek gave her that name as a joke, but the name stuck, so we kept it."

"Were you and Merek good friends?" I asked.

"Yes, most of the time. We were like brothers, really. We fought at times, but never stayed angry for too long." His eyes fell, and he looked away from me. "I would never forgive myself if I had to carry his body back to his father."

"How did you come to be his squire?"

"King Duc'Line found me after one of the high sorcerer's raids on my village. He felt sorry for me, I suppose. I was a skinny, half-naked savage in his eyes. He took me back to the castle and trained me to be a squire."

"He took you from your family?"

"Yes and no. I'm still in contact with them. They're proud of me for becoming the prince's squire."

"Did you have any say in the matter?"

"Not really."

"Does that bother you?"

He paused before answering. "I suppose it does. Sometimes I wish I could have stayed in my village and taken my father's place as patriarch, helped with the family's spice business, married an Outlander girl and started a family, but life rarely works out the way we wish. I'm grateful for the opportunities I have now. I never would've had them if the king hadn't taken me. Still, I miss my home. I miss the smell of my mother's curry spiced dumplings. I miss my family."

We continued saddling the horses in silence. I tightened Sable's girth, making sure it was secure. I wasn't sure what to think about Raj, although it seemed that he, like me, was also a prisoner of sorts. He'd been taken from his family, and I'd been taken from mine.

When we mounted our horses and rode away from the stables, night fell over the village. Flames flickered from the gaslights atop the lampposts, casting a hazy orange glow over the cobbled pathways winding through the thatched-roof buildings. A chill breeze blew past, blowing leaves and bits of straw across our path. The wind tugged strands of blue hair from my cowl. I tucked the loose hair beneath my hood, scanning the street for anyone who may have been watching. Only a few people lingered, some pushing carts with squeaking wheels, others walked with their heads down, not paying us any attention.

Good. I didn't need any attention. If anyone recognized me, it was possible they could report it to the high sorcerer. Plus, I wasn't anxious for anyone to spot me alone with a strange man.

The clopping of the horses' hooves echoed through the lane until we reached a dirt road leading away from the village and through open fields. The bright moonlight turned the grassy hills to mounds of silver. Away from the village, with only the sounds of horses' hooves clipping rhythmically over the dirt-packed road, the world remained quiet. I would have expected crickets chirping or the occasional hoot of an owl. Instead, silence shrouded the air.

Our lanterns illuminated the wagon wheel ruts and the impressions of horse hooves in the mud. Patches of fog snaked through the air, a transparent white blanket that dampened my skin.

We rode for several hours, passing no one at this time of night, which didn't bother me. At one point, Raj suggested we stop and let the horses rest. We drank a few sips of water, and then continued.

As the night wore on, my hands, though gloved, felt stiff and cold, and I wasn't sure I would be able to walk once I was off the horse. Up ahead, the shapes of buildings appeared on the horizon.

"Grimlore," Raj said, "the last village before we enter Spirit Woods. I think it best if we stay here until morning. We'll need rest before we journey into the forest."

"Fine," I said, too tired to argue.

We guided our horses off the road and onto the path leading to Grimlore. It was a bigger village than Willow Wood, with three story buildings that crowded the narrow lanes. Gas lamps shone from light posts, glowing over the glass windows of store fronts and inns.

"Where should we stay?" I asked, looking at the bronze and wooden signs hanging from poles that jutted from the wrought-iron balconies. *The Ruddy Pig, Mooncastle Inn, and The Dead Rooster's Watering Hole,* were a few of the names I spotted.

"Down the lane there's an inn away from the others. If the high sorcerer's guards are on patrol tonight, we should be out of the way."

"Are you sure about that?"

"No, but it's safer than spending the night in Spirit Woods. I, for one, would rather not be poisoned by imps while I sleep."

"Do you really think there are imps in the forest?"

"Yes, and there's worse than that, too."

"Like what?"

He shot me a dark glance. "Witches."

"Witches?"

He nodded.

"Are you afraid of witches, Raj?"

"Anyone would be a fool not to be."

I pulled back on the reins, stopping my horse. Raj glanced back at me, then stopped his own horse and turned around to face me.

"What's wrong?" he asked.

"You do realize *I* am a witch, don't you?"

"Yes, but you're not like other witches."

"How would you know that? How many witches have you met?"

He pondered for a moment. "One."

"I'm the only witch you've ever met?"

"Yes."

"Then how can you be afraid of them if you've never met them? And how can you trust me?"

"Because... I don't know."

My anger bubbled to the surface. "You don't know? You demanded I come on this quest with you when you think anyone would be a fool to trust a witch?"

"I didn't mean it that way."

"Then how did you mean it?"

"Look, we're both tired. We've been riding all night. Let's just get to the inn and get some rest, okay?"

He wasn't getting off the hook that easily. "Are you sure you want a witch to go to the inn with you? What if I cast a spell on you in your sleep and turn you into a frog?"

"You can do that?"

Oh, for goodness' sake. "Of course, I can. I'm a witch!"

"You could really turn me into a frog?"

"That's what I said, didn't I?"

"But I didn't think... I know you did that spell on the princess... you could really turn a person to a frog?"

Would he drop the frog thing already? "Frog, horse, dust mote, manure, yes. All of it. Could we get to the inn now? I'm feeling testy. I'd hate to turn you into a person who thinks."

"That's uncalled for."

"Is it?"

I kicked Sable's flanks and rode past him. Without arguing, he followed. At the end of the lane, the path branched. To the right, the road continued through the village, but on the left, trees overshadowed the narrow lane, their branches forming a canopy that blocked out the moonlight.

"Go left," Raj called.

I glanced back at him. "Are you sure this place is safe?"

"Yes. Mostly sure."

Mostly, huh?

As we turned down the lane, I spotted the gables of a whitewashed building peeking from the trees. Hazy pools of light shone from the windows, glowing over the skeletal tree branches that surrounded the structure.

"There," Raj called. "That's the inn."

When we drew closer, I wasn't impressed with the paint peeling from the shingles, the broken windows, or the fragments of glass from smashed wine bottles lying near the hitching posts. But it was away from the other inns, and I was in desperate need of sleep, so I wouldn't argue, even if it was only *mostly* safe.

We dismounted our horses and hitched them to the posts. Without speaking, we approached the inn. I had to admit I felt a little guilty for being rude to Raj. In truth, he didn't deserve my outburst, but had he seriously not realized I was a witch when he asked me to journey with him? Was he really so thoughtless? Honestly.

Our booted feet echoed over wooden planks as we ascended the stairs leading to the porch. When we reached the doors, Raj opened them for me and stood aside to let me pass through. A gentleman, huh?

Even if he was a gentleman, he was still an imbecile, and I was seriously contemplating why I was making this journey with him. Someone so naïve would easily get us killed.

Inside the inn, overheated air radiated from the enormous hearth at the back of the room. Flames cast a flickering light over the roughly-hewn tables and chairs crowding the floor. The room was empty, and the only sound came from the crackling fire.

As we stood inside the inn, sweat beaded my skin, and I had the urge to remove my cloak, but resisted. My blue hair made me easily identifiable, so I chose to keep it covered. Sometimes I hated my hair. I'd used every spell imaginable to try to change it, but nothing had ever worked.

An overweight man wearing a dressing robe and slippers entered from a door at the back. He eyed us suspiciously as he walked toward us. His slick, bald head reflected the firelight.

"It's nigh three in the morning. What on earth are you doing here at this hour?"

"We seek shelter," Raj said.

"Aye, I supposed that. Very well. I've got a room available upstairs, but you'll need to tread quietly. I've got paying patrons who don't want to be disturbed."

"I understand," Raj said. "We'll need two rooms, if you've got them."

"Two? Why? Are you quarrelling with your lover here?" He eyed me. "Seems a perfectly fine girl to me."

"We are not lovers," I snapped. "And we would prefer two rooms, if you please."

"Yes, yes, as you wish, but it will cost you more. Three-hundred shekels."

"Three hundred?" I asked, aghast. "Maybe if the beds are made of gold."

"Three hundred is fine," Raj said, pulling out his coin purse and counting out thirty coins. He hesitated before handing them to the innkeeper. "I'll pay an extra ten to buy your silence."

He frowned. "I'm not in the habit of housing criminals."

"We're not criminals, but we'd like to stay invisible, if you understand my meaning."

"Very well," the man sighed. "But it'll cost you twenty more."

I bit my tongue to keep from protesting as Raj counted out the money. At this rate, we'd be penniless in a week. Then again, Raj hadn't told me how much money he was carrying. How many shekels were in his coin purse? Maybe it was best if I didn't know.

"We'll also need our horses stabled," Raj said. "And something to eat in the morning."

The innkeeper grunted, but didn't argue as he took Raj's coins, then led us to the stairs. The steps, made of split-planked logs, squeaked as we treaded to the second floor. Antlers and animal skins decorated the walls, and a musty smell wafted from the dust-covered pieces. We reached a door at the end of a hallway. The innkeeper pulled a key from his pocket and unlocked it with a click.

We walked inside, and the innkeeper lit a lantern on a table beside a bed with a straw mattress. The room was smaller than I expected, and the only furniture was a small writing desk, a lavatory with a jug for water, and a large bucket for bathing.

"There's fresh water in the bucket. Should ye be needing anything else, it'll have to wait till morning." He turned to Raj. "You, follow me."

I watched as the two men left the room, shutting the door behind them, and leaving me in silence. An uneasy feeling settled over me. I wasn't accustomed to sleeping in strange places. I'd slept nowhere but inside the tower for the past five years, and being here now, facing the prospects of sleeping on a bed of straw, far from Rapunzel, unnerved me.

I pulled my knapsack off my shoulder and placed it on the ground, then sat on the straw mattress and began unlacing my boots. After pulling them off, I set them aside. I removed my cloak next, and though I sat alone in the room, I still felt as if someone were watching as I removed the cowl.

My mop of turquoise, windblown hair was beginning to come free of the bun, so I removed the hair pins and let it fall to my waist. Self-consciously, I removed my clothes and dressed in my nightgown, all the while thinking someone must've been watching me. Why else would I feel so vulnerable?

I crawled under the bed covers, blew out the candle, and closed my eyes tight, trying to ignore the straw poking into my back, and the sour smells of dried urine and sweat coming from the coarse blankets. Outside my window, tree limbs scratched the glass. Their leafless silhouettes reminded me of long, curving claws, making my thoughts turn to tomorrow's journey through Spirit Woods.

It wasn't until now that I seriously pondered what we would be up against. The stories always varied. Monsters and witches were said to live there.

Witches. Ha!

Unlike Raj, those ghost stories didn't bother me. I was more frightened of the actual dangers. The wolves that would rip a person apart, leaving nothing but scattered bones behind.

A knock came at my door, startling me from my thoughts. I lit the candle, grabbed my cloak, and hastily put it on to cover my hair, then tiptoed to the door.

"Who's there?" I asked.

"It's me. Raj."

I opened the door just enough to peer outside.

"What do you want?" I asked.

"I wanted to talk. It will only take a moment."

"In here?"

"Yes, if you please."

I hesitated. What if he tried something? I would be alone. But I had my knife and potions, though I didn't want to use those unless I had to.

"Very well," I said. "Come inside."

He entered, then shut the door behind him. The glint of a knife's blade shone from his hands. Startled, I stumbled back, cursing.

"Get away from me!"

"Hey, it's okay," he said, holding the knife up and out of reach. "I've brought this for you. I don't entirely trust this place, and I thought it best if you armed yourself."

"I've already got a knife."

"You do?"

"Yes, I brought it in case anyone tried anything—like entering my room with a weapon."

"Do you really distrust me so much?"

"Yes, I do. Forgive me, but I hardly know you."

"Then you should know you have nothing to fear. I gave you my word I would protect you, and I mean to keep it."

"Fine," I said. "If you've nothing else to bother me with, and as I already have a weapon, I would appreciate if you leave—"

"Gothel," he interrupted. "That wasn't all. I also came to apologize. I didn't mean to offend you earlier. I realize you are a witch and most likely a very powerful one. I should have thought before I spoke, but I have a bad habit of saying things before I think, and for that I'm sorry."

I crossed my arms, somehow still wanting to be angry with him, but he'd apologized, which showed he was humble enough to admit he was wrong. I couldn't fault him for that.

"Very well. I accept your apology."

"You do?" he asked, surprised.

"Yes, of course I do. I'm not a total witch, you know."

"Now you're teasing me."

"Maybe a little." I smiled.

"And you won't… turn me into a frog or anything. Right?"

"Only if you make me really angry."

"Ah." He forced a laugh, as if he couldn't decide if I were joking or not. "Well, I suppose I should go back to my room."

"Yes. And you can keep the knife."

"Of course." He flipped it in the air, caught the hilt, then shoved it into a sheath hanging from his belt. He turned toward the door, stopped, then turned around once again.

"Gothel, I hope I'm not being intrusive, but why are you wearing your cloak?"

"Oh, I forgot. I wasn't sure who was at the door." I pulled off the cloak and tossed it on the bed. "I didn't want anyone to see my hair—not that I've had any trouble before—but if the high sorcerer's squadrons came through the village looking for a girl with blue hair, I'd be easy to spot."

He eyed me, a curious expression on his face. My heart fluttered as he stared at me. I'd never realized how beautiful his eyes were. His dark irises reflected the soft glow of the candle, making them twinkle. He took a step toward me, and I cleared my throat, glancing away, suddenly feeling unbearably hot.

"You have lovely hair," he said.

Lovely?

He reached out and touched a strand near my cheek, his fingers nearly touching my skin. He smelled of amber and dark forests, and something else, something that reminded me of the spices the high sorcerer bought from the Outlanders—a rich, heady scent that washed over me.

My heart pounded at his nearness, but why? I'd been so angry at him earlier, and now I was feeling… strangely excited. It felt as though butterflies danced in my stomach. I desperately wanted him to touch me, but I didn't at the same time. My emotions baffled me.

"Was it a spell that made your hair this way?" he asked.

"No. I was born with it."

"Really? That's unusual."

"Yes." I wasn't sure what else to say. His nearness made me feel breathless, but perhaps any girl would have the same reaction. He was from an exotic land and squire to the prince. His mysterious nature made him attractive. Yes, that must have been it. I was only having the same reaction anyone else would have. There was nothing special between us. At least, I hoped not.

"I'm tired," I said, whispering.

"Oh, yes. Sorry." He stepped back, straightening, as if he'd only now realized that he'd let down his guard. "I'll just go. Sorry," he repeated, stumbling as he turned to the door, opened it, and left the room, shutting the door firmly behind him.

I didn't move for several seconds. I wasn't sure I could. My body felt so wound up, and I was breathing too fast. I needed to convince myself that there was nothing between me and Raj, otherwise, this quest would be a disaster.

Breathe deeply. Clear your mind.

I closed my eyes, but when I did, all I could see were Raj's beautiful eyes again—dark and penetrating—making my skin feel flushed and wonderful.

Drat. This wasn't at all working.

Climbing into bed, I pulled the blankets up to my chin. I stared at the window, listening to the sounds of the wind howling and limbs scraping over the glass.

He'd called my hair lovely.

No one had ever said anything like that to me. I'd never thought of my hair as lovely. Different, maybe. Cursed, sometimes. But never lovely.

I rolled away from the window to face the door instead. Raj baffled me. On the one hand, he seemed so kind and gentlemanly, and on the other, he acted like a fool.

As I drifted off, not even the scratchiness of the blankets or their sour odor could drive away my thoughts of Raj, so I stopped fighting it. Chances were, he wasn't even attracted to me, and I had nothing to worry about in the first place. Complimenting a person's hair was hardly a confession of love. He was only trying to be kind to me after his apology. Yes, that must've been it.

I had nothing to worry about.

Probably.

FIVE

THE NEXT MORNING, I SAT at a table, sipping something the innkeeper had called cocoa, made from a bean. I'd never tasted anything so extraordinary, and I couldn't fathom how something so good could be made from such an awful plant.

Raj appeared at the top of the staircase, and I stiffened. My stomach did that flighty thing it had been doing lately, and I couldn't decide if I liked the feeling. Honestly, I was pretty sure it annoyed me more than anything else. It made me think I had feelings for Raj when I was certain I didn't.

I pulled my cloak's cowl lower, feeling the urge to tuck my hair underneath, except earlier, I had braided it and wrapped it around my head. I told myself it was to keep it out of the way, but really, after Raj had seemed so smitten by my hair last night, I'd decided it was best to keep it out of sight.

"You're here early," Raj said as he sat across from me.

"Yeah," I mumbled, keeping the warm mug firmly pressed between my hands.

"What are you drinking?" he asked.

"It's called cocoa," I said, finally daring to look up at

him. He sat casually, and I breathed a sigh of relief. After last night, I was afraid things might have been awkward between us.

"Have you ever heard of such a thing?" I asked.

He smiled—that grin that showed his teeth, perfectly white and straight—and his lips, so full and pleasant. Oh, heaven help me. I had to stop this.

"Cocoa, yes. It comes from the Outerlands. My family had groves of the plants. We sold cocoa beans to people from all over the continent."

"Really?"

"Yes. And my nijida made the best cocoa."

"Nijida?"

"My grandmother."

"Oh."

"She's passed now. Like so many others. I doubt I would recognize my home anymore."

"I'm sorry."

"Don't be. There's nothing you can do about it. Well, except for traveling to the Ice Mountains in the northern lands to get a pair of shears, cut the princess's hair, and save the king's son from a spell so he can gain the throne. And you're already working on that, so I would never ask anything more of you."

"That's nice." I sipped my cocoa, feeling its creamy warmth as I swallowed.

A serving girl came by and placed two bowls of porridge on our table, then turned and left without a word. Quiet conversations filled the room, and a fire roared from the hearth, crackling and sputtering as it consumed the logs, filling the air with its sweltering heat. I wanted to remove my cloak, but I knew better.

I turned my attention to my food and quickly shoveled in a bite, not wanting to waste any more time before we left for Spirit Woods.

"How long do you think it will take us to travel through the forest?" I asked.

"I'm hopeful we'll reach the other side by nightfall, but that's assuming we make good time, and aren't stopped by any witch—" he cleared his throat, "by anything dangerous."

I couldn't help but smile at his slip. "You shouldn't fear witches."

"I know. I don't."

"Really?" I asked.

"You're never going to let this go, are you?"

"Maybe I will. Someday."

He sighed, looking away. "I suppose I should admit that I fear magic. I fear things I don't understand. Robbers and wild animals—I can kill. They're mortal. But those things people speak of when they mention the forest, ghost tales we know little about, enemies with powers we don't understand and don't know how to defeat. Those are the things I fear."

"I suppose I'm the opposite. It's the wolves that bother me."

"The wolves?"

I nodded.

"Why wolves?"

"I don't know. I suppose because they *are* real."

He sat back, crossing his arms. "I don't fear wolves," he said smugly.

"Then I guess we're not much alike."

"Yes. I guess so."

A tenseness fell over our conversation, and I took another sip without meeting his gaze.

"I've heard there are different types of witches." Raj said. "Light and dark, that sort of thing. Is it true?"

"There aren't really any types. But there are witches who possess natural magic and those who have to create their own."

"Which one are you?"

"I have to create my own. Natural powers only come to those who inherit it from two magical parents. Because my father had none, I wasn't born with the gift, so my mother taught me to use herbs and potions to create magic. It's not as easy as having it come naturally, but it works."

"I see."

He eyed me, as if trying to decide if he trusted me or not. I made up my mind that I didn't like discussing magic and witches with him. We finished eating in silence. As we stood, Raj mentioned saddling the horses. I agreed to meet him at the stables after gathering my things.

When I walked outside with my knapsack strapped to my back, my knife secured in my boot, and my cloak billowing behind me, I searched for the stables. My boots crunched over a thin layer of frost blanketing the dry stalks of grass.

I wrapped my cloak around me as I spotted the looming shape of the stables behind the inn, barely visible through the fog. Hulking spruce trees overshadowed me as I made my way to the entrance.

When I stepped inside, the sweet scent of hay filled the air. Raj stood saddling Tranquility, her black coat glistening under the light of a lantern glowing from a post. He looked up at me, but he said nothing. I wasn't sure what to think of his silence. Had I offended him in some way? Then again, I was most likely reading too much into it.

Sable stood behind Raj and his horse. She stood munching a mouthful of hay, a blanket thrown over her back. I approached my horse and grabbed the saddle off a wooden beam, but as I prepared to throw the saddle on her back, the shrill sound of screaming stopped me. I turned around to face the inn when more screams joined in with the first.

Chills prickled my neck. Raj stood beside me, staring intently at the inn, though we could see nothing.

"Hopefully it's just a bar fight," I said quietly.

"No way to tell unless we go check it out."

"What if it's a squadron?" I asked.

"Then we'd better not go check it out."

"And we'd better disappear," I said.

We turned back to the horses and saddled them quickly. The screaming got worse, until I was convinced that a squadron must have been inside the inn.

My heart pounding, we mounted the horses and trotted down the path leading around the inn and out of the village. As the fog burned away, a man wearing black and red armor stepped into our path. The image of a snakelike basilisk was imprinted on his breastplate. The creature's coils curved to form a clover-like pattern, with three intersecting circles.

The mark of the high sorcerer.

"Halt," the man yelled, pulling a broadsword from a scabbard at his back, his voice booming. The blade's sharpened edges glittered in the morning light.

Sable jerked her head as I pulled on the reins.

My hands shook as I held tightly to the leather straps. What good would my knife do against a sword like that?

The guardsman swung his sword in an arc. I heard its whistling sound from where I sat atop my horse.

"What do you want with us?" Raj called.

"We seek a girl!" the man yelled back. "One of the high sorcerer's own has escaped." He eyed us both, his gaze seeming to peer beneath my cowl. I had the urge to reach up and pull it lower, but that would only draw attention, and that was the last thing we needed.

"We've tracked her this far," the guardsman said. "And look what I've found. A girl!"

"Indeed," Raj replied. "There are many girls in the land. What makes you so sure you've found the right one?"

"Because I'll kill every girl in my path until I find her."

"That's an unpleasant thought," Raj called back. "Have you considered a different method for finding this girl? It seems a bit inefficient, to be honest."

The man creased his brow. "Are you toying with me?" he demanded, his voice harsh.

"I would never dream of doing such a thing. However, I will inform you that you're wasting your time with us. I've heard rumors she's headed south."

"Where did you hear that?" the guard asked.

"From the locals, of course. They know everything. Perhaps you should consider speaking to them before killing them. It might prove worthy of your time."

"Enough!" the man hissed. "The girl I seek is the keeper of the princess in the tower. She's got blue hair." He pointed the tip of his sword at me. "Remove your cowl, girl! Show me your hair."

I hesitated, frozen to the spot, trying to think logically through my fear, but all I could do was imagine how he would kill me—the pain of the blade as it slid through my heart.

But I couldn't think that way. I had to control my fear.

"No," I said, reaching into my pocket, wrapping my fingers around a satchel.

"No?"

"I won't do it."

"Then I'll remove it for you." He lunged toward me. I pulled out the packet and threw it in his face. White smoke exploded. Screaming, the man fell back. He dropped his sword to claw at his eyes. Coughing and sputtering, he staggered toward us, but I kicked Sable's flanks hard, spun her around, and galloped for the road.

The wind pushed the cowl from my head. I grabbed it and pulled it up, praying the guardsman hadn't seen my hair.

Raj followed close behind me. Our horses' hooves pounded the cobbled street, but instead of turning toward Grimlore, we took a path through the farmlands instead, avoiding the town and hopefully eluding the squadron—at least for now.

I lost track of how long we rode. We didn't slow until the dark treetops of Spirit Woods appeared on the horizon. Tightening the reins, I slowed Sable to a walk. She breathed heavily, her coat slick with sweat.

Raj also slowed his horse and rode beside me.

"What was that?" he asked. "That smoke?"

"Morrid bane. It's basically harmless. Its powdered form can temporarily disable a person. The liquid form can eat through skin. It's too volatile to carry, so I only brought the powder."

"That was brilliant," he said, beaming. "I was ready to charge him, but you reacted first. You're a hero, Gothel."

I laughed. "*Hero?* That's an exaggeration."

"It's no exaggeration. You defeated a member of the king's squadron. Do you know how many people have been killed by men like him? You must be a true warrior at heart."

"Raj, I threw some powder on him. Let's not get carried away."

"Still, you were brave, and you used your head. Not many people can keep their cool under pressure the way you did."

"Thanks," I mumbled, self-consciously fidgeting with my cowl to hide my burning red cheeks. I wasn't sure anyone had ever complimented my bravery.

Up ahead, the forest loomed closer. The hulking trees looked like a solid black mass against the sky. Rumors of the Spirit Woods surfaced in my memories. I'd never been inside, but I'd known others who had. Their stories still haunted my nightmares.

"Why are we going here again?" I asked.

"Because we're saving the prince and Rapunzel—and basically everyone in the land."

"Is it worth it?" I asked, teasing. Sort of.

He eyed me, but he didn't say anything.

A cold chill prickled my neck as we entered the forest. My horse whinnied nervously, and Raj's mare stopped abruptly, her eyes wild. He spoke quietly into her ear as he stroked her neck, gently coaxing her.

Something about the movement of his hands caught my attention—the way the tendons moved beneath his skin, the gentle strength of his fingers. I realized I was staring and quickly pulled my gaze away.

We continued into the forest until the thick canopy of trees obscured the sunlight. Silence surrounded us. Frost covered the trunks of trees—most of them dead— looking like fingers with broken nails sticking up from the moss-covered forest floor.

Frogs croaked rhythmically, their voices resonating through the woods. Pools of dark, crimson colored water appeared in patches through the gaps in the trees. I was thankful we'd filled up our canteens before entering the forest. I would have to be parched before I drank from those pools.

A sensation came to me, a prickling that raised the hair on my arms. Was it fear making me feel that way? Or something else?

A hollow laughter whispered through the forest, and the wind picked up, making the tree limbs creak.

"Did you hear that?" I asked Raj.

"Yes. It's the wind."

"Are you sure? It sounds like something else."

"Like what?"

"Laughter, maybe?"

"It's the wind," he said, as if to reassure himself. The wind faded, leaving the frogs to fill the silence.

"I don't like this place," I said. "It makes me uncomfortable."

"You and me both," Raj agreed.

Everything in the forest looked dead. The only colors were the charcoal gray of the trees, and the pools of red water that reminded me of blood. The horses pawed their feet and snorted their disapproval. When we finally stopped for a quick lunch, the sun shone above our heads, though very little light made it through the thick blanket of trees.

Raj and I sat on a log away from the main trail, our horses tied to tree trunks to keep them from bolting. I sipped water from my canteen, keeping my eyes on the forest for movement. Except for the sound of the frogs—which was incessant—I saw no signs of any other animals, not even birds.

I pulled a piece of jerky from my satchel, chewing slowly, watching bits of moss hanging from the trees move in a lazy breeze. The moldering smell coming from the decomposing wood filled the air, and I tried holding my breath as I ate, but it did no good.

As soon as we finished our meal, Raj and I mounted the horses once again and continued down the trail. The air warmed as afternoon approached, and I took the opportunity to remove my hood. I doubted the high sorcerer's guards would follow us into the forest. The chances of getting spotted were slim—at least that's what I told myself. Something about constantly wearing a cowl made me feel trapped.

Ahead, the form of something blocked our path. When we neared it, I looked into the face of a skull. My horse flinched back at the sweet, sickly scent. Flies buzzed through the air and crawled over what remained of the body. Eyeless sockets peered from a skeletal face, and only a few patches of gray flesh clung to the bones.

Across the person's chest, three large gashes split his tunic. The wounds were so deep, they cut his ribs in half, and severed bones stuck out from the wasted flesh.

With my arm held over my nose, I slowly backed my horse away, though Raj dismounted to inspect the body.

"What are you doing?" I asked.

"Trying to find out how he died."

"Something cut him open," I said.

"Yes, but what?"

He grabbed a stick and poked the body, disturbing the flies. They swarmed into the air. "Those gashes are each the same length and width, and the same distance apart. Something with claws did this, most likely."

"Claws?"

He nodded, tossing the stick aside and mounting his horse. Tranquility pranced, but he managed to grasp her reins and keep her steady.

"What kind of creature would have large enough claws to cleave a person nearly in two?"

"I don't know. I'd rather not find out."

He kicked his horse past the corpse. I followed him, glancing back at the body, praying we didn't meet whatever had killed him.

As afternoon turned to evening, with the sun sinking toward the horizon, my anxiety mounted. I didn't want to spend the night in the forest, but it seemed as if the path went on forever without end. The scenery hadn't changed at all—still the same dead trees and strange pools of red water—and I had the illogical feeling that we were riding in circles.

As the sun set, it transformed to a bright glowing ball that was barely visible through the moss-covered trees.

"Raj, we're going to make it before nightfall, aren't we?"

"Yes. We need to ride harder, that's all."

I had trouble sharing his confidence, but I didn't argue as we kicked our horses into a full gallop. My legs ached from being in the saddle all day.

The sinking sun painted orange splotches over the road. Ahead, I spotted a lump lying across the road. As we approached it, I gasped.

"Is that the same body we saw earlier?" I asked, looking at the three gashes in the exact same spots, the gray flesh, I even spotted the same stick Raj had used tossed beside the road.

"This isn't good," Raj said.

"How did this happen? We've been on the same road. There were no places to turn or take another path."

He shook his head. "Could magic be responsible?"

"If so, I don't know what kind."

"Then we've got no choice but to keep going and find somewhere to camp." He kicked his horse forward and I rode behind him. The idea of spending the night in these cursed woods made my heart tremor with anxiety.

The wind whispered through the trees with an eerie howl, raising the hairs on my arms. My heart dropped as the color drained from the already bleak world. Raj turned off the trail, searching for someplace suitable to camp. Something moved in the trees, but as I focused, in the dim light, I saw nothing. Maybe my mind was playing tricks.

The ground dipped lower. Rocky cliffs interspersed the trees.

Up ahead, a clearing opened. A sheer wall of rocks overshadowed the clearing, giving a little protection from the wind.

"We'll camp here," Raj said, stopping his horse and dismounting. I did the same. Thinking of everything that needed to be done helped keep my mind off spending the night in the forest. We stayed busy with unsaddling the horses, giving them water and a scanty scoop of oats, scavenging for firewood, building a fire, and preparing the soup.

By the time we sat in front of a crackling fire, a boiling pot of thick stew atop the coals, and the heavenly scent of boiled vegetables filling the air, I finally felt as if I could let down my guard—at least a little. Nothing had attacked us yet. Maybe we were safe.

I stretched my hands toward the fire, reveling in its warmth. Raj ladled two bowls of soup and we ate quietly. The broth was thick, as we didn't have much water to spare, but the carrots and potatoes were soft and melted in my mouth. I thought of Rapunzel as I ate. If the high sorcerer's squadrons had discovered I was missing, it meant they must've entered the tower. Had they harmed her?

She was the high sorcerer's daughter. They would've been fools to touch her. Still, I worried. I even worried about Jester, although the cat could take care of himself. He never ceased to amaze me at the amounts of lizards and birds he brought into our tower. Still, I worried about him.

"What are you thinking about?" Raj asked me.

"I'm worried about Rapunzel. If we don't get the shears and return to her, or if we're killed and never return…" I couldn't finish. Thinking of Rapunzel living forever in that tower was a depressing thought. "I'm also worried about the cat," I added. "It's silly, I know."

"It's not silly. I worry about the prince as well. But it does no good to ponder on those thoughts. We must believe we will succeed. We must imagine how it will be to have the high sorcerer overthrown, Prince Merek as our new ruler. Rapunzel as our queen. Maybe then we can live the lives we want."

"What life do you want?"

He smiled, a thin stretching of his lips that didn't touch his eyes. "What I want I will never have. I want to live with my family in the Outerlands. I want to make my father proud and carry on his name—marry an Outlander and raise a family, but I want to be a knight as well. I will never have both."

The fire popped sparks that burned bright, and then faded. I pondered Raj's words. Why did it bother me that he wanted to marry an Outlander? It shouldn't have mattered. But I wasn't an Outlander. And somehow, that seemed important.

"What about you?" Raj asked. "What will you do if you're freed from the tower?"

I didn't know what to say. I'd never pondered it before, because I never thought it was a possibility. "I'm not sure. My mother worked selling herbs and plants from her garden, but I've always been lousy at growing things. I'm not sure what's out there for me. To be honest, there aren't many options for someone like me. I guess I would go back to Willow Wood. It's the closest thing to home I know. I had some success selling potions and herbs. I could make a decent living, I think. Plus, I'd have Jester for company. It wouldn't be so bad."

"But haven't you ever wanted anything more?"

"Like what?"

"Adventure. Making the world a better place. That sort of thing."

"I'm already doing that, aren't I? To be honest, it's a dangerous way to live. I'm not sure I want to continue with it for the rest of my life."

I had other dreams as well, ones I felt were too personal to share with him. I wanted what I'd seen other women in the village have. Someday I wanted a family of my own. My father died when I was young, and my mother had made foolish decisions that eventually got her killed. I felt cheated at never having a real family, and one day, if I lived long enough, I wanted to give my own children a better life.

As the fire dwindled, Raj and I rolled out our sleeping packs, although I didn't know how I would get any sleep in a place like this. The frogs continued their incessant croaking as I laid down, pulling the blanket over me, small sticks poking my back through the thin layer of the woven mat.

Raj had offered to take the first watch. He sat hunched near the fire, his sword resting across his lap. The flames illuminated his profile—the flat plane of his forehead, the wide bridge of his nose, his full lips, and strong jaw. It wouldn't be hard for him to find an Outlander wife. He was honorable—almost to a fault—and he was pleasant to be around. I also had to admit that he wasn't bad to look at, either. Any Outlander girl would be lucky to have him as a husband. I almost wished I were an Outlander, just for that.

But I wasn't. And although he'd complimented my bravery and said I had lovely hair, I couldn't imagine him ever wanting me for a wife. I was a witch, after all. He feared witches.

I closed my eyes, not wanting to look at him any longer, feeling the tiniest bit of loneliness as I did. I hadn't admitted it to Raj, but if things were to work out the way we planned—with Rapunzel restored and Prince Merek as king—then I would have nothing left. Rapunzel was the only person I knew and cared for. After she went away to live as queen in a faraway castle, I would be nothing.

But it was selfish for me to think that way. I couldn't allow Rapunzel to continue how she was now. I would have to let her go.

Howling shocked me out of my thoughts. Before I could make sense of anything, I got to my feet, clutching the hilt of my knife, scanning the forest, my heart pounding. My hands shook as I backed toward the fire.

A blur sped from the forest and into the clearing—all inky blackness, fur, and glowing yellow eyes.

The creature stood taller than Raj. It had the lean appearance a wolf—though only by definition. The animal was a behemoth, a monster. Snapping its teeth, it stood over Raj.

The beast lunged so fast, it must've been using magic. All I saw was a blur of black, and then Raj hit the ground hard, his sword falling out of reach. Bone crunched as the monster snapped Raj's shoulder.

Raj cried out—a sound so pain-filled it made tears spring to my eyes. Reacting on instinct and adrenaline, and certainly not sound judgment, I grabbed a long stick from the fire, its tip ablaze, and sprinted toward the monster.

I impaled the beast's flank. The monster yelped, rounding on me. Its heated breath washed over me, and its maddening yellow eyes burned with rage and fury, much more intelligent than any ordinary wolf.

Behind the wolf, Raj lay writhing on the ground.

I held the fiery stick between me and the wolf. In my other hand, I clutched my knife. Neither weapon would do any good.

SIX

THE WOLF SNAPPED ITS MASSIVE jaws at my face. Firelight reflected off its wicked sharp teeth, dripping with saliva. It knocked me down and pinned me to the ground, its heavy paws on my chest, making it impossible for me to draw in a breath.

I stabbed my knife into one of its paws, and it howled, releasing me. I took the opportunity to scramble out of its reach. The flame extinguished from the stick I'd been carrying. I sprinted toward the fire, hoping to find another one—any sort of weapon would help at this point.

When I reached the fire, I grabbed another stick, but as I rounded, the clearing remained empty. Raj limped toward me. Blood seeped from punctures in the metal plate covering his shoulder. He dragged his sword behind him as he walked toward me.

"Where's the wolf?" he asked, his voice ragged.

"I don't know. You're hurt!"

"Yes. It's not bad."

"I can heal you."

"No time."

He made it to my side, and we faced the forest. Tree limbs rustled. Howls echoed, angry and insistent. The horses shrieked, their eyes wide as they attempted to pull free from the trees.

"There are more out there," Raj said.

"Yes, but where?"

Behind me, the fire felt as if it were burning my skin, but I didn't dare step away from it.

Blurs appeared in the forest. A half dozen wolves appeared. Chills prickled my neck as the pack stared us down. How would we ever defeat them all? There were too many. We'd barely survived one.

Raj took a step forward and raised his sword.

"Raj, what are you doing?"

"I told you I would defend you. So I will."

He charged the wolf closest to us. His battle cry reverberated as he swung his sword. The animals swarmed like hornets.

Raj moved on lithe feet, his sword flashing as it reflected the firelight. He stabbed one wolf, dodged an attack, then stabbed another. Each movement was like a dance, fluid and with purpose, every action deliberate. He swung the sword in an arc, keeping the beasts from attacking while driving them away.

One of the wolves dove at him, but he stabbed its chest. Its scream ripped through the air as it retreated into the trees. More came at him, but he drove them away.

I watched in awe.

He said he would defend me. I had no idea what talent he had with the sword. If I'd known, perhaps I wouldn't have hesitated to travel with him.

The wolves retreated in a matter of minutes.

"Raj..." I said as he stood before me. His eyes were dark and intense. Blood splattered his breastplate as he breathed heavily. I stood in stunned silence. He wasn't talented—he was a master of swordplay. I felt unworthy to stand in his presence.

A shadow moved behind him. He rounded as a wolf padded into the clearing. Unlike the others, this beast was of average height. Its silvery gray fur sheathed its sleek body. An empty socket replaced one of its eyes. It was also missing a paw, and it limped toward us, keeping its front left stump tucked protectively under its chest.

The wolf circled the clearing, keeping its one eye focused on us. Raj and I didn't move. I couldn't imagine battling the beast. It was already wounded so badly that killing it seemed like a spiteful thing to do.

When the wolf reached the edge of the firelight, it stopped, then whined. Raj and I exchanged glances. I took a step toward the wolf.

"Careful," Raj said.

"It's okay. I don't think he'll hurt us."

"But it could be a spirit of some sort. You never know in a place like this."

I carefully stretched my hand toward the wolf, allowing it to sniff my fingers.

"There," I said soothingly. "You're not so bad, are you?" I turned to Raj. "He's all right. I think he's a friend."

"Are you sure?"

"Yes, I'm—"

Light blinded me. The wolf's coat shimmered as if it were on fire.

"Gothel, get back!"

I stumbled away from the wolf as its shape changed. Fur morphed to skin and clothing. Wiry gray hair and a beard grew from the humanlike head. A dwarf man lay where the wolf had been. He wore a patch over one eye, and a wooden peg replaced his left leg.

Coughing racked the small man's body as he lay huddled on the ground. Raj approached him, gripping his sword, his eyes narrowed with suspicion.

"Who are you?" Raj demanded.

The dwarf cursed, his voice gravelly, growling, almost wolf-like.

"Put down your sword," I said to Raj. "He won't hurt us."

"The witch is right," the dwarf said.

"How can I be sure? He's a creature of magic, isn't he?" He waved his sword at the dwarf. "Who are you?" he demanded.

The dwarf snarled, his wrinkled face scrunched, making him look menacing.

I stepped between the two. "We don't mean you any harm," I said.

"Tell that to the big guy," the dwarf growled.

I glanced at Raj. "Put your sword down, all right? I can handle this."

Raj looked as if he wanted to argue, but he backed away, sat by the fire, and placed his sword on the ground. I turned back to the dwarf.

"Who are you?" I asked gently.

The dwarf stood tall and straightened his wrinkled tunic. Dried splotches of mud covered his shirt and breeches, and dirt caked his one boot. His good eye focused on me, the whites tinted yellow, looking wolfish.

"I am a cursed man, as you may have noticed. A witch changed me years ago. Took my eye and my foot, too. And if that wasn't enough, she took my name."

"What do you mean?"

"Stole it from me. My own name. Took it."

"You don't know your name?"

He shook his head.

"What are you doing in these woods?" I asked.

"Watching. Waiting."

"Waiting for what?"

"Another witch. And it looks like I've found one."

"Do not harm her," Raj called.

"I've no intention of harming the one who will restore me."

"You want me to restore you?" I asked.

The dwarf nodded.

"How?" I asked.

He shrugged, then limped to our fire and sat. "That's for you to figure out."

I followed him to the fire where he stretched his gnarled fingers toward the flames. Raj winced as he sat up, and I decided I couldn't be distracted by a shape-changing wolf any longer.

I found my pack near my sleeping pallet and brought it to where Raj sat. I fumbled through my bag's contents, looking for a bottle of cleaning ointment, a needle and thread, a small pair of scissors, and a satchel of healing herbs. As I searched, the dwarf cleared his throat.

"Fendelick. Nurburton. No. Bustlewort. No, no, no."

"What are you going on about?" Raj asked.

"My name!" he called back. "My name, my name!"

Raj and I traded glances. I gently unbuckled the metal plate from Raj's shoulder. He winced as I lifted it off. Blood soaked his shirt, and I cut away the fabric until I could pull it apart. Gaping holes tore through his flesh.

The raw, iron-rich scent of blood filled the air. My stomach soured, but I pushed aside my queasiness and focused on wiping the skin clean.

"Have you anything to eat?" the dwarf asked.

"Not right now," I said. "Sorry, I'm a bit busy."

"Ah well, I thought I would try."

"How long are you staying here?" Raj asked, trying to keep a straight face as I cleaned one of the wounds.

"As long as it takes. When your witch cures me, I shall be on my merry way." He laughed, an awkward giggling that made him wheeze and start coughing.

"How did you know she was a witch?"

"Been following you since you entered the forest. That hair gave her away. No one's got hair that color unless there's magic in their veins. I knew she must've been a witch. So, I decided she'd be the one to heal me." He burped, loud and low, then pounded his chest with his fist. "I'm a might gassy. You'll have to pardon me."

"Heal him soon," Raj whispered through clenched teeth.

"I don't know how," I whispered back.

"You don't?"

"No idea."

Raj sighed. "I don't trust him."

Reluctantly, I had to agree with Raj. He hadn't harmed us, but there was definitely something off about the dwarf.

"Ouch," Raj said as I poked the wound with my cloth.

"I know. I'm sorry, but it needs to be cleaned."

He nodded, breathing deeply. I didn't envy him having to go through this, but there was nothing to be done about it. When I finished cleaning, I inspected the gashes. Blood no longer seeped free.

"I think you'll be okay. The wounds didn't puncture your life vein. But I will have to stitch the flesh back together."

I grabbed up my needle and thread. The metal gleamed in the dim firelight as I held it up for him to see.

"This will hurt," I said.

He only nodded, gritting his teeth as I began stitching his flesh back together.

"Oi, if that's how you're to heal me, then I want no part of it." The dwarf laughed again, amused by his own words. "I'm only joking, of course. I can't stand another day without me eye or leg—and losing me name was the worst. The worst. Have you ever lost your name? You'd know if you had. It sits in the back of your mind, taunting you always, like a fly waiting to be swatted, buzzing, buzzing, buzzing, but never to be caught. Nivelbrick, Jundlewort... No. No. No."

"You doing okay?" I asked Raj, who held completely still as he focused on the flames.

A slight nod of his head was the only answer he gave.

"Almost done," I said.

I tied off the last knot, then wrapped his shoulder in a roll of clean fabric that I got from my pack.

"That's it," I said, smiling. "I'm done."

He inspected his shoulder, running his fingers gently over the rolled fabric.

"Be careful before fighting with wolves next time," I said.

"I'll keep that in mind." His voice was soft, low, and caused heat to rise to my cheeks. I quickly glanced away, busying myself with putting my healing supplies back in my pack.

The dwarf yawned, stretching his arms over his head. "If you two don't mind, I think I'll switch back. It's easier to sleep when I don't have to worry about what I'm called. Easier as a wolf, you see."

"Very well," I said.

Raj sat up, scrutinizing the dwarf with narrowed eyes. "You should know that we're on a dangerous quest to the Ice Mountains in the northern lands. We're preparing to meet two awfully mean witches who can kill you with a mere glance. Tagging along with us could very well lead to your death. Plus, not to cause offense, but we can't afford to be slowed down. If you can't keep pace with us, I'll kindly ask you to find another witch who's not busy trying to save our lands from a maniacal, murderous sorcerer."

"No need to be concerned. I'm quick on my three feet when I'm a wolf, sure enough. You'll not even notice I'm here. Plus, you might be interested to know that I can lead you out of this forest."

Raj sat up. "You can?"

"Yes, yes. You'll see. I'll get you out of these woods in no time at all."

"How?" I asked. "We wandered through the woods all day and only went in circles."

"Ah, my lady, for something like this, you just need to know the right person." He gave me a sly grin, as if he knew something I didn't. "Now, if you'll please excuse me. I'd like a bit of a nap." Light shone from his skin as his body morphed from that of a dwarf back to a wolf. The beast sat on its haunches, then got to his feet, and trotted around our camp, sniffing, until he found a spot by the fire. He laid down with his chin resting on his only front paw.

"I prefer him in this form," Raj said.

"He's not so bad."

"He's following us all the way to the northern lands unless you cure him first. Please cure him."

"I can't."

"Why not?"

"Because whoever put that spell on him will have to do it. He's missing a leg and an eye, which means she holds power over him. It also means I can never use any magic on him."

"Then you need to tell him you can't do it. Otherwise, he'll keep following us."

I glanced at the wolf, his eyes closed, ears relaxed. Could he hear what we said?

"There may be a way," I said.

"Yes, how?"

"His name. She removed it for good reason. If he were to remember it, one could use it in a spell to restore him."

Raj sighed, looking disappointed. "Isn't there another witch he could pester about this?"

"Yes, if you can convince him to find one. In the meantime, I'd like to get some sleep. Who knows? Maybe he'll be true to his word and help us find our way out of this forest."

Raj grunted. "It makes me wonder why the witch cursed him in the first place. What did he do to deserve it?"

I shook my head. "Some witches can be spiteful and petty. He may have done nothing more than steal vegetables from her garden."

"Or he may have done something really awful."

"Yes, that's also a possibility. At least he agreed to guide us out of the forest."

"Let's hope he does it."

I watched the sleeping wolf, seeming at peace as he rested by the fire, wondering if he were someone to be trusted and could get us out of these woods. I stood and turned toward my sleeping pack when Raj caught my hand. Warm, callused skin cradled my own. His touch didn't feel how I'd expected, which made me wonder, had I been expecting him to touch me?

"Gothel, thank you for healing me."

"It was nothing."

"No." He stood close to me. His warmth radiated around me, making my heart flutter. He brushed his hand over my cheek, pushing a strand of hair behind my ear. "You deserve my thanks. I've never met anyone with talents like yours."

"Oh," I mumbled, my insides twisting. I couldn't look into his eyes. What would happen to me then? No. I couldn't do that. I stepped away from him. "Good night, Raj."

He looked confused, hurt maybe, as I backed toward my sleeping pallet, but I wasn't sure what to make of my feelings, and being so close to him was difficult. I laid down and stared up at the stars, but it didn't stop my heart from pounding. Raj made me feel things I'd never experienced before. My mother had never prepared me for any of this. Maybe she would have if I'd been a little older. We could have had those talks that women gave to their daughters, but all I knew of them were the brief conversations of the cooks in the castle kitchens, or the passing words of young girls in the streets of Willow Wood. I knew nothing of men, or what they could do, or why Raj made me feel the way he did. Was it normal?

Perhaps it wasn't. Maybe I'd come down with a sickness.

I rolled to my side, looking out over the forest. With my back to Raj, I listened to his footsteps as he walked back to the fire, and the creaking of his armor when he sat on the log. For some inexplicable reason, I wanted him near me. I wanted to feel his warmth again. What would it be like to lay with his arms around me?

Squeezing my eyes shut, I willed the feelings to go away. They couldn't be good, or normal.

My mind wandered, and finally, my heart stopped racing, allowing me to drift to sleep.

SEVEN

THE MORNING ARRIVED GRAY AND dreary as we rode our horses down the forest path. I hadn't slept well. My dreams had been plagued with nightmares of giant wolves, and a certain man with dark, exotic eyes and gentle hands. I'd only spoken a few words to Raj all morning. In truth, I felt too awkward to speak to him casually. What if everything I said sounded ridiculous? For whatever reason, I didn't want to sound ridiculous. I wanted to sound smart and witty. But all I felt was awkwardness, so I remained silent.

The wolf trotted ahead of us. He moved with determined focus, his head held low, nose sniffing the ground as he paced down the trail. We'd rode through the same scenery of dead trees and red pools of water, and I was beginning to lose faith in him.

My horse snorted, pinning her ears. I patted her neck to keep her calm, though it seemed the only thing to put her in better spirits would be to leave the forest.

We crested a hill. The wolf stopped, looking out over the landscape. Beneath us, the trees thinned, and I spotted the first greenery since we'd entered Spirit Woods. Pastureland replaced the dreary monotony of dead trees, and I breathed a sigh of relief. Was it possible? Were we finally leaving?

The wolf sat on his haunches and sniffed the air.

"Good job, Wolf," I said. "You did it."

"But how?" Raj asked. "We wandered in circles all day yesterday."

"I don't know." I glanced at the wolf. "I guess you just have to know the right person."

He gave a playful yelp, then led us down the trail. I half expected the forest to swallow us up and send us back to the beginning of the trail, or giant wolves to jump out and attack us, but nothing happened, and we finally approached the edge of the woods.

The world brightened as we left the enchanted forest behind us. Green grass rolled in waves along either side of the road. The air held the scent of sunlight. Feeling it again on my skin was more exhilarating than I thought possible.

I cautiously pushed the hood off my head, letting the sunlight bathe my hair that trailed behind me as we rode. I wasn't sure I'd ever felt so free. The sensation was foreign to me. I'd been locked away in the tower for so long, and being out on the open road, with the wind and the sun on my skin, was a new experience.

In Willow Wood, I hardly ever traveled during the day. My hair stayed hidden in the darkness, and that was the way I wanted it.

Raj had asked me what I wanted to do with my life, and now I knew the answer.

I wanted freedom.

The unexpected emotions caught me off guard, and I glanced back at Raj who trailed behind me. Watching me, his curious gaze lingered on my hair. Reluctantly, I pulled the cowl back over my head, covering my hair, resuming my sentence in the shadows once again.

Raj rode up next to me and kept pace with my horse.

"Why do you wear the cowl now?" he asked.

"I've told you before."

"No. You said it was for protection—to stay hidden from those who might harm you. But why do you wear it now?"

I didn't know what to say, so I said nothing.

"Is it because of me?" he asked.

"No..."

"You fear me?"

"I don't. Not exactly."

"Then what?"

I fisted my hands around the reins, the leather straps smooth and warm, wishing he would've just stayed behind me and not decided to have a conversation.

"I don't fear you, but maybe I don't trust you, either."

He nodded, his jaw clenched, as if unhappy with my answer. "What can I do to earn your trust?"

"I don't know. Maybe you can't."

"What does that mean?"

I pondered his question before speaking. "I've never known many men in my life, and the ones I know, like the high sorcerer, are hardly people I trust. I barely knew my own father. I've been in a tower with a cat and a half-sane companion for the last five years. I guess I don't know how to trust anyone, to be honest."

And I'd just opened up to him. I certainly hadn't meant to. What had happened to staying quiet? Not only had I spoken, but I'd divulged an intimate piece of myself that I'd never told anyone before. I'd almost admitted to him that I was a miserable, lonely wretch. This was going too far.

"I thank you for your honesty," he said.

Don't get used to it.

"Why did you leave me last night?" Raj asked.

"Leave you?"

"Yes, I was trying to thank you for healing me, and then you left. This morning, you've hardly spoken a word. Why?"

I looked away. "I don't know."

"I only meant to compliment you. I don't understand why you're avoiding me."

"I'm not avoiding you," I said without much conviction.

"Have I offended you somehow? Are you upset because I was injured by the wolf and didn't protect you as I should have?"

"What? Of course not! You saved my life. I didn't realize how incredible you were at wielding a blade. You really are an amazing fighter, and very talented, and amazing. You're really… amazing." I was stumbling over my words, so I stopped talking and took a deep breath. "You're very good with a sword," I stated, enunciating so I wouldn't stumble, an edge of formality to my voice.

He grinned. "You think I'm an amazing fighter?"

"Yes, but don't let it go to your head."

"Oh, I won't." He winked.

I swallowed hard, fighting that flighty feeling deep in my stomach. I kicked my horse ahead, hoping he hadn't seen my burning cheeks. As I left him behind, I didn't want to contemplate a romantic relationship with him, because I knew logically, it could never happen. Heaven knew he'd gotten too close already. Maintaining my distance from him was the only option I had. I couldn't allow myself to open up to him again.

The grasslands gave way to sloping hills. When the sun crested the sky's zenith, the dark shapes of mountains appeared on the horizon.

"The Wrallic Mountains," Raj said, riding his horse beside mine.

"Yes. We're almost to the old castle," I said. "It's in the valley just beyond the mountains."

Sable pranced, and I pulled her to a stop. Raj halted his horse beside mine. Uneasiness settled over me. It had been five years, but sometimes it felt like yesterday when I lived there. I knew it wouldn't be the same, but the memories of that place still haunted me.

"Are you okay?" Raj asked me.

I glanced at him, remembering my vow not to open up to him. "Yes, I'm sure I'll be fine."

"You are? You don't look fine."

I sighed. This wouldn't be as easy as I'd thought. "It was my home once. I guess I'm anxious about returning."

"I understand. I suppose I'll be faced with the same problem once we reach the Outerlands. It's not easy going back to a place with so many memories when you know it will never be the same."

I only nodded, and we continued down the road. Trees dotted the path, their limbs creaking in the breeze. Leaves tumbled across the road, bringing the scent of fall. Ahead, I spotted a tree, its limbs heavy with shiny red fruit.

"Apples," I said.

"Yes. We should stop here for our midday meal. Our supplies are low as it is," Raj said.

We pulled our horses to a stop. As we dismounted and tied them to the tree, my gaze snagged on the looming mountains, jagged purple spires against the sky.

Beyond those mountains was the castle—the place I had once called home—the place my mother had been killed. I wasn't sure I was ready to face those memories, and I wasn't sure I would *ever* be ready to face them, but if I wanted to save Rapunzel, I didn't have a choice.

I pushed my misgivings aside and approached the apple tree. Some of the fruit had fallen to the ground, some of it rotten, other pieces still pristine. I gathered a few of the unbruised apples, excited by the prospect of eating fresh fruit, when Raj approached me. I couldn't find it within me to look at his eyes.

"I spotted a stream down the hill," he said. "I'm going to refill our canteens and take the horses to get fresh water. Do you mind gathering a few extra apples for our journey?"

"No, I don't mind." I cleared my throat, still refusing to look up at him.

"Gothel, is something wrong?"

"Wrong? No." I reached for another apple.

"Then why won't you look at me?"

"Because I'm busy."

He lingered a little longer, but he didn't push the issue as he turned and walked away. I breathed a sigh of relief. I wasn't sure what was worse—opening up to him about my feelings or avoiding him.

He grabbed the horses' reins and untied them, then paced down the hill and out of sight behind the brush. The wolf trotted to me, his tongue lolling, and sat at my side. I patted his head, his fur wiry and matted with burrs. His one good eye smiled up at me.

As I began collecting apples, the wolf stayed at my side, sniffing some of them. I picked up a few and placed them in a pile. The wolf stood beneath the tree, and the air filled with light as he transformed, his fur morphing to skin and clothing, gray hair sprouting from his head and growing along his jaw in an unkempt beard.

The dwarf snorted as he lay on the ground, patting his pockets, and adjusting the patch over his eye. It was going to take some time for me to get used to that.

"Hello," I said.

He only snorted, his mouth puckered, as if he'd eaten something sour.

"What are you doing?" he asked.

"Collecting apples—"

"No, no. I mean, what are you doing with that whelp?"

"I beg your pardon?"

"That young man—the one you've been avoiding?"

"Avoiding?"

"Yes. Avoiding!"

I placed my hands on my hips. "You've been spying?"

"Observing. And let me tell you something—you're a daft fool."

"What?"

"Yes, you heard what I said."

"How dare you—"

"Blind, you are. Stupid, too."

This was going too far. "Listen here," I snapped. "You asked for me to heal you. We've allowed you to accompany us on our journey. If you would like to continue, then I suggest you behave civilly. Name calling is unwelcome."

"I've more names to call than that. If you keep it up, you're likely to end up like me. Alone and cursed. You don't realize what you're doing, so I'm forced to point it out. If you reject him, he'll take it hard, and you'll never have another chance. Some maids think because they have charm and wit, they can afford to reject a man, and that he'll fight to get them back again. It isn't true. A man like your squire will not come back once he's been rejected. He's too honorable. He wouldn't want to be pushy. He'll leave and not return. Do you understand?"

My blood boiled, and I had to force myself to stop breathing so fast. He was one person, after all. Why should I let his words hurt me so much?

"You've no right meddling in my affairs," I said.

"I've every right."

"Sir," I said, tempering my voice to keep from snapping at him. "Let me remind you that I didn't ask for your advice. What goes on between me and the squire is my business. Plus, he's an Outlander, and he wants nothing to do with a person like me. He told me himself he prefers Outlander girls. It would be vile and wrong of me to lead him on when I have no right doing such a thing."

The dwarf grunted.

"Plus, I don't even like him."

"Ha! That's the boldest lie you've told yet."

Frustrated, I turned away from him to continue collecting apples. How dare he intrude on my personal affairs! I was tempted to send him away this moment, as I was sure I couldn't tolerate him any longer. His words made no sense. Lying? I hadn't told a single lie to anyone since I'd started this journey.

The dwarf's mind was obviously cracked. He was a lunatic for sure.

Fire burned in my chest, and the anger made tears

spring to my eyes. I used my apron to wipe them away.

You'll never have another chance.

Was it true?

Wasn't it enough that I had to leave Rapunzel behind to go on this quest? To be confronted by feelings I'd never asked for only complicated matters. Worse, the stupid dwarf was right, and I knew it.

Somehow, the feeling of being apart from Raj frightened me. Did I love him? Of course not. What an absurd notion. But I didn't want to be separated from him either, and the more I pushed away from him, the quicker it would happen.

Still, I couldn't allow the dwarf to keep up with his ramblings. Would he say the same things to Raj when he returned? It would completely mortify me. This had to stop, and I knew what I had to do.

"Dwarf," I said. "Tell me again—what's your name?"

"I've told you I bloody don't know it."

"Was it Alfinstock? Musklewort, maybe?"

"No." His gaze wandered to the treetops, seeming as if the gears in his head were shifting focus. "Hifflewump. Ah, what was it?"

I smiled inwardly. Was it wrong of me to manipulate his weakness to get him off my back? No. After what he'd called me.

No.

Raj returned with the horses.

"I've gathered a few apples," I said, sitting on the grass.

"Good. I've got fresh water." He held out a canteen and I took it from him. Although I tried to avoid it, my fingers brushed his, making butterflies flit through my stomach, and I ground my teeth.

He sat across from me, his eyes on the road as he began eating an apple. We didn't speak, and I was fine with that.

As we finished our meal, dark clouds blocked out the sunlight, and we quickly mounted our horses. The dwarf stayed under the tree, still mumbling one name after another.

"How long has he been transformed?" Raj asked.

"Not long. He's been mumbling names this whole time. I pity the creature." I hoped the goddess forgave me for omitting the truth, but there was no way I could tell Raj of the poison the dwarf had been spouting. I would be humiliated for the rest of eternity.

"I see." He narrowed his eyes at the dwarf. "I'm still not convinced he's friendly."

"I'm starting to agree."

"You are?"

"Yes. But unless we can think of what do with him, I'm afraid we're stuck."

Raj mounted his horse. I stayed back with the dwarf. Still mumbling, he sat under the tree, too caught up in his own thoughts to pay us any notice.

Could I leave him here? He'd more than deserved it. He'd been rude and demanding. Then again, I wouldn't feel right leaving him here alone. Grudgingly, I spoke up.

"Dwarf," I called. "We're leaving."

He looked up, eyes wide, as if coming out of a trance. "Aye, I can see that," he snapped. He got to his feet. With a flash of light, a wolf stood in his place. I mounted my horse, then kicked her to a trot to catch up with Raj. The wolf followed on quiet feet, keeping pace beside my horse, his tongue lolling.

The afternoon turned chill as thick clouds blanketed the sky. The road grew steeper as we approached the mountains. Sable had trouble keeping up with Raj's Arabian mare, who seemed more suited to steep inclines.

Walls of granite covered in vines lined the roadside as our horses climbed. My fingers were growing numb as I held to the reins. Sounds of the horses' hoof steps, coupled with their exhalations, broke up the silence.

My thighs ached as I clung to the saddle. My thin riding breeches were the only thing to keep me from chafing. I'd never ridden so much in my entire life, and I couldn't say that I was anxious to do it ever again.

As afternoon turned to evening, we finally crested the mountain range. I stopped my horse next to Raj's, who stood looking out over the valley.

The old castle sat at the valley's center, tall spires reaching toward the sky, reminding me of my sewing needles, sharp spikes that seemed to poke through the hovering, misty clouds gathered around their tops. Vines encased the castle, making it seem as if the structure were part of the ground. The remains of the town surrounded the fortress, though only ruined structures remained. I was shocked at how five years of neglect made the place look so old. Nature had a way of reclaiming its own.

Memories flooded back as I looked at the castle. I remembered looking back as the high sorcerer took me away to the tower. He'd tied my hands together, and I still remembered the sting of the ropes as they left blisters on my skin, although I'd been too afraid to run even if I could have. I thought I would never return, yet here I was, prepared to enter again.

Without speaking, we took the road descending into

the valley. Cobblestones appeared in patches beneath the grass. At one point, this had been a major thoroughfare leading to the castle, but now, it was nothing more than a footpath, barely visible beneath the weeds.

The wind picked up, slow at first, but gaining strength until it blustered so hard I had to tug on my cowl to keep it from flying off. Strands of blue hair beat against my face. The air smelled of rain, and cold droplets splashed my skin as we weaved between the dilapidated buildings and approached the castle gates. I searched for our old cottage but couldn't find it. Maybe it was better that I didn't see it. Too many memories I needed to forget.

We neared the end of the lane where the castle loomed over us. Behind it, the backdrop of the gray sky reflected off the parapets, making them blend in with the approaching darkness. Vines with thick bark and thorns the length of my ring fingers encased the castle. Stones crumbled beneath the vines. The drawbridge was barely visible through the mass of woody growth, and the incessant wind shrieked through the open portcullis.

The wolf trailed behind us as Raj dismounted his horse, and I did the same.

"What should we do with the horses?" Raj called over the wind.

"We can leave them in the old stables," I answered. "Follow me."

Grasping Sable's reins, I walked around the castle. The stables sat away from the towering walls. Parts of the thatched roof had collapsed, but the wooden posts remained standing, and inside, the stalls were dry. The air held the scent of moldy hay. Rats scattered, their tiny feet pattering, as I tied Sable's reins to a post. Outside, the wind shrieked, but in here, the air remained calm. The wolf sat just inside the entryway, keeping to himself.

"Will the horses be safe here?" Raj asked.

"They should be safe enough."

"Very well. Do you know where to find the radish?"

"Yes, we'll have to follow the vines. When my mother cursed the king, she planted it in the castle's dungeons, then caused it to grow the vines that you see everywhere. If we find the source of the vines, we'll find the radish."

"Good. I'd like to get this over with as soon as we can. That castle gives me a bad feeling."

"You're not the only one."

I shuddered as I thought of entering the castle. What would we find? Would there be bodies?

I'd heard rumors of what had happened after I'd left— of the townsfolk rioting and trying to take the palace, of them being slaughtered by his squadrons inside, of the thieves that lived there now. I'd never known whether to believe the rumors.

We left the stables and rounded the outer bailey. Facing the looming drawbridge, I took a deep breath before entering. I'd already made up my mind to do this. Now, I'd have to live with that decision, even if it cost more than I was able to pay.

EIGHT

OUR FOOTSTEPS ECHOED AS WE walked into the massive entryway. Raj grabbed a torch from one of the sconces, then lit it with his flint rock. Flames crackled and sputtered as they flared to life. The acrid scent of smoke filled the air as we continued through the cavernous, arching chamber.

Vines twisted around the walls, seeming to consume them. Smashed vases covered in dust lay on the ground. Some of the cracked remains still held onto their colors. I spotted painted pink cherry blossoms on one of them. The sight brought back memories of running down this hallway with the vases lining either side, wishing I could've touched one, afraid of getting whipped if I did.

I knelt beside a crushed piece and placed my fingers atop it, laughing to myself. Well, at least I'd finally gotten to touch one, though now the once treasured piece was nothing more than discarded rubble, left to turn to dust along with the rest of the castle.

After standing, I continued with Raj and the wolf at my side. Our bootsteps crunched over the debris on the floor. Firelight flickered over the walls. Some of the portraits were still visible beneath the vines. Empty gazes stared from the canvas. Most depicted the royal family, people who lived so long ago, I couldn't recall their names.

We made it through the main foyer and into a hallway that led to the stairs. The air became staler as we took the stairs to the dungeons. The scent of rot lingered when we stepped off the staircase and onto the bottom floor.

The dungeons spread out before us, though the vines had grown so thick, it appeared as if they'd replaced the walls completely. It seemed as if nothing remained of the bricks and mortar, and we walked through a strange forest of thorns. We stepped over the growth crisscrossing the floor as we paced through the dungeons.

Unlike the area above, in some places, the snaking plants here grew with green shoots that fluttered as we walked past. My mother had created the vines to be impervious to flames, and to never need water, air, or sunlight—they were basically impossible to destroy. High Sorcerer Varlocke had found out the hard way.

The wolf followed us on silent paws. The glow of the torch's flame highlighted the rusting gates barring the cells. A rotting corpse lay on the ground in one of the cells, the tunic and cape chewed by rats, the face little more than a skull. My insides squirmed at the sight of the human remains. He must've been abandoned in this place when the vines had forced the high sorcerer from the castle. I couldn't imagine enduring such a death—to be locked away, left to starve and die.

We stepped into a hallway that branched in either direction.

"Which way?" Raj asked.

I glanced at the green shoots growing from the vines. To the right, only a few sprouted, but in the passageway to our left, they covered everything.

"I think we should follow the shoots. There will be more growing around the radish."

We turned and followed the hallway, stepping carefully over the brambles that grew thicker the farther we went. The flame from our torch sputtered, casting a hazy glow over the woody bark covering the twisting plants. Sounds of rhythmic beating came from up ahead, reminding me of the drumbeats I'd heard on the high sorcerer's battlefields many years ago.

The hallway opened to form a circular chamber. Cells lined the walls, and in the center of the floor sat what could have once been a well, with intricate stonework etching the marble. Greenish light shone from the well's interior, and a single vine rose from the well's opening. The gnarled protrusion grew with long spiky thorns.

We approached the well. I arrived first and looked inside. Pulsing green magic shone from a radish about the size of a human heart.

Raj stepped beside me and looked inside the well. "This is it?"

"Yes, I think so. It's been altered by my mother's magic."

I removed the dagger from my boot. "I'm going to cut a piece from it, but I'm not sure what will happen when I do. Keep a watch out."

Raj nodded, unsheathing his sword and holding it at the ready. Greenish light reflected off his mirror-smooth blade.

As I lowered my hand into the well, the magic warmed my fingers. Its familiarity made me pause.

This was my mother's magic. It conjured images of

sitting next to her while she read from her spell books, her beautiful golden hair spilling down her back and over her shoulders. I remembered playing with her hair as she worked, and how she'd chide me if I pulled on it. I also remembered the magic—the way it felt as she read the spells, light on her tongue, powerful magic escaping with the words she spoke, like music.

Sometimes it seemed she'd never died. Those days were the worst.

I pushed my memories aside and reached for the radish, cutting through the red skin, revealing the pearl-white flesh beneath. Its sharp fragrance filled the air as I removed a sliver.

Holding the slice, the radish felt light in the palm of my hand. It pulsed with magic ever so faintly. I pulled a handkerchief from my knapsack, wrapped the piece inside, and tucked it into my bag.

"That was easy enough," Raj said.

Above us, the ceiling groaned. Vines moved overhead, making small pebbles fall to the ground.

"Or not," Raj added, looking up at the writhing vines.

"Now you've done it," a man's deep voice grumbled from the darkness. I rounded, searching for the source of the voice, when I spotted a tall silver-haired elf standing inside a cell, his bone-white fingers grasping the rusted bars. He had a dangerous look about him—his eyes dark and brooding, his hunched shoulders held in a defensive posture.

"Who are you?" I demanded as the vines continued to move.

"My name is Drekken Von Fiddlestrum, my lady. And you are about to be disemboweled by enchanted thorns."

"What?"

"You removed a piece of the magical radish. You didn't think it would let you leave with it, did you?"

Larger pebbles rained down on us. One of them hit my shoulder, leaving a bruise for sure. I moved toward the elf's cell.

"How did you get in here? How do you know about the radish?"

"So many questions. As you're about to be killed, I don't see why I need to answer."

"Answer her," Raj growled.

The elf glanced at Raj, taking in the Outlander warrior. With his height, his sword drawn, and his dark eyes, Raj made an impressive presence, though if it came to a fight, I had no doubt the elf could hold his own.

"Very well," the man said, the tone of his deep voice sounding brusque. "I was imprisoned because I, too, tried to stea—to *take*—a piece of the radish."

Vines moved behind us, blocking the path leading out of the room. I cursed under my breath. This was my mother's magic. I should've known something like this would happen.

"How do we get out of here?" I asked the elf.

"You don't. All I can tell you is that I hid inside one of these cells when the vines came after me, and that is how I survived. You cannot leave this place."

"That's rubbish," Raj said.

A vine snaked behind us. Raj turned and lopped it in half. The severed pieces fell to the ground with a thud, though more vines struck out at us. Spike-like thorns lashed out. One of the vines whipped toward me. I stabbed it with my knife, and it retreated, though more took its place. The wolf growled at my side, snapping at the vines, ripping them with his teeth, though it only stalled them.

Raj and I backed toward the cells. A hand reached out and yanked me back as the vines hissed and writhed like vipers. I fell back and landed inside the cell alongside Raj and the wolf. The elven man, Drekken, stood over us. He rounded and slammed the cell door behind him, trapping us inside.

Raj got to his feet, and I followed. Outside, vines whipped at the metal bars, but as they touched the iron, they retreated. Soon, the vines retracted. They resumed their place on the ceiling, looming over us, as if watching.

We stood in the cell alongside Drekken.

"Welcome to my home," he said. His large stature, dark eyes, and unusual clothes made a tremor of fear race through my heart. He wore leather pants, a black doublet, and a silver skull-shaped pendant around his neck. His pointed ears, almond-shaped eyes, and silver hair that fell in a straight wave to his waist denoted him as elven, but what was he doing here—and why was he dressed like that? The skull-shaped pendant had me worried. Was it some sort of magical talisman?

"I'm sorry we have to meet like this," he said in a deep, smooth voice, as if to put me at ease, unlike the curt tone he'd used earlier. Perhaps he'd seen the fear in my eyes. "Normally, I would break out the ale whenever I had guests such as yourselves, but I lost my flask to the vines, and I've got nothing to offer but a bit of watered wine. Would you like some?" He held up a waterskin.

"No, thank you," I said. "I'm more interested in finding a way out of here."

"If that's what you want." He took a long draw from

the waterskin. "Just so you know, it's not possible to get out. The vines won't let you leave. I've tried for two days with no luck. Our only choice is to sit and starve to death—or die in a drunken stupor, which I much prefer." He gave me a sly smile, took another draw from his waterskin, then grimaced. "Blasted watered wine. Where is my flask?"

"There's got to be a way out of here," Raj said.

"There isn't," Drekken said. "Nothing but my lute will tame them. But it's missing a string, so it's useless."

"Your lute?"

"Yes." He moved to the back of the cell where a wooden stringed instrument sat atop a bag. He picked it up, cradling the rounded wooden bowl and narrow neck. I noticed it was painted black, and a skull with flames bursting from its eyes and mouth had been painted on the back of the bowl. Odd. And a bit creepy. Who was this elf?

Drekken ran his fingers lightly over the strings that glowed silvery white.

"Is that a magical instrument?" I asked.

"Not exactly. These strands are unicorn hair. Whenever I play it, I can calm the most savage beasts, even these vines, if I could find that blasted string."

He strummed the instrument, and it played with an off-kilter sound. Beside me, the wolf whined. I patted his head.

"You see?" Drekken said. "It won't play a thing without that string. Curse my elven luck."

"Where did you lose it?" I asked.

"Near the well. I was hunched over it trying to remove a piece of the radish when those vines stole my lute. I managed to grab it back, but not before they tore off a string. Blast it all—I had the perfect plan, too. I was going to cut a piece from the radish, then use my lute to calm the vines while I escaped, but those bastard plants must've known what I was after. I never got a chance to remove anything from the radish."

"What if we were to search for the string?" Raj asked.

"Possible, yes. Will you live? No."

I stood at the bars looking out. In the pulsing, greenish glow cast from the well, the floor and walls seemed to be underwater. The dim lighting made it hard to spot anything, especially a thin strand of unicorn hair.

"It's a bloody shame," Drekken said, gently running his fingers over his lute's strings, "I could create the most beautifully haunting music. It would've brought tears to your eyes had you heard it."

"Then we'll find that string," Raj said. "If you can calm the vines with your music, it's our only chance of escaping."

"How?" I asked. "If we go out there, the vines will kill us while we're searching."

"I don't know yet," Raj said, staring intently at the well, and at the single vine growing from it.

As I stood trapped inside the cell, I racked my brain, trying to think of a way out. The image of the corpse in the dungeon surfaced in my memory, and I wasn't sure our fate would be any different from his.

But I couldn't think that way. There had to be a way out. I just needed to concentrate and come up with something. This was my mother's magic after all, if anyone could beat it, then surely, I could, except I knew my mother's powers had far surpassed mine. I possessed no natural magic. If I practiced and trained the rest of my life, I would never become as skilled as she had been. Magic was a part of her soul, a piece of herself. What chance did

I have of defeating it?

Raj paced the cell behind me, his face pensive, as if he were deep in thought. Drekken sat on the floor, his back to the wall. His fingers moved deftly over his lute's strings. He didn't play, keeping his fingers just above the strings, yet his faraway expression told me he must've heard the music, even if no one else could.

An idea struck me, so I walked to him and knelt at his side.

"Drekken," I said, "what if you were to use some other hair besides unicorn hair?"

He shook his head. "No. For the magic to work, it has to be unicorn hair."

"But what if I could create something so similar, you couldn't tell the difference?"

His eyes narrowed. "You could do that?"

"I think so. I can't promise I'll be successful, but I think it's worth trying."

He straightened. "Very well. Try it. We've got nothing to lose."

I picked up my pack. Searching through its contents, I found a vial of yarrow oil, some twine, and a satchel of dried lemon balm leaves. I used my knife to cut the twine and laid it on the floor, straightening it out until it formed a line.

Grasping the vial, I pulled out the stopper. The faint, floral scent tickled my nose.

"What's she doing?" Drekken asked Raj.

"What she's best at," Raj answered.

I looked up at Raj. He stood over me, a faint smile tugging at his lips, and I couldn't help but smile back. As our gazes connected, my heart skipped a beat.

Blast it all.

Raj was nothing but a distraction—an attractive, swoon-worthy distraction.

Looking away, I concentrated on the enchantment. The glass vial warmed in my hands as I held it. I placed my finger atop its opening, tipped it over until a drop of liquid moistened my finger, then I ran the oil along the twine, whispering a spell.

"Into the light, change your form…"

Chanting over and over, I watched as the twine began to glow. It was almost imperceptible, and took longer than it should have, yet as I continued with the spell, the twine glowed brighter.

I placed the vial aside and grabbed the satchel of lemon balm leaves. Pulling open the drawstrings, I reached inside and grasped a single leaf. I held the brittle leaf carefully to keep it from breaking. Gently, I brushed it over the twine.

"Out of the earth you come, from twine to a unicorn's hair, make us see what is not there…"

Magic pulsed from the leaf and into the twine. It was a simple spell. I'd seen my mother use it so many times, I'd memorized it and didn't need her journal. Still, the magic came strongly as I continued to chant, running the leaf from one end of the twine to the other.

White light blinded me as the twine transformed completely. I sat back, clutching the leaf as the intense heat of the magic radiated from the twine. As the light dissipated, I crawled toward the twine, no longer made of wool, but appearing to sparkle with the silvery glow of unicorn's hair.

Drekken stood over me. "Is it really unicorn hair?"

I gingerly picked up the strand. "Not exactly. But it's close. Let's hope the vines can't tell the difference."

He took the hair from me, running it through his fingers, looking suspiciously at the silver strand.

"Only one way to know for sure," he said, then turned to his lute. He ran the strand through the missing space, tightening and wrapping the long end until it held firm.

"Go ahead," Raj said. "Give it a try."

He looked up at us, hesitating as he held his fingers over the strings. "I don't think I should."

"What? Why not?" I asked.

"My music is bold, to put it lightly. I doubt you've heard anything like it. Plus, it has a strange effect on people. I'm not sure you're ready for it."

"We've heard music before," I said.

He shook his head. "Not like this."

I placed my hands on my hips. It had been a long day. I'd been nearly killed by vines, and before that, attacked by wolves, traversed the Spirit Woods, slept on the ground, forced to leave my home, and fought an attraction to an Outlander who was far too good looking to trust as my traveling companion. Plus, I missed my stupid cat.

I had no patience left, especially not for an elf with an apparent case of stage fright.

"I've created that strand so you can play your lute and free us from this place," I said. "You will play it, and you'll do it now, or I swear as the goddess is my witness, I will place the vilest curse imaginable on you. Now you'd better do it!"

Raj and Drekken looked at me with awestruck expressions.

"Please," I added.

"Fine," Drekken snapped, "but you can't claim I didn't warn you."

He strummed a chord on his lute, producing the most peculiar sound. It had a metallic, electric clang, though I knew no better way to describe it.

As he played one chord after another, my arms prickled with gooseflesh. The most haunting, strange melody filled the chamber. I either had the urge to clamp my hands over my ears or cry tears of joy.

He plucked a few more chords, then launched into a song with a dizzying cadence, the metallic sound making me feel strangely giddy.

"Is this music?" I called.

"No, it's not!" Raj answered. "But he did warn us."

"I think I like it."

"You do?"

"It takes a bit of getting used to, but yes."

The wolf stood beside me, whining, and I patted his head. Drekken played a final chord, then stood still.

"That was… different," I said.

"Unicorn hair," he said. "That makes the difference."

"Do you think it will work to make the vines stop attacking us?"

"There's only one way to find out," Drekken answered.

"Then we have to try," Raj said.

I gathered my things and slung my pack over my shoulder. Facing the barred door, I breathed deeply, praying Drekken's lute worked to keep the vines from killing us. Clutching my dagger, I waited as Raj and the elf gathered their bags, then we walked to the door.

Raj stood with a straight back, holding his sword, his cloak cascading down his back.

"Open the door and I'll play," Drekken said to me. I nodded, then faced the barred gate. Grasping an iron bar, I pushed the door open. Metal hinges squealed. The vines reacted, writhing over the ceiling, sending small pebbles smashing to the ground.

Drekken plucked the strings gingerly, playing a light tune. As the elf's magic filled the room, its power made my skin tingle. The pulsing light of the radish stilled, and became a slow, rhythmic cadence rather than a harsh, pounding beat.

We stepped out of the cell. The vines remained on the ceiling. I paced toward the exit, though vines still blocked the path.

"Not that way," Drekken said. "It'll take us forever to leave through the main castle. I found a shortcut through the old irrigation duct. Follow me."

I traded glances with Raj, but neither of us argued as we walked in the opposite direction. The vines moved overhead, but none of them attacked. I held my knife in a firm grip, my hands clammy, as I studied the long dagger-like thorns protruding from the woody bark.

A doorway sat beneath a tangle of vines. We had to duck to walk underneath. My cloak snagged on a thorn. It wriggled, but with Drekken's music filling the chamber, it could do nothing but remain on the wall, so I pulled my cloak away.

"Wait," Drekken whispered. The music stopped. I rounded to find him reaching for a silver flask on the ground. The vines reacted, writhing, then diving at us.

"Drekken, play," Raj shouted.

"Not without my flask!"

He snatched it up. The vines tore off a chunk of the

ceiling. Stones sailed at us, pelting our heads and shoulders. The plants raged with fury as they surrounded us. Raj hacked at them, his weapon slicing through the air.

Drekken started playing once again, giving us barely enough time to race through the exit before they trapped us. We sprinted through a dark tunnel, though in places, sunlight shone through cracks in the ceiling. The walls crumbled, and roots clung to the loose stones.

Our path sloped upward and ended at a wooden ladder that led to an opening overhead. I ascended first and climbed into the sunlight. As I stood on a grassy hill, I breathed a sigh of relief. I had to shield my eyes from the brightness, but it felt so wonderful to be out in the fresh air once again. A grove of cottonwood trees stood beyond the castle's walls. A few yellow-gold leaves still clung to their branches, though most of the leaves lay in heaps on the ground.

Behind me, Raj and the wolf climbed out. Drekken crawled from the hole last.

As he stood, he attached his lute to his pack. After getting situated, he straightened to his full height—nearly as tall and broad as Raj—and smiled at us. It was then I noticed a rim of red surrounding his blue irises, made apparent by the bright sunlight.

My stomach turned.

He must've been a dark elf. No wonder he'd been lurking through the castle's dungeons, wearing such an odd pendant, looking for a bit of the radish to steal.

"You're a dark elf?" I asked.

"Ah, yes. You noticed, did you?"

"It's hard not to, now that I can see properly."

I half expected him to pull out his knife and demand

we give him the radish I carried in my bag, but he only smiled.

"Don't be so shocked. I may be a dark elf, my dear, but that doesn't make me an evil person, does it?"

"Perhaps not, but you still owe us an explanation. What were you planning to do with the radish you hoped to steal?" Raj asked.

"Sell it, of course. An item like that would fetch a hefty price."

"And… you aren't going to try to steal it from me?"

"I would never dream of doing such a thing."

"Really?" I asked.

"Yes, yes, however, there is one thing I do require, seeing as how I've saved both of your lives."

"Barely," Raj said. "You almost killed us when you went for your flask."

"Yes, and it was so worth it." He smiled slyly, then removed his flask from his tunic pocket, unscrewed the lid, and took a long swig. "Now, about this business of repayment. There is one small thing I'd like to ask of you."

"What is it?" Raj growled. "Coin? I'll have you know I carry only enough money for traveling."

"Nothing like that. I merely want to join you on this journey. Wherever you're going, I want to come."

"Not possible," Raj said. "We've already taken on one stray. Two would push my limits."

"But I've saved your lives. You owe me."

"*Barely* saved our lives," Raj repeated.

"Why do you want to come with us?" I asked. "You don't even know where we're going."

"True, but I'll know who I'm traveling with, which is ever so much more important."

Raj groaned. "I've had enough of tagalongs."

"You still didn't answer my question," I said to Drekken. "Why do you want to come with us?"

"Fine. I'll tell you this. My people hate me. I didn't turn out the way my parents wanted. I had no interest in the dark arts, so they banished me. I've been on my own ever since. My sole wish is to perform music people will enjoy, and hopefully to stir their souls a little. That's all. But I've learned doing such a thing on my own is a dangerous way to go, as you may have noticed in the dungeons. I need help. In exchange for companionship, I promise I will use my lute to defend you against the vilest of creatures. Unfortunately, that's all I can offer. I have nothing else. But if you let me journey with you, I give you my oath that I won't cause any trouble. That is, unless we come upon a comely lass or two." He winked, then took another swill from his flask.

I looked at Raj. He worked his jaw back and forth, the way he did when he was deep in thought. I tried not to notice how handsome he looked when the muscles in his jaw flexed that way.

"May I speak with Gothel alone?" Raj asked.

"Of course, I'll wait under that copse of trees just over the hill." He turned and walked to the grove of cottonwoods, out of earshot from where we stood, and the wolf followed him.

When Drekken reached the trees, Raj turned to me. The autumn sun picked up the copper tones of his skin, and I had the urge to reach up and touch his face. I banished the thought. The last thing I needed was to do such a thing, although a hint of a beard sheathed his jaw, only serving to make him look more masculine.

"What do you think?" Raj asked me.

"Think? Oh, yes, about Drekken." I straightened, trying to sort out the emotions running rampant through my head. Curse Raj and his unnatural good looks. "I'm not sure he can be trusted, although his lute is impressive. Having him with us may not be such a bad idea, especially as we've still got to travel through the wastes of the Outerlands, with who knows what kind of creatures lurking there."

"I agree. The last time I traveled the Outerlands, the sand demons were multiplying. Perhaps it wouldn't be a bad idea to keep him with us. Still, he doesn't have a horse, and he'll be another mouth to feed. I'm not sure this would be a prudent decision."

"We can get another horse in the next village."

"I still don't like it. Plus, I don't trust him."

"Do you trust anyone?" I asked.

"Yes, I trust you." He spoke with a deep baritone tenor to his voice, causing my insides to flutter.

"You trust me?" I asked, looking up at him.

He met my gaze, which only served to make the fluttering worse.

"I trust you with all my heart, Gothel." The way he said my name sounded soft, sincere, but with an intensity that made my knees buckle.

"Why do you trust me?" I asked, my voice almost a whisper.

He carefully moved his hand to my face, where he brushed his thumb over my cheek. My insides ignited with wildfire. What was I supposed to do? Did I push him away? Did I remind him that I wasn't an Outlander?

My mind turned to mush, and all I could think about

was him, and how close he was, and how much closer I wanted him to be.

"Raj, what are you doing?"

His lips quirked into a smile, showing his teeth, and I was hit with the urge to kiss him.

No, no, no. Stop thinking that way!

"I'm admiring your eyes. They match your hair. Blue, with a touch of green. I've never seen anything like them."

He cupped my cheek. His hand was warm, and the skin smooth. He smelled of spices, ones I had smelled before when visiting the Outerlands with Rapunzel and her father. The scent conjured images of deserts and sunsets and sprawling tent cities with every sort of exotic spice and oil available—the Outerlands—the place he was meant to be, surrounded by the people he was meant to be with.

I placed my hand over his and moved it away from my face, though as I did, the dwarf's words echoed through my head. I pushed my misgivings aside. I was doing the right thing.

"Raj, I'm an ordinary person, and not worth anyone's time, especially yours. Now, let's tell Drekken the good news, shall we?"

"Good news? Have we made a decision?"

"Yes, we're bringing him with us."

"Is that so?"

"I think it would be in our best interests to have someone like him with us. He stopped those vines with his lute. If he can do the same for the beasts we're sure to meet in the desert, I think we should have him with us."

"I can defeat sand demons just as well as him."

"Maybe so." I said, unable to hold back a smile.

"You're smiling. You don't believe me?"

"Quite the opposite, really. You're a talented swordsman."

"Then why do we need the elf?"

I sighed. "Fine. Maybe we don't need him, but he has no one else."

"So, we're helping him?"

"Yes, we're helping him."

He sighed, glancing at the sun as it dipped westward, toward the desert. "Very well. We'll bring him with us. But if he crosses us, don't blame me."

"I won't."

We walked to the grove where Drekken and the wolf waited. The elf sat beneath a tree, his lute held carefully on his lap as he plucked the strings. The metallic sound clanged yet seemed to calm me with its strange sound.

"Have you made a decision?" he asked, looking up at us, continuing to play. The lute's sound made me pause, and I forgot why I'd come to the grove. Couldn't I just sit down and rest for a moment?

"Yes, we've made a decision." For the life of me, I couldn't remember what it was. The music lulled me, its harsh beats seeming to put me in a trance.

"Will you stop?" Raj asked, pressing his hands to his ears. "That music is making it hard to concentrate."

"Ah." Drekken lifted his fingers off the strings. "Yes, sorry. Sometimes I forget what an effect my music has on people."

I straightened, the quiet air seeming to bring me back to my senses. "We've made a decision," I repeated. "We've agreed that you can come with us."

"I can?"

"Yes, if you'll stay true to your promise and help us defeat any creatures we encounter. Also, you should know that we're traveling to the Ice Mountains in the northern lands, to a castle where my aunts dwell. They're dangerous, and they have magic that could kill you instantly. Plus, we'll have to travel through the Outerlands to get there. If you decide you no longer want to join us, I'll understand."

Drekken stood, fidgeting with his skull-shaped pendant. "No need to worry. I'm a dark elf, after all. I hail from one of the most feared places in the realm. I'm not afraid of Ice Mountains."

"But what about the Outerlands?" Raj asked.

"No need to worry about those either. I fear nothing as long as I've got my lute and my flask."

Oh, for goodness' sake. Why were we bringing him with us again? A drunken elf and a shapeshifting, sour dwarf hardly made useful traveling companions. Who would we pick up next? No, I didn't want to know the answer.

"Your ale will do nothing to help where we're going," Raj said. "And you should know that if you slow us down or cross us in any way, you'll pay the price. I've no idea why you're choosing to come with us. Anyone with half a head of sense would be wise to fear the desert. Unfortunately, that's where we travel next."

NINE

EVENING APPROACHED AS WE TRAVELED west toward the Outerlands. After passing through a small village, we'd managed to barter a horse from a farmer. Drekken rode a gray nag whose ribs protruded, and had a swayed back. If we were attacked, I doubted the horse could keep pace. Still, he had a horse, which was more than he'd had before, although I wasn't sure if he deserved it. Something about the man made me uneasy, yet I pitied him at the same time. Either I was making a new friend, or I was trusting a complete cheat. I would most likely find out soon enough.

After leaving the village, the landscape changed. Grass grew in clumps amongst the rocks. The trees disappeared, replaced with sage brush. Color drained from the world. Greens and reds and yellow were replaced with the faded hue of the sand. Even the plants took on the same color, as if the sand had drained all the brightness away.

"We'll not make it to the border before nightfall," Raj said. "We'll have to make camp."

"Where?" I asked.

"Maybe we'll find a cave."

"Or an inn," I said with a sigh, "with a hot meal and a bath drawn."

Raj laughed. "There'll be no chance of that the closer we get to the Outerlands."

"One can wish."

"I suppose so."

Our horses' hooves echoed through the expanse as the sun approached the horizon, leaving only a few rays to light the world. The wolf plodded alongside us, not making a sound, moving forward as if in a trance. He hadn't taken his dwarf form since we'd met Drekken, and I wondered how the elf would react to having a shapeshifter as a traveling companion. Maybe we should have warned him of it, but I doubted he would have changed his mind.

As we rode, the wind blew stronger, its howling drowning out all other sounds. On the horizon, a dilapidated hovel and a stable appeared. Rotting wooden timbers and crumbling stones formed the outer walls, and the thatched roofs had collapsed in places. We stopped our horses and scanned the area. There were no animals about, and all that remained of the fences were a few posts peeking from the sand.

"It looks abandoned," I said.

"I agree," Raj said. "I doubt anyone's lived here in years."

"Do you think we should stay?"

"Yes. We'll not find anywhere else this far out."

"What if it's unsafe?" I asked over the wind.

"If it is, we'll find out."

I wasn't thrilled by his answer, but anything was better than staying outside in the sandstorm, so I dismounted.

The soreness in my legs was still present, but it seemed my muscles were growing accustomed to riding. I walked with the others toward what had once been the stable but was now a ramshackle structure with a half-collapsed roof.

Inside, stalls lined either side of the walkthrough, and we stabled our horses in them. We'd purchased a few scoops of grain from the previous village, and though it wasn't much, especially for three horses who'd been traveling so much, it made me feel better that we had at least a little to give them.

After leaving the horses, we made our way to the house. The air had grown cold. My skin shivered with goose bumps, and the biting wind only made the chill worse.

When we got to the hovel, Raj grabbed the door handle and, with a shove of his shoulder, pushed it open. We entered a musty smelling room. Stone and timber columns supported what remained of the thatched roof. My boots treaded quietly over the hardpacked dirt floor. Broken clay pots lay strewn about. Outside, the wind beat against the walls, but inside, without the wind, it was a little warmer, though I still couldn't shake my chills.

In the light of Raj's lantern, I spotted a spinning wheel sitting near the room's only window which was covered in furs. As I looked at the room's back wall, I spotted a rocking chair and a broken baby's cradle near the stone fireplace. Raj stepped toward the hearth, and his lantern's light glinted on an iron cooking pot hanging over the empty coals. Gray ash was scattered about, and tiny footprints, like those of a rat, were visible in the dusty cinders.

"What do you think happened to the people?" Drekken asked.

"Whoever they were, they must've come upon hard times," I said.

"Do you think we'll find their bodies?" A gruff voice

said behind us.

We turned around to find the dwarf sitting on the floor. He looked on us with a bloodshot eye as he arranged his eye patch.

"What in the—" Drekken stumbled back and hit the wall. "Who's that?"

"Drekken, meet… umm…" I started. "Meet our wolf. He's a shapeshifter."

"Shapeshifter?"

"Aye," the dwarf said.

"But… how?" Drekken asked.

"Long story," I answered. "It involves a witch's curse. He also can't remember his name, so don't bother asking."

The dwarf grumbled. Drekken's eyes darted from me to the man on the floor, as if he couldn't decide if he liked what was going on.

"I'm pleased to meet you," he said, formally, almost forced, as he gave a stiff bow.

"Save it," the dwarf bit back. "No dark elf is pleased to meet me unless they've laid eyes on my coin purse."

"Ah," Drekken said darkly. "I assure you, I've no interest in the coin purse belonging to a dwarf. Probably full of cursed gold."

"What?" the dwarf spat.

"You heard me, Dwarf. I've known enough of your kind to know your capabilities."

"I'll break your legs, you filthy elf."

"Will you? With what weapon? Your peg leg?"

"Why you—"

"Dwarf," I interrupted. "That's enough. If you'd like to continue on this journey with us, I'd ask that you respect our traveling companions. That goes for you as well,

Drekken. If we could get a fire going, would you be inclined to play a tune or two?"

His eyes lit up. "Play for you? You really want me to?"

"Yes, I would love it."

"Then I shall acquiesce," he said with a formal bow.

"I think a tune by the fire is a wonderful idea," Raj said. "I suppose we can use what's already here for fuel. Dwarf, Drekken, would you mind helping me with this chair and cradle? Gothel, you can dismantle the spinning wheel. We'll use them all."

He placed his lantern on the floor, unsheathed his sword with the quiet sound of metal rubbing against leather, and hacked the cradle in two. I cringed. It seemed wrong to so casually destroy an object that had been used to hold someone's infant, but we needed warmth, and as the cradle was already broken, I put aside my misgivings.

Removing my knife from my boot, I walked to the spinning wheel and began cutting away the spokes. We worked without speaking until we'd dismantled the wooden furniture. After we arranged the wood in the fireplace, Raj lit the fire. A cheery orange flame burst into existence, chasing away the shadows, seeming to lighten the mood. As I sat on the floor beside the blaze, my skin warmed.

It didn't take long for the fire to chase the chill from the small room, and as we sat near the hearth, we ate a dinner of sausages—that we'd managed to buy in the last village—and some cheese and vegetables.

After riding all day and eating very little, the food tasted divine, and I savored every bite. The others made small talk, and I was grateful Drekken and the dwarf no longer argued, though I was too exhausted to keep up with the conversation. I huddled under my cloak as the smell of wood smoke filled the air. Flames crackled as Drekken pulled out his lute and began playing.

He plucked a tune, a melancholy sound that conjured images of my past. Varlocke killing my mother. Standing over her broken, bloody body, her too-cold hands pressed between mine, not accepting that she was really gone.

Later, my sadness had grown to anger. Why had she been so petty? If she'd escaped him and left Rapunzel alone, she would've lived, and I wouldn't have been an orphan, forced to protect the person she'd cursed.

"Are you going to sleep?" Raj asked, jarring me out of my thoughts. I glanced around the room. Drekken had stopped playing and now lay sleeping on his bed roll. The wolf also slept curled in a ball near the fire.

"Sorry," I said, rubbing my eyes. I stood and grabbed my pack, untied my bed roll, and placed it on the floor. I wished I could've found an actual bed to sleep in, but there wasn't one in the room. There weren't many things I missed about the tower, but my soft feather mattress was one of them.

I laid atop the worn blanket and pulled the woolen coverlet over me. Raj lay not far away, closer to the fire, and I tried to ignore the way the firelight reflected on his smooth, bronzed skin. I failed, and my heart gave its usual flutter. He laid on his back, and I gazed at his profile: a broad forehead, straight nose, and strong chin.

He rolled to face me, and his eyes opened. I quickly looked away, feeling my cheeks grow hot with embarrassment. Had he seen me looking at him?

"You're awake?" he whispered.

"Yes," I answered, looking intently at the thatch and wooden planks comprising the ceiling. I wouldn't dare glance his way again.

He scooted closer to me, and I froze.

I wanted nothing to do with Raj being close to me or with the tingling feeling that prickled my skin as he drew nearer. No. I wanted to go to the other side of the room, but for the life of me, I couldn't bring myself to do it.

"Gothel," he said, his voice quiet, almost seductive.

"Yes?"

"Tell me, what do you know of the destruction of Al-Maar?"

"Al-Maar... the Outlander city? Don't you know?"

"I know how it happened, but I don't know why. They say the high sorcerer's father had good relations with our people. He visited King Bajar often. They got along. But his son... No one knew why Varlocke hated our people when his father didn't. Now, we travel those lands again, and since you lived in Varlocke's castle, I wondered if you knew the answer."

"Yes," I whispered. "I think I know. It may have been because of his father."

"What do you mean?"

"He hated him. Varlocke confessed many things to my mother, and some of those things I overheard. One time, I remember Varlocke sitting in my mother's chamber. He spoke quietly, so naturally, I snuck toward the door and listened. I was young. Seven, maybe, but I remember he said that when he was a child, his father had taken all his possessions and sold them to the Outlanders for Al-Maarian ore and spiced wine. Everything. His toys, his pony, even their stores from the kitchens. He had nothing to eat for days at a time. The kingdom suffered because of the king's obsession, and Varlocke hated his father for it."

Raj rubbed his eyes, as if trying to erase his memories. "If it's true, then that's a petty, sorry reason to destroy an entire nation of people. I lost loved ones in his wars, Gothel. My baby sister and my uncle and all his family. I can never get them back again. I can never get my home back again."

I pondered his words. "I'm sorry for your loss."

"Thank you," he said, his voice reserved, and I felt my words did nothing to give him comfort.

"That's not all true," I said.

"What do you mean?"

"He took your sister and uncle, and all his family, yes, that's true. But he didn't take your home."

"He burned nearly every building in Al-Maar."

"Yes, but they're just buildings. They can be replaced. You can find your home again."

"Find it again? Do you not understand what my people went through?"

"I understand, but I also know you need to move forward. You can't hold on to the past forever."

Anger simmered in his eyes. "I can't do that."

"Why not?"

"Because," he said, "I have to kill Varlocke first."

I watched his face, the clenching of his jaw, the anger that I saw so rarely.

"You really mean to kill him?" I asked.

He nodded.

"Is that what this quest is all about? Not to save the prince and free Rapunzel, but to take your revenge on Varlocke by killing him?"

"I thought that was intuitive. If we succeed and free the prince, Varlocke will have to be dead for the prince to marry Rapunzel and take the throne."

"So much of what you just said bothers me. Killing and forced marriages? Is that really what we want?"

"It's not like that."

"Then what is it like?"

He couldn't answer, so I rolled away from him. The fire crackled, and my heart squeezed painfully tight. I didn't like arguing with Raj, but I also didn't like the idea of killing Varlocke. Yes, he was misguided and evil, but I'd known him as a real person who loved his daughter. I wasn't sure I liked the idea of killing him.

"Have I upset you?" Raj whispered, his breath warm on my cheeks.

"I don't know. Maybe."

"I always have a way of upsetting you. I'm sorry."

He trailed his finger along my cheek. Tingles spread across my skin. Did he have any idea what that did to me?

I rolled toward him, intent on asking him to politely shove off, when his eyes met mine. Dark and exotic, with a hint of wildness about him, I couldn't make my mouth work. The scent of curry and amber lingered on his skin. My heart could have pounded out of my chest.

"Don't push me away this time," he said, his words soft, and his eyes pleading.

"But…"

"No." He pressed his finger to my lips. "Will you let me kiss you?"

My mouth went dry. How did I answer? "I don't know."

"Please."

A tightness grew in my chest. He'd told me before that if he married, he wanted an Outlander wife. I was nothing. A nobody. If he wanted to kiss me, it meant he only wanted to use me. But that didn't seem like Raj, did it? He'd been nothing but honorable to a fault.

I pressed my hand to his chest, feeling the pounding of his heart beneath my fingers.

"Have you ever kissed anyone?" he asked.

"I've been locked in a tower for five years, remember?"

"Right."

He licked his lips, and my eyes went to his mouth. What would it feel like to kiss him? Maybe I should just do it and get it over with. It was only a kiss, after all.

I leaned toward him, and he brushed his lips over mine.

A fire ignited within me. I could hardly think, hardly move. He held me in his arms and deepened the kiss. His lips felt soft and warm against mine. Kissing him was better than I'd ever imagined. Stars danced in my vision as he pulled away.

"Well," I said breathlessly. "So that's a kiss."

"Yes." He smiled, and I couldn't mistake the devilish look in his eyes. "That's a kiss."

TEN

I LAY AWAKE AS I listened to the crackling fire. Staring at the ceiling overhead, I couldn't sleep with the memory of Raj kissing me. Like a gentleman, he'd moved away from me and slept near the fire. What was I supposed to do now? There was no denying there was something between Raj and me, but it could never go anywhere. He was an Outlander. I was a witch bound to a tower. Unless we succeeded.

If we succeeded, if I was finally free of the tower, would he still want me?

No. I was overthinking this, as usual. I needed to forget him, forget the kiss, and move on with my life.

But something inside me fervently resisted that notion. I liked spending time with Raj. I liked his smile and his simplicity. I liked his optimism. When I was around him, I felt happiness unlike I'd ever felt before—I felt hope. No one else made me feel that way.

The wind's incessant howling sounded like a shrill wail. A low thud pounded the wall outside. I tensed. It was most likely the wind battering a loose object.

A nightmarish scream pierced through the air. I bolted upright. Raj also sat up, his eyes wide as he grabbed for his sword.

"What was that?" he asked.

"I don't know. I think someone's out there."

He got to his feet and I did the same. We stood at the window, moved the furs aside, and peeked out. An orange glow appeared from the stable. Other than that, we saw only blackness.

"I'm going out there," Raj said.

"I'm coming with you."

I expected him to argue, but he said nothing as I grabbed my knife off the floor. The wolf and elf both slept soundly, and I decided not to disturb them as I followed Raj outside.

As we pulled the door shut behind us, the wind blew so hard it threatened to knock me over. I had to close my eyes against the onslaught of sand. It blasted my skin, rubbing it raw. The ground chilled my bare feet. I cracked my eyes open as best as I could, using my cloak to shield my face. Raj walked away from the hovel and I followed.

We approached the stable. Flames roared from the thatched roof.

My heart stopped.

The horses were inside.

"We have to save the horses," I yelled over the wind.

"It's too dangerous," Raj yelled back.

"But we can't let them die."

Despite Raj's hesitation, I pushed forward through the wind. When I made it inside the stable, heat blasted me. The rafters smoldered, and thick, yellowish smoke choked the air. The horses shrieked from their stables.

As if on impulse, I raced to the gray nag's stall—the closest one—and tore the gate open. The horse bolted outside, running faster than I thought possible.

Raj's mare stood in the next stall, and I repeated the process of yanking open the gate. The horse galloped out of the stall and away from the fire.

I turned toward Sable's stall when someone entered behind me. I turned, thinking it was Raj, shocked to come face to face with the guard I'd faced at the inn.

Cold, glaring eyes met mine as the man stood straight, firelight reflecting off the basilisk carved into his breastplate. He held his claymore between us. I yanked the knife from my boot, its small blade reflected in the firelight.

"How did you find me?" I demanded.

"I tracked you, love. Did you really believe you could escape me? Now I've found you, I'll take you to the high sorcerer. You'll never leave that tower again—assuming you survive the journey back." His laugh made a cold chill creep up my spine. "Accidents have been known to happen."

"You'll kill me?"

"Aye, if you give me trouble."

I couldn't let him take me. I refused to be his prisoner. I refused to let Rapunzel continue to suffer. This ended now. He would never have me.

"You'll never get the chance."

"Is that so?"

He took a step toward me. In one swift motion, I flung my dagger at him, turned, and sprinted for the exit, but the ceiling collapsed. Sparks sprayed the air and burned my face. I fell back, my hands smacking the ground.

The guardsman bellowed behind me. I twisted around as he closed the distance between us. Blood streamed from a wound in his shoulder where the handle of my knife peeked from the joint in his armor.

Rage fueled his movements as he barreled toward me. I tried to stand, but he moved too fast, flinging the cowl from my head and grabbing me by my hair. My scalp screamed with pain as he hauled me to my feet.

"You'll regret that," he hissed in my ear, his stale breath making me queasy.

I fought back, jamming my elbow into his ribcage so hard, I heard something pop. He screamed, releasing me for just a moment, long enough for me to scramble out of his grasp.

Fire blocked the exit, so I backed into a stall, bumping against the wall. Sable shrieked as her stall filled with flames, burning the hay around her. Tears stung my eyes. I stood against the wall, trapped like Sable.

Embers flitted through the air, giving a strange, glowing sheen to the guardsman's blade. Lightning fast, he stabbed the blade through my middle. Pain exploded through my entire body. A shuddering scream filled my throat as he pulled the blade out, wet with my blood.

Behind him, Raj appeared. I fell to the ground, unable to think or move, except to clutch my hands over the wound. Warm blood seeped between my fingers, and I inhaled shuddering gasps.

Raj fought the guardsman, but he was too late. I would never survive. My gaze went to Sable. Fire engulfed her stall. I could no longer see her, but her pain-filled shrieks filled the air. Painfully slow, I crawled toward her. Every movement was torture. I had the selfish urge to curl into a ball and pass out, but I couldn't let Sable die, so I crawled, slowly, gaining one inch, and then another.

Smoke stung my nostrils and burned my eyes. The

tears stinging my eyes made everything look blurry. I made it to her stall, but as I reached up for the latch, my wound sent fresh waves of pain through my body.

I cried out, cradling my stomach, trying to think through the pain.

Save Sable. Open the stall.

Fire crackling with hellish fury around us, I ground my teeth, reached for the latch, and opened the gate.

She burst out, running through the flames and out into the night just as I collapsed.

The blackness took me.

ELEVEN

"GOTHEL."

My whispered name broke through my consciousness. I heard his voice, rich and silken, a low baritone that felt comfortable and familiar.

I wanted to open my eyes. Behind my eyelids, I saw splotches of yellow and red, but making my body respond to my command wasn't working, so I relented, and went back to the place where I had been—the darkness where I couldn't feel the pain.

"Gothel, wake up, please."

The voice came again. This time, I managed to open my eyes. An oilskin tarp was the first thing I saw. It fluttered back and forth, revealing a flap that opened to a landscape of white sand dunes and a faded pink sky. I breathed deeply, hoping to make myself wake up. Dry, desert air filled my lungs.

Someone squeezed my hand. I turned to find Raj sitting beside me.

"Gothel," he breathed.

I reached for him when pain lanced through my middle, so I held still.

"Where am I?" I barely recognized my hoarse voice.

"She needs water," another voice said beside me, and I turned to see Drekken opposite me. He held a flask to my lips. I hesitated before drinking.

"Is it water?"

"Of course," he said with mock indignation. "What else would it be?"

I was too thirsty to argue, so I drank from his flask. Thankfully, cool water coated my parched throat.

"We all thought you were dead, lass," another voice said. The dwarf walked toward me. His shoulders were hunched, and his mouth was stuck in its usual frown, yet I saw a hint of relief, perhaps a look of compassion, in his eyes.

"What happened? Where are we?"

"Raj killed the guardsman," Drekken said. "After that, we found the horses and escaped into the desert."

"Killed him?" I asked Raj.

"No," Raj corrected. "I injured him, but he escaped. We're not sure if he's dead."

"With the wounds Raj gave him, he must've bled out," Drekken said.

"We should still be wary," Raj said. "There are other guardsmen out there. They'll be looking for Gothel, too. We're not safe, even now that we've entered the desert."

"How far are we from Al-Maar?"

"A day, at most. Assuming we're able to travel without being attacked or slowed down. Since you saved the horses, we should make good time," Raj said.

"The horses are okay?"

"Yes, they're fine. We found them on the edge of the desert."

I sighed, looking at the canvas overhead as I did my

best to ignore the throbbing pain in my midsection, wondering how it was I'd managed to survive the guardsman's attack.

"Raj was about to tend your wound. We'll wait outside," Drekken said. "There's an oasis nearby, and we need to collect more water if we wish to make it across the desert today."

Drekken and the dwarf left the tent, leaving me alone with Raj. I rubbed my forehead, feeling a dull headache throbbing through my temples. I wasn't thrilled with the idea of Raj tending my wounds, but I hardly had the strength to argue.

He smiled, but it didn't touch his eyes. It wasn't the carefree look I'd become so accustomed to.

"Gothel, please allow me to apologize. I should not have hesitated to follow you into the stable. After you left to save the horses, the guardsman attacked me, just enough to incapacitate me so he could enter the stable behind you, I thought…" he swallowed. "I thought he would kill you. He almost did."

"It's okay. You didn't know the guardsman was following us."

"True, but I should have known he was the one who set the fire. I should've realized he was trying to ambush us. He could have killed you."

He looked away from me, swallowing hard, as if trying to control his emotions. "I'm sorry."

"You don't need to apologize. The guardsman injured me. Not you."

He only nodded, and I wished I could've said something to ease his regret, but what? I didn't blame him for my injury. How could he have known the guardsman would ambush us? Neither of us had known.

"Will you allow me to tend your wound?" he asked. "I know it won't make things right, but I feel I need to do something to help you."

What other choice did I have? "Very well," I said.

He nodded, removing a rolled linen from his pack and a vial of ointment. Rosewood, perhaps?

"You carry rosewood oil with you?" I asked.

"Yes. All the king's soldiers keep it with them for injuries on the battlefield." His fingers hovered above my waistline. "Are you ready for this?"

Despite being stabbed through the gut, the butterflies returned. I'd hoped being sliced open would have gotten rid of the annoying feeling deep in the pit of my stomach, but no such luck.

"I'm ready."

He gently lifted the fabric of my riding gown, which I noted had already been cut open. Bandages lay across my abdomen, just below my ribcage. They were soaked through with dark blood.

Raj lifted them away one at a time. The iron-rich scent of my own blood filled the air. I wanted to gag, but held still as he removed the last bandage, revealing a cut that perfectly severed through my flesh in a straight line. Jagged black thread crisscrossed the wound, sealing it shut.

"You stitched it?" I asked.

"Yes, as you can see, I'm not as proficient as you."

"It looks fine."

"I guess so. The good news is that you didn't injure any vital organs, and the bleeding has stopped, but I fear that if we don't keep the wound clean, taint could set in."

He picked up a bowl filled with water. After wetting

a cloth, he lightly dabbed the wound.

I balled my fists against the pain. Though he worked gently, fire burned through my skin, as if I'd been stabbed all over again.

Sweat beaded on my brow, and my agitated stomach twisted, threatening to heave up the little bit of water I'd managed to drink.

After cleaning away the dried blood, Raj picked up the vial of rosewood oil, and dabbed a few drops onto my wound. The scent of roses and herbs filled the air. I forgot to breathe as he worked the oil into my skin, his warm hands calm and gentle, though the stab wound ached. He placed the vial aside and covered the wound with strips of white cloth. After finishing, he pulled a blanket over me. His eyes met mine, and his pain-stricken face revealed his turmoil.

I knew he felt responsible for my injury, for my pain, for my near death caused by the guardsman. He grabbed another cloth, soaked it in water, and wiped the sweat from my brow.

"I'm so sorry, Gothel. I swore to protect you, but I failed."

The feel of his warm hands calmed my beating heart and soothed my pain.

"Raj, I don't blame you. I shouldn't have run into a burning stable. It was a reckless thing to do."

"You were being brave. More so than me."

He smoothed the cool cloth across my forehead. My pain eased, and I relaxed under his gentle hands. I never wanted to move from this spot. Raj's presence calmed my fears. Closing my eyes, I imagined what it would be like to have him always close.

He moved the cloth away, then pushed a strand of hair away from my face. I moved his fingers away, suddenly reminded of the guardsman grabbing my hair last night. Panic welled up inside me. I hated the guardsman for stabbing me, but I hated him almost as much for pulling my hair.

"Do you not want me to touch you?" Raj asked.

"No. It's just that last night, the guardsman grabbed my hair and nearly pulled it from my scalp. It's not a pleasant memory, and now I can only imagine what my hair must look like."

"Would you like me to comb it for you?" Raj asked.

"You don't have to. I can manage."

"It's no trouble."

"You're sure?"

"Yes," he said. "I'm sure it still hurts for you to move."

"It's not too bad." And by that, I meant it hurt like hellfire with every inch I moved. "But I suppose my hair must look frightful."

"You'll let me comb it, then?"

"Fine," I relented. "There's a boar hair brush in my pack." I was letting him get way too close, yet I seemed incapable of doing anything about it. Sighing, I decided since I was injured, surely it was okay to let my guard down. Just this once.

Raj gently lifted my head and pulled my matted mess of hair away from my neck. He carefully ran the brush through the strands, working the tangles out as he went. I wasn't sure how to react to his familiarity. Aside from my mother and that accursed guardsman, no one had touched my hair, let alone brushed it. I'd always been too self-conscious. The greenish-blue strands stood out. My hair made me feel exposed, so most of the time I kept my head covered. To have Raj's fingers in my hair, working away at the tangles, unnerved me. Despite his familiarity, I couldn't find the willpower to ask him to stop. He'd enchanted me, and I was powerless to resist him.

Calmness settled over me. He worked the brush toward my scalp, never pulling, working gently. He couldn't have realized how awkward this was for me. No one touched my hair. Ever. But he held me under his spell, and I remained on the pallet, staring at the oilskin tarp overhead, listening to the sounds of the bristles running through my hair, removing one tangle after another, one barrier after another, taking away all my defenses, until he left me exposed and vulnerable, and oddly content.

Sighing, I closed my eyes as he moved the brush up to my scalp, brushing from top to bottom, long, elegant strokes—a painter creating a work of art.

He placed the brush aside, then gently ran his fingers through the long strands. My breath stilled, and I lay frozen, not wanting him to stop. He moved to sit beside me, his hands still moving deftly through my hair.

"You should never hide your hair."

"Why?" I asked.

"It's too beautiful to be hidden."

"I disagree. It makes me a target."

"You've never told me why it's blue."

"I haven't told you because I don't know. When I asked my mother, she told me it was my father's fault, but I never understood what she meant."

"Do you remember him very well?"

"Not much. I remember my mother's face when he returned from his journeys. Those were some of the only times I saw her happy. But he died when I was very young, and I only remember brief images of him. He was very handsome, and he always brought the most beautiful flowers when he returned. Although now, I realize they were only wildflowers."

His eyes lingered on my face, and I desperately wanted him to kiss me again, but I knew a second kiss couldn't possibly feel as good as the first. If it did, I might lose my head completely and never be the same. No, a second kiss couldn't be half as good.

He leaned closer to me, his dark eyes drinking me in, and I could do nothing but stare into the bottomless depths—dark and mysterious. Exotic.

The scent of sage and dark forests clung to his skin and hair, and a hint of a beard shadowed his jaw. I reached up and touched his face, feeling the prickly hair beneath my fingers, a subtle masculinity that set my insides on fire.

He placed his hand atop mine. Warmth seeped from his skin, melting the chill in my fingers. Leaning toward me, he focused on my lips, but as he drew closer, voices came from outside the tent.

Raj sat up straight, and I pulled the blanket to my chin as Drekken and the dwarf entered, each carrying several large canteens. The sound of sloshing water came from their containers as they set them on the sand.

"Sun's getting higher," the dwarf said. "We'll need to hurry if we want to make it across the desert before nightfall."

"Do you think you can travel?" Raj asked me.

The thought of sitting on a horse wasn't a pleasant one, but what choice did I have? "I'll manage."

Raj took my hand and helped me sit up. I expected

the wound to hurt, but with the rosewood oil numbing the pain, I only felt a slight prickling sensation. Raj held my hand a second longer than necessary, still looking at me with that guilty expression.

I let go of him to grab my pack. Lifting it off the ground pulled at my wound, so I carefully bent and maneuvered the strap over my shoulder. The canvas whipped back and forth as the breeze picked it up, and the others worked to dismantle the makeshift tent.

I stepped away from them to take in my new surroundings. The sun was a hazy white dot far on the horizon. I shielded my eyes against the brightness, looking out over the dips and gently curving slopes of white sand dunes. Arid desert air rushed past, brushing my cheeks, holding a slight salty scent.

Our horses lingered nearby, and I made my way toward Sable. Her coat was shiny and covered in sweat, and the distinct scent of wet horse caught my senses. Although I never wanted to confront the guardsman again, I felt grateful that I'd at least saved the horses.

"Hi girl," I said, stepping to her and patting her velvety nose. Sable looked at me with her wide eyes, snorted, and walked away, seeming oblivious to the fact that I'd saved her life. Animals.

We worked to gather our things and saddle the horses, and soon, we were riding across the vast expanse of desert on an ancient highway. The horses' hooves clopped over what was left of the cobbled road. Broken stones lay in the dirt, though some places were completely erased by the sand. To think that only a decade ago this had been a major thoroughfare for traders was a sobering thought.

In the distance, white dunes rose and fell against the

backdrop of a cloudless blue sky. I kept my cowl pulled over my head to shade my eyes from the sun, which beat down on us relentlessly and burned my cheeks. Sweat drenched my neck and the palms of my hands where I held to the reins.

As the day wore on, we only paused a few times for a sip of water or to tend the horses. I reapplied the rosewood oil whenever I could, and it helped to numb the pain, but the jostling motion of the horse wasn't helping.

As afternoon turned to evening, with the sun sinking closer toward the horizon, we stopped near a rocky outcropping. I slowly slid from the saddle, gingerly climbing to the ground.

The wolf sniffed the sand as I crossed toward Raj and Drekken, who both sat on rocks. I sat, slowly, trying not to let them see me grimace. Raj's eyes met mine, and I glanced away, instead busying myself by removing a bit of bread and sausage from my pack.

"How do you feel?" Raj asked me.

"I'm well enough," I answered.

He only nodded, his expression riddled with guilt. I wished he would've stopped acting that way, especially since he had nothing to be ashamed of. It was the guardsman's fault I had this wound, not his, but how could I make him understand?

I tore off a piece of bread and fed it to the wolf. The air cooled as the sun approached the horizon. Bands of pink and lavender stretched across the sky.

"We've got at least another hour before we reach Al-Maar," Raj said. "Stay watchful. The sand demons will be out once the sun sets."

Drekken played a few notes on his lute as we rested. I focused on the sun as it descended beyond the hills. Though the desert was dry and desolate, it held a certain beauty. The vast expanse reminded me of how small I was in comparison to the world around me. It made me realize how much existed out there that I didn't understand or comprehend, how much magic was left to be discovered. I'd only ever seen a small portion of the world. The rest I'd read about in mother's atlases, and those were mostly speculations of what lay beyond.

"What will Al-Maar be like?" I asked Raj. "Do you think your family will be there?"

"They'll be there. They have nowhere else to go. The city was once the most beautiful place in all the land. There were hanging gardens, flowers and fruits you would have never seen before. It was a magical, colorful place. Now, there isn't much left. But it will be good to see my father and mother again, and all my nieces and nephews. They will love you, Gothel."

Apprehension settled in my chest. What if they didn't? What if they hated me? How could Raj be so certain they would like me? Better yet, why did it matter?

Suddenly it did matter. It mattered a lot.

No longer hungry, I tossed my last heel of bread to the wolf, who swallowed it whole. Did we have to go to Al-Maar? Wasn't there a way to pass it by on our journey to the Ice Mountains?

Drekken plucked another tune, a simple melody that made me think of fairies flitting over a pond, helping to calm my worries. Whether Raj's family liked me didn't matter. He wanted an Outlander girl, and most likely, they wanted the same thing for him. I had nothing to worry about, because I'd never had a chance with him in the first place.

We finished our meal—if one could call it that—and returned to our horses. Raj came to me as I fed Sable a handful of oats.

"I've said something again, haven't I?" he asked.

"What makes you think that?"

"Just a hunch, I suppose."

I glanced up at him. "I guess I'm nervous about meeting your family."

"Why?"

"I don't know. I don't have a good reason."

"You've got nothing to worry about. They'll love you. Especially my nieces, who'll most likely fawn all over your hair."

He ran his fingers through strands of my hair that had blown around my face. I self-consciously tugged on the cowl covering my head, and he moved his hand away.

"Do we have to go to Al-Maar? I know it would take longer if we go around, but I don't have a good feeling about it. I'm pretty sure they'll all hate me."

"Don't say things like that. You've never met my family."

I sighed. "Yes, you're right." But the nervousness settling in my belly didn't go away. If anything, it got worse.

Raj rested his hand on my shoulder, looking intently into my eyes.

"How are you feeling? Tell me honestly this time."

I rubbed at the wound needling through my skin. Riding all day had made it hurt more, but I refused to slow us down, so my only option was to push through it.

"I haven't succumbed to the chills, so I suppose I'm fine."

"You suppose?"

"Yes. I'm uncomfortable, of course, but that's to be expected. As soon as we get to Al-Maar, I hope to get some rest, and then I should be healed and ready to ride again."

"You don't have to be brave."

"What else can I be?"

He opened his mouth but didn't answer immediately. "Good point."

"I've managed to ride all day, haven't I? What's an hour more?"

He looked as if he wanted to argue, but only nodded after a moment's pause, then turned away and walked to his mare.

Tranquility pranced as he mounted. His Arabian looked suited to the desert, and Raj looked regal atop her. Sometimes I forgot how different we were. I was a prisoner bound to spend the rest of my life in a tower. He was a squire trained by the crowned prince.

A few stars appeared as we set off across the desert, the last rays of sunlight draining from the world. A bloated orange moon rose, turning the sand to copper. Heat radiated from the sand, but as the light disappeared, the air cooled, and I stayed huddled under my cloak.

A gentle breeze gusted, carrying clouds that billowed into the sky like a curtain across the stars. The moon rose higher, turning from orange to silver, and I stared in awe at the sky.

Millions of tiny dots glowed, creating a tapestry of twinkling lights, more than I'd ever seen in my life. I could hardly comprehend the enormity of the stars. How could there be so many? The entire universe sprawled before us, and I felt smaller—yet somehow larger—than I'd ever understood. The light from the heavens glowed over the sand, reflecting it so brightly, we didn't need lanterns.

I'd thought of the desert as a desolate, colorless place until now.

The sound of a piercing howl interrupted my thoughts. I stared across the dunes, thinking it was perhaps the wolf, but he trotted alongside me. The howl had come from straight ahead. We halted our horses.

Another wail echoed, making my skin prickle. I grabbed the knife from my boot. Its warm handle conformed to my palm. Searching the desert, I saw nothing but billowing sand against a backdrop of stars.

Something rose up over us. At first, it appeared to be another cloud of sand, but the air was too still. Fear made my hands grow clammy as the thing gained substance. It stood taller than two men, and it had no shape other than a silhouette of a head and shoulders.

Eyes the color of two simmering coals glowed from the area that should have been its face.

Raj cursed. "A sand demon."

TWELVE

"SPREAD OUT!" RAJ SHOUTED, TRANQUILITY shrieking as she reared up to face the sand demon. I backed Sable away from the shadowy form. Only its eyes stood out against its black, smoke-like form. How were we supposed to fight such a thing?

The wolf snarled and launched at the creature. Tentacle-like fingers whipped out, slapping the wolf across the chest. A yelp of pain ripped from the wolf's throat. He landed with a thud on the sand. The demon loomed over the wolf's body, and before I could think, I jumped from my saddle, ran to the wolf, and dragged him away from the demon.

Raj's horse raced past me. The glint of Raj's sword caught the moonlight as he stabbed its tip into the demon's form. Its inhuman shriek filled the air. Perhaps our blades had more effect on it than I realized.

A mass of tentacles rose up and swiped at Raj's seated figure, but Raj's horse moved light on her feet and avoided the ropy appendages. Raj swung his sword, severing several tentacles that landed on the ground with wet thumps. Blood seeped from the snakelike remains.

Blood was a good thing. It meant the creature could

be killed.

A tentacle whipped past me. I stabbed it with my knife, opening a wound that leaked bright red. The creature hissed, coming closer. Lashing out, it slapped my chest. I fell, losing my grip on my knife, hitting the ground hard. The wind escaped from my lungs.

Gasping, I rose to my hands and knees, searching for my weapon. From the corner of my eye, I watched Raj charge the monster. He aimed his sword for the head, but a tentacle lashed out, striking his horse.

Tranquility shrieked, showing the whites of her eyes as she toppled over. Raj leaped out of the way, still holding to his sword as a massive storm of tentacles launched toward him. Fear flooded my veins as I watched the tentacles writhe toward Raj. How would he ever stop so many?

A frantic tune played from the darkness, a sound of desperation. The vibrations of the lute strings stirred the air, creating a symphony of sound. The song increased in volume. The tentacles slowed.

Raj took his opportunity and lopped off several tentacles, then more and more, and finally drove his sword into the monster's head, right between its two glowing eyes.

The creature shrieked, its eyes burning with rage. Its covering of smoke faded away and floated into the sky. A gray hairless body fell to the ground. Getting to my feet, I finally spotted my knife, grabbed it up, and limped toward the creature. As I walked, the pain in my midsection throbbed, feeling as if my stitches had reopened.

Raj stood over the creature. Drekken and the dwarf, no longer in his wolf's form, also walked toward the thing on the ground.

"So that's a sand demon," Drekken said, gingerly nudging the limp body with the toe of his boot. It was the size of a hound. It had gray, leathery skin and the remains of tentacles for feet.

The dwarf cursed, calling the creature every vile name imaginable, some words I'd never heard before—and could only imagine what they meant. How many "sons of" and "wifeless mother's" he spouted about I lost count.

"Dwarf," I said, cutting him off. "That's enough. We all agree. Thank you."

He grunted but remained silent.

"It uses the smoke to hide its true appearance," Raj said. "They kill with their tentacles, then eat their victims, taking everything, even bone, leaving nothing behind. They've killed many travelers along this road, and no one can seem to stop them. They're vile creatures, and unfortunately, their numbers have grown exponentially ever since the high sorcerer destroyed our city."

"How far are we from the city?" I asked, flinching at the pain in my midsection, grateful for the darkness so Raj wouldn't see me grimace.

"Just there." He pointed at a ridge, and beyond, the faint glow of lights lit the sky. "We're nearly there."

"Good," I said, gasping as the wound tore at my flesh. Sable walked toward me and nudged my shoulder. I held tightly to her reins, not having a clue as to how I would climb atop her.

The others got to their mounts, but all I could do was stare up at the saddle, which seemed much higher than I remembered. With a deep inhale, I stuck my foot in the stirrup and attempted to climb up, but my midsection felt as if it had caved in on me—as if I was being stabbed all over again, and with a cry, I fell to the ground.

Stars danced in my vision as I stared overhead, cursing the stupid guardsman for stabbing me, the sand cold beneath my back.

"Gothel," Raj said, rushing to my side. His eyes widened as he looked at my wound. A large spot of dark blood stained my riding gown. He moved the fabric aside. Every touch sent waves of pain shooting through my insides, but I held my tongue. I refused to let him hear me scream.

"Your stitches have opened," Raj said. "You're losing a lot of blood. Drekken," he called. "Bring me bandages!"

The elf hurried to Raj's pack and pulled out strips of white cloth, then brought them to Raj.

"How badly is she hurt?" Drekken asked.

"It's worse than I thought," Raj said. "She may be bleeding inside."

The stars wouldn't hold still as I stared overhead. I blinked to make them stop moving, but it didn't help. The sound of Raj's voice faded. I thought he called my name but couldn't be sure.

A cold cloth dampened my forehead, helping bring me back to reality. The scent of rosewood oil hung heavy in the air. Where I felt pain only a moment ago, I now felt a tingling numbness.

"Gothel." Raj's voice brought me back to reality, and I focused on him.

"Yes," I said, my voice so weak I barely managed a whisper.

"We're going to take you to the healer in the old city. Hang on."

I nodded, and he scooped me up in his arms. The warmth of his chest enveloped me, and his taut muscles held me steady. I placed my hand on his chest to keep stable, feeling the beating of his heart beneath my palm. A strong rhythm thumped beneath my fingers.

He lifted me atop his horse, and I threaded my fingers through Tranquility's mane to keep from falling off. He climbed behind me, pressing his chest to my back, and holding me firmly around the middle, just below my breasts so as not to touch my wound.

"Does this hurt?" he asked, his mouth pressed to my ear.

"No," was all I could manage.

He kicked Tranquility's flanks. The horse loped toward the glowing horizon while the others followed us. I grasped Raj's forearms to keep steady as he held my waist. Wind rushed past, making strands of my hair batter my face. I held tightly to Raj, my consciousness fading in and out.

Keeping my gaze on the lights ahead was my only link to reality. I had to stay awake. If I was losing blood, falling asleep meant I might not wake again. Holding onto Raj's arms, I blinked slowly, the world fading in and out, the sounds of hooves pounding the sand, echoing in cadence with my heart beats. Tranquility loped with long, smooth movements, not as jerky as Sable had been.

"Almost there," Raj said, his voice deep, reverberating from his chest.

The lights grew closer. Flames flickered from torches and camp fires. Tents were interspaced among the ruins of a massive city that was nothing more than hollowed-out domes and towering sandstone structures, their windows empty and devoid of life.

Two men wearing rags around their heads and carrying spears blocked our path. Raj pulled back on the reins, stopping his horse. My head spun. Though the wound didn't ache as badly as it had earlier, I felt so dizzy, it took all my fortitude to keep from passing out.

"Raj Talmund? Is that you?"

"Yes, Babak. I've returned, but I need help. This is Gothel. She's a girl from the south who's aiding me on my quest to restore our lands, but she's been injured, and she's bleeding out. Where is Anahita?"

"She's in the healer's tent. Would you like me to lead you there?"

"Yes, straightaway."

"You frightened us," the other man said. "We weren't sure what demons approached us. We're glad you've finally returned."

"It won't be a long stay, I'm afraid. We're journeying to the Ice Mountains."

The man's eyes narrowed between the strips of cloth. "Gods forbid. Why would you go there, brother?"

"It's a long story."

"Very well. Tell it to us over the fire tonight."

"I will, as soon as the girl has been tended."

The man nodded. "Very well. Follow me this way."

One of the men turned and led us into the village. Smells of wood smoke rose up from the fires. Stews bubbled in cooking pots sitting atop coal beds, steam rising and mingling with the desert air, and I caught the scent of curry.

As we passed by, people wearing bright robes and sparkling beads gathered around us. Gasps came from the crowd. Small rubies shone from the foreheads of some of the women, and the children ran on bare feet covered in layers of dust.

I tried to take it in through blurry eyes, but it was all so different, and I had trouble thinking past the dizziness.

We stopped when we reached a tent that looked no different from the rest—square shaped with a point rising to an apex, its oiled fabric matching the tan color of the sand.

Behind me, Raj dismounted the horse. Without the warmth from his body, my skin bristled with chills. I wasn't expecting such a lack of warmth, such a shock without his presence close to me. I threaded my fingers through Tranquility's mane, holding tightly to keep my balance.

He reached for me, and I knew I had no choice but to release the horse's mane. I let go and fell into his arms. I hated that Raj had to see me this way. If I thought of it too much, it would mortify me. I'd always thought of myself as a strong, independent person, and to have to be reliant on him was more than I wanted to contemplate.

Still, as he cradled me in his arms, I couldn't think of anyone else I wanted near me.

Raj turned to the wolf and Drekken before entering the tent.

"I'll take her inside. Stay close by. Find some food if you can. Everyone here is more than willing to share."

Drekken nodded. "Can I do anything to help her?"

"Only the healer can help at this point."

The wolf stared up at me with his yellow eyes. I couldn't be sure, but I thought I saw a hint of concern.

Raj turned away from our companions and faced the tent. I breathed a sigh of relief as we ducked under the flap and entered a warm space lit by glowing orange lanterns and rugs strewn across the floors.

The scent of spice hung heavy in the air. Jars and clay pots crowded the shelves lining the room's walls. Raj placed me atop a bed of pillows. A woman entered from an adjoining chamber. She wore colorful robes of crimson trimmed in golden fringe that rustled as she moved toward us. Wrinkles lined her skin as she smiled warmly at Raj.

"Raj, blessed be, is that really you?" she asked.

"Yes, Anahita. I've returned, but only for a short time. This girl is called Gothel. She's aiding me in overthrowing the high sorcerer, but she was stabbed by one of his guardsmen. Can you help her?"

The woman knelt beside me and took my cold hands between her warm ones. Her touch made me think of my mother. Though she was a bit older and more filled out, it must've been the compassion in her eyes that reminded me of her, and brought me back to my childhood, when I'd been abed with a fever and she had tended me.

"Would it be all right for me to examine your wound, child?"

I managed a nod. Her eyes widened as she took in the blood staining my gown. With gentle fingers, she moved the fabric aside.

"It's not putrid, which is good, but the bleeding needs to be stopped and quite soon." Her eyes met mine. "I'm going to prepare a sleeping draught. It will help you rest while I stop the bleeding inside your body."

Again, I only managed to nod. I wanted to thank her for her kindness but couldn't find the strength to speak.

She stood and crossed to the shelves. Raj helped her fill a clay mug with hot water and herbs. The scent of mint and lavender mingled to fill the air.

When they'd finished, Raj knelt beside me. Anahita stood over us, holding the cup.

"I'm going to help you sit up," he said. He placed his hands under my arms as I raised into the best sitting position I could muster. Keeping one hand on my back to support me, he took the mug from Anahita in his other hand, then carefully brought it to my lips.

I sipped it, noting the strong taste of mint which helped mask the more bitter flavors. As the warm liquid filled my belly, my eyes grew heavy. I wanted to warn Anahita that this might not have been a good idea—that if I slept, I wouldn't awaken, but that thought faded, and I lost focus.

The last thing I saw was Raj kneeling over me, a sad smile creasing his lips, worry filling his eyes, his strong hands lowering me onto the pillows.

THIRTEEN

SUNLIGHT WARMED MY FACE AS I woke to an empty tent. My throat felt dry as I sat up and stretched my legs, surprised that my wound didn't ache as I moved.

Anahita entered through the flap. Steam rose from a wooden bowl she held between her hands. The scent of chicken broth filled the room.

"You're awake," she said, smiling.

"Yes, and apparently I'm alive, too."

She laughed, then knelt at my side and held out the bowl. "I imagine you'll be quite hungry after such an ordeal. I've made some soup. Do you think you can take a few sips?"

"Yes, I think so. Thank you."

She only smiled as she handed me the bowl. I took it from her, the heat emanating from the smooth wood warming my hands. Taking a sip, the salty broth filled my belly. After a few more sips, I felt full, and I gave the bowl back to her.

She took it from me, then placed it aside.

"How long have I been sleeping?" I asked.

"Many hours. It's afternoon now."

"Afternoon?" I'd lost almost a whole day. This wasn't

147

good. If we wanted to make it back to the tower before the spell killed Prince Merek, we'd have to hurry. But I was only starting to feel normal again.

"Where's Raj?" I asked.

"He went to visit his family."

"His family?" My insides roiled, and I wasn't sure if it was from my wound or my nerves.

"Yes, they've planned a feast tonight to celebrate his return. Are you feeling well enough to attend?"

"I'm not sure." I stretched my arms, my fingers, shaking out my legs, testing out my body's strength.

"I managed to stitch your wounds internally. I also applied a curing tincture made from the magical zahra blossoms growing in the frost fields. Without it, you would have bled out. You had already lost so much blood, I'm surprised you made it this far. But now, you should be quite recovered."

I glanced at my clothing. I still wore my dirty questing robes. The blood had dried on my gown and stiffened the fabric. Smoothing the hair away from face, the greasy strands tangled in my fingers.

"Anahita, would it be possible for me to bathe? Is there a river nearby?"

"I've a bathing chamber in the next room. Perhaps we're not as unsophisticated as you might think." She winked.

Embarrassment made my cheeks grow hot. I hated being ignorant.

"I'm sorry. I'm afraid I know very little of your people or your ways after the wars."

She took my hand. "There is no need to apologize. We're a lost civilization for sure, and we're not the sophisticated people we once were, though I should say, we still like a warm bath if we can have it. I shall have hot water and clean robes brought to you, if you'd like."

"Yes, that would be wonderful."

"Very good." Looking from my face to my hair, she pursed her lips, as if deep in thought. "Blue robes, with silver trim, yes that would do nicely."

"My clothes don't need to be fancy," I said.

She gave me a knowing look, as if she was privy to a secret. "Oh, but I believe it should be special for you."

"Why?"

"Because I've known Raj since he was a child. He would run through the streets with bare feet and that smile that lights up his face. You know the one, yes?"

I had to laugh. He had a charming smile. Sometimes too charming. "Yes, I know, but what's this got to do with my clothes?"

"He's never looked at a girl before, much less cared for one the way he cared for you."

My heart pattering, I glanced away from her. "Then you misunderstand. He was only trying to save me. He would've done that for anyone."

"Nay, child. I saw the way he looked at you."

I exhaled to steady my breathing. "He doesn't think of me in that way. He told me he prefers Outlander girls."

"No. He prefers you, that is why he shall see you the way he ought to—in the robes of an Outlander. You will look splendid." She tapped her chin. "The turquoise jewels for your hair. Yes, that will do nicely."

I wasn't sure I liked where this conversation was going. "But I'm not an Outlander. Dressing as one won't change that."

She only smiled. "We'll see."

She took the bowl and left the way she'd come. I stared at the canvas overhead, wondering how I'd gotten to this point. Our journey hadn't gone at all as expected, and my feelings for Raj had grown deeper than I cared to admit. Did I love him? I didn't know, but I knew I cared for him—probably more than I ought to.

Anahita thought he cared for me, and I didn't disagree, but I had no clue if his feelings ran deeper, or if I was a mere infatuation until he found a more suitable Outlander girl.

It did no good to worry about it, so I attempted to put Raj from my mind. Several women entered the room carrying buckets with steam rising from their surfaces. They gave me polite smiles as they held the buckets and crossed to the opposite chamber. Sounds of pouring water came from the room.

Gritty sand coated my skin and clothes, and I only hoped I got the opportunity to burn my gown and breeches at the earliest opportunity. After the women left, I pushed up from the pallet, my muscles weak and protesting. I managed to sit upright, then stand, and walk across the room.

As I moved, the exertion helped clear the fog from my head. I lifted the flap leading to the next chamber, and stepped into a warm space, where a copper tub sat amidst stacks of folded drying cloths. Shelves sat around the room's perimeter, their timbers lined with jars of soap pearls that shone iridescent in the firelight coming from a fire pit opposite the tub. The honeyed, smoky odor of incense hung heavy in the air.

I searched the stacks of soap pearls, testing each one,

some smelled like spice, others like flowers. I settled on a bottle of blue-colored pearls that smelled of jasmine, then turned to the tub.

Removing my clothing was more of a chore than I'd anticipated, and I winced at every movement. Although my wound no longer ached, my sore abdominal muscles felt as if they'd been torn apart.

After tossing aside my last shred of clothing, I stepped into the tub and sank to the bottom, the water level with my chin. I wasn't sure if anything in my life had ever felt so heavenly.

I soaked until my fingertips turned wrinkly, and then decided I'd better wash before the water went cold. Picking up the glass of soap pearls, I poured a handful into the water, then worked them into my hair until I created a lather.

The dirt and grime of the past week of traveling sloughed off—and I imagined letting all my past pains go—my insecurities at leaving Rapunzel, my fear from losing my mother, my vain hopes of having Raj be a part of my life. I let them go and simply enjoyed the moment.

When I felt ready, I left the tub and dried off. Wrapping a drying cloth around me, I entered the opposite room and spotted a stack of shimmery fabric folded atop my pallet.

As I lifted the cloth, I wasn't sure I'd ever felt fabric so silky and light. What was it made from? The blue robes were trimmed in silver brocade with crystals worked into the pattern.

Turning the robes around, I wasn't sure how I was supposed to put them on. Did I wrap them around me? Were there fasteners of some sort? And what were the smaller pieces for? Were they undergarments?

I shifted the fabric around, putting pieces together atop the pallet until I arranged them to look like some semblance of clothing, with the smaller, form fitting pieces beneath the larger robes.

I pulled on the top piece first, then the bottom, then the smaller robe that fell to my knees. The final piece—the larger robe, was the only clothing that remained. I lifted it, turning it from front to back, then threaded my arms through the long, dramatic sleeves. Its hem swept the ground.

A brush also sat on my pallet, and I picked it up, then combed through my long strands, working through the tangles until my hair shone.

"Are you ready?" Anahita's voice came from outside the tent.

"I think so," I called to her.

She entered, carrying a handful of jeweled necklaces and bracelets that glinted in the candlelight. She placed them on the pallet, then straightened to look at me.

"Have I put them on correctly?" I asked.

She smiled. "Almost. The re'hushka is backwards. Here, let me help you." She removed the larger robe, then the smaller one, turned it around, and put it on me again.

"There," she said, standing back. "Perfect. I've brought a few things for you. See what you think?" She picked up the handful of jewels and held them out for my inspection.

"They're lovely, but I can't wear any of these. They must cost a fortune."

"They're of little value to anyone anymore. Outlander jewels have grown out of fashion everywhere but here. What about this one?"

She picked up a piece that could have been a necklace, yet it was too complicated, with long golden strands and turquoise jewels that formed two points, holding all the strands together, almost like a spider web.

"This goes on your head. Like this." She lifted it up and placed it on my head, then straightened one of the jeweled pieces to fit at the center of my forehead, with the golden strands looping behind me, and the other jeweled piece resting at the back of my head.

"Beautiful," she said. "I've a mirror somewhere." She searched through the stacks on the shelves until she pulled out a mirror of polished copper. I took it from her and looked into it. Gasping, I hardly recognized myself. Turquoise crystals glinted from my headpiece, matching my hair and eyes. I glanced down at my dress that flowed around my feet, rustling as I moved, the silver brocade shimmering. The bodice hugged my waist and chest, and the V neckline, embroidered with the same silver thread, plunged to just above my breasts—not enough to be revealing, but more formal and daring than anything I'd worn before.

"I should let you know," Anahita said, "Raj is with his family now, but they're celebrating in our village gathering place. Your other friends are with him. Shall I take you there?"

"Yes, except I think we've forgot one thing. I have no shoes."

She waved her hand in a dismissive gesture. "You've no need of shoes here. But I have brought this." Searching through her pile of jewels, she held up a band that looked like a bracelet. Small silver discs jangled as she held it up.

"Do you dance?" she asked.

"Dance? No. Not really."

"I think you should like to try. Everyone dances here. Would you like to wear this?"

"Okay." I held out my arm, but she chuckled quietly, then knelt and attached the bracelet to my ankle, looped a leather strand through my toes, then attached it to the piece around my ankle.

"There," she said, standing. "I believe you're ready. Follow me." She turned and exited the tent. I followed, feeling a bit foolish for wearing so much jewelry and sweeping, colorful robes. I'd never been so decorated in my life, and I felt a bit like a jester in a costume.

The ankle jewelry jangled with every footstep as I left the tent and entered the village. The sights and smells barraged my senses from every direction. As evening descended over the village, I realized I was finally getting my chance to experience the city of Al-Maar.

People and children talked and laughed, crowding around their tents or fires, wearing robes of all colors. Purples, oranges, and blues jumped out at me. A gentle breeze carried the spiced scent of curry. The peppery aroma seemed to come from everywhere, not only from the cooking pots sitting atop the fires, but from the air, the sand, the clothing, and oilskin tents. It was as if the spice had infused with the culture, flavoring it with its brilliant burst of life.

Lazy rays of orange sunlight stretched across the sky, lengthening from one end to the other, not rushing to set as I followed Anahita through the tents, and then to an area that led into the old city.

Not much remained of the towers and spires that had once risen over the city. Most lay in ruins, piles of rubble that Anahita deftly moved around, her hips swishing back and forth. I followed slowly, still feeling weak, although none of the pain lingered. I had that to be grateful for.

Sand shifted beneath my bare feet as we entered an area that could have once been a town square. Skeletal buildings rose into the air, their windows empty as they stared down over the small crowd of people. Music played on unfamiliar string and wind instruments, and those gathered danced to the lively tune.

I spotted Drekken and the wolf standing on the edge of the crowd. Anahita and I approached them, and the elf gave me a charming smile.

"You had us all worried," he said. "I'm glad to see you've recovered."

"Thank you. Have you seen Raj?"

"No, but I'm sure he's in the crowd somewhere."

The wolf gave a playful *bark*, and I scratched his head. With his tongue lolling, he looked happier than I'd seen him in a long time. Al-Maar had a way of getting into your blood and making you feel at home.

Anahita stood beside me. "Raj is most likely in his family's chambers. It's one of the only remaining structures in the city. Come, I will take you to him."

She started walking toward the crowd, but my nervousness kept me rooted to the spot. Was I ready to see Raj again? And his family?

Of course I was. I would do it because Raj was a friend, and nothing more, and I had no reason to expect anything else.

We moved through the crowd. I reached up to pull a cowl over my head and cover my hair, but remembering I had none, I balled my fists instead. In this place, I would have to get used to being without my protection.

I followed Anahita to the other end of the square where we stepped onto a road paved in cobblestones that led toward a semicircle of two-and three-story sandstone buildings. Only a few piles of rubble blocked our path as we made our way to the tallest one.

In the evening light, the mosaic of colorful tiles decorating the structure's façade shone with brilliant gemstone colors—emerald, ruby, and opal. The square-shaped tower was several stories tall, with the mosaic decorating the outer walls, trailing up toward the top floor in a pattern of vines and flowers.

The desert blooms here.

"My goodness," I said, stopping short. "Did all buildings look like this one before the war?"

"No," Anahita said, her eyes smiling sadly. "They were much larger and more beautiful. This is only a taste of what was here before."

I stepped to the structure, running my fingers over the glass tiles, the surface warm and smooth.

"Raj lives here?" I asked.

"He lived here, yes. This is his family's home. Come, I will show you inside."

She brushed past me and walked toward the entry. The doorway was impressively tall, with the top of the arch tapering to a point. I followed her into the building.

The sound of running water echoed through the open rooms, and flowering plants and cacti potted in large painted jars lined the corridors. We entered a round space with a fountain situated at the center. Water streamed from the top of the fountain, flowing around petal-shaped platforms jutting from the center, then pooling in the basin at the bottom.

The same colorful tiles I'd seen outside had also been worked into the fountain's construction, lining the sides of the basin in jewel-toned colors that glinted in the sunlight streaming inside.

As I looked up, the ceiling opened all the way to the top of the building. A circle of faded blue sky peeked from the top of the opening. Below it, railings lined the floors overlooking the fountain. Plants in colors of verdant green hung from the balconies, their trailing tendrils stirred by a gentle breeze.

"This is an amazing place," I said, looking from the fountain to the top of the open-air dome. "It's magical."

"Not magical, my dear, but close enough. Come, they will be leaving soon to join in the celebration."

I hurried as Anahita walked past the fountain to an open doorway. As we crossed through, we spotted a staircase and took it up to the next level. Animated voices came from above. We stepped off the staircase and entered a long hallway. Children's laughter echoed as we walked toward a doorway at the hallway's end.

The familiar feeling of nerves pinching my insides returned, and I ran a hand over my gown, self-consciously smoothing the wrinkles that weren't there to calm the turmoil in my mind.

If I was being honest, I held out hope that I had a chance at a life with Raj. The thought made me happier than anything I could imagine. It made my head feel light and my heart race with a feeling of euphoria. Perhaps that was why I wanted so badly to shut those feelings away, because if a relationship never worked out, I wouldn't be crushed.

Exhaling nervously, I followed Anahita through the doorway and inside a brightly lit room. Bodies crowded the space. Some sat cross-legged atop pillows covering the floor. Others stood in the corners talking quietly, while children raced through the open spaces.

I spotted Raj across the room. He wore the clothing of an Outlander, with dark, plum colored robes thrown around his shoulders, accentuating his broad frame. His black pants and shirt were adorned with a simple golden belt. Without his armor, he looked like a true Outlander. His feet were bare, and his dark hair, washed and combed, fell in soft waves to his chin. He'd shaved, and his smooth skin glowed in the waning sunlight streaming inside through the room's many windows.

He smiled as he looked up at me, setting my insides on fire. His brilliant countenance lit up the room. I couldn't draw in a breath of air, and I had the urge to leave as quickly as I'd come. But I hadn't come this far just to turn away.

"Gothel," he said, crossing the room in three strides. He stood before me like a prince of the Outerlands, and I was positive this couldn't have been the same man who'd traveled with me, went without bathing, slept on the ground, and ridden through sandstorms until we'd both been covered in dirt. No. This was someone else entirely. Someone noble.

"I'm so glad you've come," he said, sounding like the Raj I remembered, slightly giddy and boyish. He took my hand and kissed my knuckles. His soft lips lingered only a moment, yet it was long enough to set my skin tingling.

"You look breathtaking," he said, a mischievous twinkle in his eyes as he reached out and touched my hair. This time, I didn't flinch.

"Thank you," I replied, not knowing what else to say.

"Are you feeling better?" he asked.

"Yes. The pain is gone. I'm only a little weak, but I'm sure that will pass."

"Good. I knew Anahita would heal you. She's a miracle worker."

Anahita smiled. "Bless you, child, for returning to us. We needed you here."

"Only for a short time."

"Yes, but a short time is better than none. It's not the same without you."

"Someday, I hope to stay longer."

"I should hope so. Have you spoken to your mother?"

"Only briefly. She wants to speak to me tonight."

Anahita cleared her throat, and I detected a hint of sadness in her eyes, but I wasn't sure why. "Good. You must speak to her, but wait until after tonight, after the dancing."

"I will, but I don't understand. What's so important that I must wait until tonight?"

She patted his hand. "You will see." She smiled, though her voice took on a melancholy tone. "Now, let me greet the others. I believe Gothel is anxious to see you again, so I will let you be."

She wandered away from us to speak to the others. Confused, I watched her go.

"What was that about?" I asked.

"I'm not sure. When I arrived, my mother asked to speak to me tonight, but she wouldn't tell me why."

"It must be important if she's waiting all this time to tell you."

"I agree. Most likely it's about my inheritance. They always bring that up every time I visit."

"Your inheritance?"

"Yes. They want me to stay and rebuild our city. Get married. Claim my inheritance and eventually take the throne."

My insides squirmed. "Take the throne? What do you mean? Are you a—a prince?"

"Prince of a decimated city. Yes."

Suddenly dizzy, I sat atop the nearest pile of pillows, my ankle bracelet jangling with an unceremonious clatter.

"Gothel, what's the matter?" He knelt beside me. "Are you unwell again? Let me fetch Anahita—"

"No." I grabbed his arm. "Raj, why didn't you tell me you were a prince?"

"Does it matter?"

"Yes! Don't you understand—that's the reason the curse didn't affect you when you went inside the tower. I wondered why the prince fell under the spell and you didn't. I thought it was because you weren't of noble blood. But that wasn't the reason. It's because you're the prince spoken of in the foretelling. You're the one who will free Rapunzel. And…" I couldn't finish. Some things I'd never spoken of, and for good reason.

"And what?" he asked.

I shook my head.

"And what?" he repeated.

"And kill the witch who guards her," I whispered, my voice haunted.

"What?"

"That's what the foretelling says. I'm sorry, Raj."

"Don't be. That's ridiculous. I would never kill you."

"But I'm a witch. You're a prince. Foretelling or not, that's how these stories end."

"No." He took my hand. "That's not how our story ends."

I swallowed hard. He'd said our. "You mean that?"

"Absolutely. I swore to protect you and so I shall. I swear to you that I will never harm you."

He smiled, showing his dimples, and I couldn't help but reach up and cup his cheek. "Why didn't you tell me sooner?"

"I supposed it wasn't all that important. I'm hardly a prince. Not anymore. How can one be a prince if they have no kingdom?"

"But you still have your people."

"A very small number of them. That's true."

"I don't understand. Why did you leave the Outerlands when you could have stayed here to become their king?"

"Because I knew that if our people were to survive, I'd have to know more about the world. I couldn't let what the high sorcerer did to us happen again, so I swore I would learn everything I could about war and swordplay. If he came at us again, we would have a fighting chance. Becoming Prince Merek's squire wasn't my first choice, as I was willfully coerced into doing it, but it suited my purposes well enough, so I went along with it."

"But if you're truly a prince and you broke Rapunzel's spell, that means you're destined to marry her and rule our kingdom."

"Then I won't marry her. I'll let Prince Merek do that instead."

"No, you can't. Don't you see? The only way this works

is for the one who breaks the spell to marry Rapunzel. That's the only way to free her from the tower."

"Why?"

"Because that's the way my mother's curse worked. I'm sorry, Raj, but if you're truly the prince who freed Rapunzel, then to save our kingdom from Varlocke, you have to marry her."

He sat up straighter, his shoulders taut, the smile gone from his face. "All these spells and curses are rubbish. Why can't we just live the way we want to without being manipulated?"

"Because that's the reality of the world we live in."

He turned to me, sighing, then took my hand in his. "Then let's ignore all that for now. I say we enjoy the evening."

I couldn't contain my smile. There was something about Raj that was so welcoming and genuine. He put my mind at ease unlike anyone else. "I agree."

He stood and held out his hand. I took it, standing, doing my best to shrug off the unease of our conversation. I walked with him through the room, and he introduced me to one person after another. Cousins, aunts, uncles, and dozens of giggling nieces and nephews.

"There are so many. How do you keep track of them all?" I asked.

He laughed. "I suppose it's different from what you're used to."

"Very different. I was an only child. I never knew my family except for my aunts, and my memories of them were brief and hardly ever pleasant. This is like a new world to me."

"Yes, I guess it must be. Come, let me introduce you

to my mother."

He took my hand and tugged me across the room. A woman dressed in golden robes stood talking to a small group. She was shorter than me and had a slight, fragile frame, though her firm voice carried through the room.

"Mother," Raj said. "Please meet Gothel."

The woman turned her gaze on me. Black, intelligent eyes met mine. Wrinkles lined the skin of her small, angular face. She didn't smile as she nodded in my direction, but her eyes shone with kindness, reminding me of her son.

Her smooth hands clasped mine, and she nodded respectfully.

"*Sharo abedlin,*" she said.

"Sorry," Raj said, "she only speaks the native language. She says welcome."

"Thank you," I answered.

She nodded, a small smile creasing her mouth. In that one gesture, my fears melted away. I'd been so worried about meeting his family, and especially his mother, but maybe that was because I'd never had any good experiences to compare it to. It made me realize there were good people in the world, and not everyone was self-absorbed.

"*Makis. Laroohonti ami.*"

"She wishes us good luck on our journey," Raj translated.

"*Hania letti. Alliah damada upa edora.*"

"She apologizes that my father is unable to meet you. He's gone on a hunt."

"*Abu ledia.*"

"But she hopes we enjoy the dancing tonight."

"Tell her we will," I said.

Raj spoke to his mother in their language, then shared a smile and a quiet chuckle, making me wonder what they were saying.

"Come," Raj said, taking me by the elbow. "Let's get to the dance before it's over."

We walked away from his mother and toward the doorway leading outside. As we stepped into the hallway, the conversation and laughter faded, replaced with the sound of our footsteps as we walked along the balcony overlooking the fountain. Even from here, I could hear the musical sound of the water as it trickled over the stone petals.

"What were you saying to your mother?" I asked.

He smiled, a look of mischievousness glinting in his eyes. "She told me to be careful with such a beautiful girl."

Heat rose to my cheeks. "She must have been exaggerating."

"No," he said, taking my hand. The warmth of his skin made my fingers tingle. "She wasn't exaggerating in the least. She saw what I've always seen."

"You're teasing me."

"Why would you say that?"

I shrugged, feeling awkward and embarrassed at our conversation. He brushed a strand of hair from my face, his fingertips lingering on my skin, and my breath stuttered at his touch. Why did he have to make me feel so alive and amazing? Especially now since I'd found out who he was?

When we made it down the stairs and to the bottom floor, he still grasped my hand. I had the urge to ask him to let go, but he held my fingers in a firm grip, and I couldn't find it within me to release him.

Warm wind brushed our cheeks as we left the building. The last rays of sunlight descended over the once beautiful city, making the shadows lengthen into long, painted streaks, dark against the light.

Tonight, I decided to let go of my fears and worries. I would enjoy my time with Raj and quit worrying about the future. Tonight, I would choose to be happy.

FOURTEEN

THE MUSIC CALLED TO ME. I'd never heard anything so lively and exhilarating. As Raj led me to the town square, the glow cast from the bonfire reflected off the forms of dancing people wearing colorful robes. Raj kept my hand in a firm grasp as he led me into the group.

"Do you dance?" he asked.

"Dance?"

"Yes," he answered, a twinkle in his eyes. "Dance with me."

I quickly scanned the faces of the people surrounding us. Wouldn't they notice? He was their prince, after all. Would it bother them that he was dancing with an outsider? Plus, I hardly knew how.

"Raj, I don't dance."

"What do you mean?"

"I've only danced a few times before, and that was a very long time ago. I'll make a fool of myself."

"Nonsense."

Raj led me through the crowd. With the warmth of his fingers gripping mine, I did my best to push aside my fears and follow him. We stood near the bonfire, its heat flickering over my blue robes as Raj took a step away from me, then gracefully bowed. When he straightened, he placed one hand on the small of my back. With his other hand, he gripped my fingers. Butterflies danced inside me at the feel of his skin on mine.

"The steps to the dance are pretty simple," he said. "Front, side to side, back, front again, repeated. That's it."

As he guided me, it took me a few tries to make my feet work in concert with my body, but Raj gently corrected me, and soon, we moved together in harmony.

"I think I'm getting it," I said.

"Yes, you're a natural," Raj said, smiling. With his arms holding me firmly, my remaining fears disappeared. He danced with a strong yet gentle command as he held me closely.

"You seem at home here," he said.

"I suppose so, but you have to remember, I don't really have a home. The tower isn't somewhere I'd like to stay permanently."

He sighed, glancing up at the hulking, empty buildings encircling us. "I'm not so sure this is my home either. To be honest, King Duc'Line's castle feels more like home than here. But it is nice to see my family again."

"I agree. Your mother and nieces and nephews seem like good people."

"They are. Most of the time."

"Most of the time?"

"Yes, they're family. Love them one minute and can't stand to be around them the next, but I would never choose anyone else. You know how it is."

I wasn't sure I did. I had nothing to compare it to.

As we danced, a cool breeze caressed my cheeks, and I stared up at the stars. "I wish we could stay here forever."

"Me too," Raj answered, his voice quiet.

My mind wandered, and I imagined what it would be like to live in the city restored to its former glory. I couldn't picture a more beautiful place. But staying here wasn't an option. I still had a piece of a magical radish in my pack that I hoped to use to barter for a pair of enchanted shears. Perhaps one day, when all this was done—assuming I survived and wasn't killed by the man I was falling in love with—I would return to the once great city of Al-Maar.

"What are you thinking about?" Raj asked.

I shrugged. "Just wondering what I'll do when this quest is over. Do you think I could come back and visit?"

"Yes, I don't see why not." He smiled, and the amber firelight flickering in his eyes made heat rush to my cheeks. What would it be like to spend my life here—with him? The thought seemed absurd in every way possible, and I couldn't imagine such a future becoming reality. He was supposed to rescue the princess and kill the witch.

When the song ended, Raj led me to the edge of the crowd where we found Drekken and the dwarf waiting. The elf held his lute, his fingers twitching over the strings. The dwarf stood with his usual scowl.

"We've been waiting hours for you," the dwarf grumbled. "When are we leaving this place?"

My heart sank. I didn't want to ponder it.

"Soon enough," Raj answered. "We'll leave in the morning as soon as possible. I trust you've enjoyed your stay here?"

"I have," Drekken chimed in. "It's important for me to learn of all types of music and instruments. What a wonderful land you have here! The music is unlike anything I've heard before."

The dwarf crossed his arms. "It grates on my nerves."

"You're welcome to leave at any time," Raj said. "You've no need to hang around here. Our journey will only grow more dangerous as we leave this land to travel through the northern wastes."

"Nay. I'll not leave while this curse is still plaguing me. Your witch must cure me."

Raj and I traded glances. "There's a chance that may never happen," I said. "The witch who did this to you stole your name for good reason. She knows if you can't remember it, no one will have the power to reverse the spell. I don't know how you expect me to help you."

"Because I will remember my name. That's how. Once I do, I expect you to fix this curse." He turned and walked away, his wooden leg tapping the cobblestones as he went.

My shoulders slumped. He expected the impossible.

"Well," Drekken said with a swig from his flask. "I should leave as well. I want to know more about the instruments here. Plus, I may have spotted a comely lass or two." He winked. "If you'll excuse me." He walked away, slinging his lute's strap over his shoulder, humming a tune as he walked.

Raj grunted. "He's nothing but trouble."

"I agree. But you have to admit, his lute comes in handy."

"Yes, there is that."

Raj led me to what appeared to be a bench, but as I studied the large block of chipped stone, I realized it must've been part of a building. As we sat, I noticed the crowd had thinned, and only a few people danced near the fire. The music drifted—softer now—and its melody lulled me. I'd never been to a more perfect place.

"Gothel," Raj said, "I hope I'm not being too forward, but I feel I need to admit something to you."

"Admit what?"

He took my hands in his, and the intensity in his dark eyes caused me to catch my breath. "I'm falling in love with you."

A gasp escaped my mouth. "What?"

"I know this is horrible timing. There's a chance we'll never survive this quest. The high sorcerer's squadrons are trying to kill us. We don't have a certain future, especially if one were to believe in foretellings. But I can't keep my feelings inside any longer. I want you to know how I feel about you."

His confession shouldn't have come as a surprise. I'd suspected it for some time, yet shock overrode my senses. I didn't know what to say. I'd never been put in such a situation before. My pounding heart felt as if it would break through my chest. But I knew I had to be honest with him. The dwarf's words came back to me, and I knew I may never get another chance.

"Raj, I feel the same way."

"You do?"

I nodded. He smiled—that brilliant expression that stole my breath. I wasn't sure I'd ever felt happier, here in this place, where my worries seemed so far away. The fire crackled as Raj pushed a strand of hair out of my face. He leaned closer and pressed a kiss to my lips. My heart swelled. He tasted of peppermint, and the scent of wild curry and masculine spice enveloped me.

When he pulled away, I forgot to breathe. He squeezed my hand. "Will you wait for me? I've got to speak to my mother, and I'm already late. It shouldn't take long."

"Yes, of course." I realized then that I would always wait for him. No matter where he went or how far away he was, I would always wait for him. He gave me another quick kiss, then stood and walked away.

I sat on the bench and tried to breathe. I could hardly make sense of how I felt. Surely these sorts of feelings couldn't be normal. They were too overpowering, too all-encompassing. Was this what love felt like?

I pressed my hands to my cheeks, feeling the heat radiating from my skin. Raj had admitted he loved me, and I'd admitted the same. Was it wrong to feel so happy? My own mother had lost her husband after only a few years of marriage. What if the same happened to me?

But I was overthinking this as usual. He'd admitted he loved me, not that he wanted to marry me, and that was a big difference.

I stood and wandered to the fire where only a few people lingered. They cast curious glances my way, but I dodged them as I walked by, stopping as I reached the outskirts of the city. I didn't go far, as the city wasn't much more than a village. Standing on a hill overlooking the desert, a dry breeze rushed past, stirring my hair.

Orange light flickered from campfires scattered about the desert, giving a little illumination to the darkness. We'd come so far. We'd secured a piece of the radish and were on our way to the northern lands. I was so ready for this quest to be over and Rapunzel to be free of her tower—and for our world to be free from the high sorcerer, but nagging worries plagued me, and I wasn't sure what would happen once we confronted the high sorcerer. He'd killed so many people. What would stop him from killing us?

Heavy footsteps came from behind me. I turned around. Raj trudged toward me, his shoulders slumped, his face downcast.

"What's the matter?" I asked.

He shook his head as he stood at my side. In his hand, I noticed he clutched something.

"What's that?" I asked.

"I…"

"Raj, what's the matter?"

He opened his hand to show me a dagger. The blade was curved oddly, in a serpentine shape, and red jewels glinted from the golden handle.

"This was my father's," he said, then looked up at me. Sadness shone in his eyes. "He's dead."

"Dead?"

He only nodded.

"What happened?"

"Killed by a sand demon a month ago. They already cremated his body and placed it in the hall of our ancestors. I didn't get a chance to pay my last respects."

I didn't know what to say. What could I say to someone who just lost their father?

"They want me to take his place," Raj said, his voice detached.

"What does that mean?"

"Nothing for now, but eventually, I'll have to return and take my place as the king. I can't believe he's gone."

"I'm so sorry."

He nodded but didn't move from where he stood. "I just can't believe it. He was fine when I saw him last. I never thought it would happen. I always felt as if he would live forever." He breathed heavily, running his hand through his hair.

I hated to see him so upset. But what could I do to help him? I felt so completely useless.

"I should go. I need to make sure my mother is well. Will you be able to find Anahita's tent on your own?"

"Yes, that's no problem."

"Good." He took my hand, squeezing it gently. "Thank you for understanding."

"Of course."

He gave me a sad smile, then turned and walked away, his footsteps shifting in the sand until the sound disappeared. My heart broke for him. I turned and walked toward the city of tents, my thoughts on Raj—on the sadness I'd seen in his eyes.

I had few memories of my father, and I didn't remember his death. I had little to compare it to, but I knew the pain must've been overwhelming.

Wandering through the tents, I spotted Anahita's at the end of the row. When I entered, the room was empty except for my cot. Sitting on it, I pondered the evening I'd spent with Raj, and the extent of emotions that went with it. He'd confessed his love to me, and I'd done the same, but the evening had ended on a sad note. Would his father's death affect our journey to claim the shears? I hoped it didn't.

I rested my chin in my hands, wishing I could be with Raj now, but feeling helpless as to how to help him. Perhaps spending time with his family would help. Tomorrow, we would have to travel to the northern lands. I hoped he still wanted to go. What if he decided to stay here?

Rubbing my eyes, I knew I needed some rest before tomorrow's journey began. I removed the headpiece from my hair, and the jewelry around my ankle, then placed them on the pallet in front of me. An oil lamp burned on a bedside table, and the jewels reflected under the light of the flickering flame, sparkling with the deep color of turquoise blue.

I took the jewels in my hand, weighing heavier than they appeared, and ran my thumb over the facets warmed by my skin. I could never imagine owning such things. Holding them reverently, I stood, then carried them away from my pallet. Shelves with healing potions sat on the opposite side of the tent, and I placed them on an empty ledge. I reached out to touch them one last time, but hesitated, instead deciding to step away.

When I returned to my pallet, I sat without glancing at the shelf.

They weren't mine. They never had been. No matter how much I might've wished otherwise, nothing in these lands belonged to me.

FIFTEEN

OUR HORSES PRANCED AS WE stood on the outskirts of Al-Maar, looking northward. Mountains loomed just above the horizon, their peaks capped with snow. Raj sat atop his Arabian mare, the wind tugging at the dark strands of his hair. He hadn't spoken much this morning, only giving me a brief hello.

The wolf paced nearby, his one good eye scanning the desert. Drekken also sat atop his horse, sipping from his flask. His face looked more apprehensive than I'd seen thus far as he stared out toward the mountains. I supposed even his ale wasn't enough to chase away his fears of the northern lands. I didn't blame him. Few traveled there and survived.

Some of Raj's family members stood near us. As we started across the desert, they waved goodbye, though no one spoke. The red jewels of Raj's father's knife glinted from the sheath at his hip, a constant reminder of the parent he'd lost, and of the mantle he would take up once this journey ended.

We rode in silence, over the curving slopes of sand, until the city disappeared behind us. When we stopped for a brief lunch, I kept my pack close, glancing inside to make sure I still had the piece I'd cut from the magical radish.

In my bag, the radish glowed with a faint green light. I only hoped I could hold onto it until we reached my aunts' palace—and hoped it would be enough to trade for the shears.

As we packed up and continued northward, the wind changed direction, bringing the moist air from the north. I knew soon, we would approach the border to the north-lands. I glanced at Raj who rode ahead. We hadn't spoken of anything of substance all day, and I decided that need-ed to change.

I spurred my horse forward until I reached his side.

"Hello," I said.

He smiled—a look of forced happiness that didn't touch his eyes—and offered no greeting.

"We've made good time."

"Yes."

"I think we'll make it to the mountains tonight if we keep up this pace."

He only nodded.

"Raj, I'm sorry about what happened to your father. I wish I could offer you some kind of comfort."

"You already have." He smiled again, and this time, it almost touched his eyes. "I'm glad you're with me now."

"You are?"

"Yes, I am."

When his eyes met mine, I was reminded of his confession that he loved me. Was it really true? Or had I dreamed it all up?

"I'm ready to leave the desert," he admitted. "Al-Maar was once my home, but the desert is no place to live, where sand demons take your family. Whenever I'm done with this quest and return home, I will move them from the desert."

"Do you think they'll go?"

"Yes, I hope so. If it means they'll be away from the sand demons, then I'm hopeful they will."

"But last night you seemed so happy to be home again."

"Yes, that was before I found out about my father." He sighed, his shoulders sagging. "I miss him so much. I hadn't seen him in years, yet it seems so permanent now that I realize I'll never see him again. Never talk to him again."

"I'm so sorry. I can't imagine what it's like. I hardly remember my father. Losing my mother was hard, but I felt so much anger, it distracted me from my sadness—for a time, at least. Afterwards, I had Rapunzel to tend, and I didn't have time to ponder it much. Still, sometimes when I think of it, the pain can be overwhelming. It's hard to lose someone you love."

"Yes, it's good to know I'm not alone. Thank you, Gothel."

I smiled, hoping he knew that I understood. The wind blustered, bringing clouds of sand that blocked our view of the mountains. I hoped we reached them before night—and before the sand demons appeared.

We spurred our horses forward, only stopping for brief rests, until the sun began to sink behind the peaks. As the light drained from the world, we reached the foot-hills of the mountains. The air grew chill as we rode over the curve and dip of the landscape.

Scrub bushes and vines grew along the ground. Boulders pocked the landscape, some of them covered in moss.

As time passed, the landscape turned green, with a soft carpet of grass beneath our horse's hooves, and scrubby trees grew, some of their limbs heavy with fruit.

Ahead of us came the sound of running water, and we stopped before a shallow river flowing over smooth stones. The water reflected the pink and purple evening sky. Downstream, I spotted a waterfall tumbling from a high precipice that sparkled in the last rays of sunlight, then dropped to a pool of dark water.

We guided our horses to the pool and dismounted. The air felt different here—crisper and tasting of the spray hovering above the waterfall.

"Look." Drekken pointed to the pool. "Fairies!"

I followed his line of sight and found tiny orbs of green light bobbing above the pool's surface.

"I hate fae folk," the dwarf muttered behind me. I turned around to find him wearing his human form. He adjusted his eye patch as he studied the water.

"Hate them?" I asked. "Why would you say such a thing?"

"Nasty little critters. Always meddling in other people's business."

"I've heard they're a good omen," Drekken said.

I rounded to focus on the fairies once again, mesmerized by the soft glow cast from their bodies, and the quiet hum barely audible over the splashing water. On the shore, Raj unsaddled his horse, and I thought it best to do the same.

An hour later, we sat in front of a cheery campfire popping bright orange sparks, a skewered rabbit roasting on a spit above the flames. As the fire warmed me, I realized I was happy. I knew I had every reason to be unhappy and apprehensive—we were getting ever closer to my aunts, after all, but I couldn't help but feel content in this place, with the waterfall splashing behind us, and fairies over the water.

Drekken played a quiet tune on his lute, and its magic enchanted me. I sat with my chin in my hands, watching his fingers move deftly over the strings. Raj sat beside me, and hesitantly, he wrapped his arm around my shoulders. His warmth calmed me, and I quietly inhaled the scent of cedar spice.

I didn't want to move. I wanted to stay here with his arm around me. I would never want for anything again. I'd been honest and admitted my love for him, but was there more to it? Had he somehow bewitched me? Was this really how love felt? Or was something wrong with me? I would ask my aunts as soon as I got the chance—assuming they let us near them without killing us first.

After the song ended, we ate our meal in silence, listening to the sounds of the water.

"Tomorrow," Raj said, "we ride over the mountains."

An uncontrolled shiver coursed through my body. I feared the mountains more than I feared the Spirit Woods. If the cold didn't kill us, the monsters would. Luckily, we had Raj with us, and Drekken's lute. We also had my magic, though how much use it would be, I wasn't sure.

We also had the dwarf with us. If anything, his foul mood could repulse the nastiest beasts in the northern lands. Those creatures didn't stand a chance.

As we rolled out our packs, I glanced at the water, watching the fairies' lights reflect off the dark, glassy surface. Raj walked toward me and placed his sleeping roll on the ground next to mine.

"Mind if I sleep beside you?"

"Of course not."

"Good." He unrolled his blanket and spread it over the ground. Perhaps I should've been wary of his nearness. Was it proper for him to be so close? But here in this place—a place of magic—those worries didn't seem to matter. Besides, with Drekken and the wolf so close, it wasn't as if anything improper could happen. Not that I wanted it to happen. Not at all. Right?

In truth, I wanted him to kiss me again. I wanted it so badly, I could hardly comprehend it. But since he learned that his father had died, he'd been distraught and distanced, and the only thing I wanted right now was to be able to comfort him.

"How are you feeling?" I asked as he settled beside me.

"As well as can be expected. I'm grateful for this journey. It keeps me distracted from thinking too much about my father."

He unsheathed the knife from his belt, its red jewels glittering faintly in the firelight. "At least I have this to remember him by."

"Yes."

"He was the best man I've ever known. He treated my mother well—never raised his voice at her once. I don't remember him ever being angry. I wish I could be more like him."

"You're more like him than you think."

"What do you mean?"

"You're a good person. You've got a kind heart."

"That's nice of you to say."

"It's the truth."

He sighed, looking at the stars. "What do you know

of this place where your aunts live? Have you been there?"

"I only know of what my mother told me. My aunts live in an ice palace. It's supposed to be very beautiful."

"What can you tell me about your aunts?"

"I've met them only briefly. They visited Varlocke's castle when I was younger. Their names are Neleia and Gwynna. They were nice enough to me, fawning over my hair and giving me sweets. They even gave me a new dress with a blue ribbon. But they didn't get along with the castle staff. They killed the page boy with a mortis spell for misplacing their trunks. They laughed as he gasped for breath and died. After that, they never came back to visit again. Not that anyone wanted them to."

"They sound like monsters."

"They are—but they've been alive a long time. They don't think like us. They don't value life the way we do."

"Do you think we'll survive this?"

"I hope so, but you knew how I felt about this journey from the beginning. We've managed to make it this far, so maybe there's a chance. But I won't deny that my aunts scare me. They have no concept of right and wrong. They only do what's best for them. If they decide to kill us, nothing we can do will stop them."

"Then let's pray they don't decide to kill us."

"I agree."

He reached out and placed his hand atop mine, his skin warming me. "When we get through this, I hope we'll have a future together."

Future? What did he mean by that? I didn't want to read too much into it, so I decided to act as casually as I possibly could. "I hope so too."

A chill breeze rushed past, so I pulled my blanket up

to my chin. Raj released my hand, and that faraway look returned—an expression of sadness, as if thoughts of his father had returned once again.

He turned away from me, so I lay staring overhead, at the boughs of the trees swaying in the wind, wondering how we would manage to convince my aunts to not only let us live, but also help us.

I hadn't admitted it to Raj, but I'd remembered what else my aunts had done while staying at Varlocke's castle—and of what they'd told me. Something I would never repeat to anyone.

I went to sleep listening to the waterfall, hoping its calming sound would chase away my nightmares.

Sixteen

Morning sunlight shone through the tree branches as we mounted our horses. I hadn't slept well. Despite Raj's presence beside me, nightmares of my aunts had plagued me. I wasn't ready to see them again—or ever.

The reality of seeing them began to set in. For some time, I thought perhaps we'd never reach their mountains. In all truth, we should have been dead by now. I almost preferred death. Raj had no idea of the danger we were about to face, and I was certain I hadn't warned him well enough. But what more could I tell him? We couldn't turn back now. We had no choice but to move forward.

We rode away from the waterfall and followed the stream until we were able to cross. I lamented leaving the peace of the clearing where we'd slept. After we started up the mountains, I wasn't sure where we would find shelter again.

The air turned cooler as we climbed up the slopes. We found a narrow trail and followed it. Despite my fears, the scenery took my breath away, and all I could do was stare at the soaring granite cliffs, dramatic waterfalls sparkling in the sun, and flocks of chattering fairies as they flitted through the air.

As we climbed higher, the greenery faded, replaced with patches of snow. We crested a steep hill and rode to a ledge overlooking the jagged landscape punctuated with large boulders and snowy plains. Far on the horizon sat the jagged line of the Ice Mountains. Wedged between the cliffs was a glittering blue jewel, merely a speck from this perspective.

"That's the palace," I said, pointing.

"Are you sure?" Raj asked.

"Yes, I've seen paintings of it. That's got to be it."

"Then that's good. It means we're close. A few more hours of hard riding and we should make it before nightfall."

"Yes. Good." Although I wasn't sure I could fully agree.

I pulled my cloak around me to shield my body from the biting wind as we set off down the mountain. Our horse's hooves echoed as we reached a canyon with walls that rose like jagged spires on either side of us. We stopped briefly for a lunch of cheese, nuts, and a few sips of water, then continued onward once again.

We rode until my legs burned, and still we kept going. Night approached as we cantered our horses onto an open plain. Snow lightly fell around us, blanketing the world in white. Beyond the open landscape, the crystal spires of a castle rose before us. Even from this distance, the palace was unimaginably larger and more sprawling than I had envisioned.

Blue light sparkled from the spires that seemed sharp enough to cut through the sky. The deep purple evening reflected the towers. The scene was deceptively beautiful.

We stopped when we reached the moat surrounding the castle. Glacier blue water churned through deeply carved tunnels, and large blocks of ice bobbed in the waves. I tasted salty flecks of foam on my tongue.

"We'll have to get them to lower the bridge," I called over the rushing water.

"How do we do that?"

"I'm not sure."

The wolf paced along the moat's edge, his thick fur bristled along his back. Drekken kept his strange red eyes locked on the drawbridge rising above the moat, its ice walls studded with frost-coated spikes.

We dismounted our horses and paced the shore near the moat. Frozen crystals danced on the wind. Snow and ice crunched under my boots as I paced, staring overhead at the towering spires that reminded me of knives.

Anxiousness weighed on me. I didn't want to be here, but it was too late to turn away now.

"What do we do now?" Drekken's voice echoed over the churning water.

"Maybe we could find a cave of some sort that would lead us inside?" Raj suggested.

"I doubt we'll find anything like that. My aunts used magic to construct this castle. They wouldn't have created any way inside except the ones they wanted."

We continued pacing, but as the light faded and our limbs grew numb with the cold, I began to lose hope.

What if we didn't find a way inside? Would we have to camp here? Would we survive the night?

I balled my fists, feeling my fingers cold and stiff inside my gloves. The horses whickered nervously, and I walked to Sable, patting her neck. The last rays of light faded, and it seemed my hope drained away with it.

I had no doubt my aunts knew we were here. They

wouldn't let us inside unless they wanted to.

Drekken, Raj, and the wolf walked to me.

"What do we do now?" Drekken asked.

"I can think of only one thing. I was hoping to use it to barter for the shears, but that might have to wait." I knelt and opened my pack, carefully lifting out the piece of radish. The greenish glow encompassed my hands, warming them.

I stood, holding up the radish as the icy wind battered my face. "I come with a gift," I yelled. "Let us in!"

Only the sound of the wind broke the silence. I glanced at Raj, and the pinched line between his brows revealed his unease, which didn't help my nerves. Either we entered this castle, or we stayed here and made camp—either way, death was a likely possibility.

A noise caught my attention. The drawbridge shook, as if the chains were loosening, and then began to lower.

"Well, I guess we know what they want," Drekken said.

The gate lowered with the sound of metal links clicking through gears, then landed with a boom, causing clouds of snow to billow. When the air cleared, we stood at the lip of the drawbridge.

The wolf stepped onto it first, sniffing it, as if he weren't sure he could trust it. When he seemed satisfied, he trotted to the other side. After replacing the radish in my pack, I grabbed Sable's reins and guided her to the bridge. The others followed. I held tightly to the leather straps as I led my horse behind me. Our footsteps thudded as we crossed.

When we reached the other side, we stepped off the bridge and entered an open courtyard. Behind us, the gate began to close.

I stared around the courtyard. Flames flickered from ice crystal sconces, though I wasn't sure how the fire didn't melt through. It had to be magic. We walked toward a set of doors, and as we approached, they slowly swung inward.

The dark hallway leading inside was too narrow to allow our horses to enter, so we tied them to posts in the courtyard.

I patted Sable's muzzle. "Take care out here."

We left the horses behind and entered the castle. The ice walls surrounded us, reflecting a faint bluish light. Our booted feet echoed as we entered an immense domed chamber. A crystal chandelier hung overhead, reflecting in the pool of turquoise water directly beneath it.

Two dramatic winding staircases circled the pool's shore and led up to a raised dais where three thrones sat. Intricate snowflake patterns comprised the silver chairs. Two women sat on the seats. My aunts.

"Gothel," Aunt Gwynna said, her porcelain face flaw-lessly displaying a wicked smile. She wore her raven hair in braids that she twisted around her head. Her age was starting to show. Gray strands intermingled with the black, and lines wrinkled the skin around her eyes and mouth, though she looked no less dangerous. "Do come inside. We've been expecting you."

"You have?"

"Of course," Aunt Neleia said, waving her arm, mak-ing her golden robes trimmed in purple satin rustle. She looked even older than her sister, as her crop of white hair was covered with a crown, and most of it had fallen out.

Both women had an air of danger about them, and I swallowed my fear before I spoke.

"I've come for your help."

"Yes, we know," Aunt Gwynna said.

"Then… will you help us?"

"We haven't decided yet."

"You haven't?"

"Don't rush us, child. We've let you into our home, haven't we? Now, leave the radish with us and be gone. Return in a decade, and perhaps by then, we'll have agreed on a solution to your quandary." Aunt Neleia tapped her fingers on the throne. "Though why we should be so charitable is a mystery to me."

"Family," Aunt Gwynna said with a sigh, looking at her fingernails. "We owe it to her mother."

"Excuse me," I said, butting in. "But I can't wait a decade for you to decide."

"Why ever not?"

"I need you to help me now."

Aunt Gwynna leaned forward. "Careful, child. We don't look kindly on demands."

"Yes, I know. I'm sorry. But I've brought a gift to barter with." I reached into my bag and pulled out the wrapped piece of radish.

"Yes, yes, give it to us."

I held it close to my chest. "But this is for bartering. I want the magical shears to cut Rapunzel's hair."

"I see you have much to learn, child. The radish is not to be used for bartering." Aunt Neleia leaned forward, her eyes dangerously narrowed. "It's to keep us from killing you."

She snapped her fingers, and magical blue ropes appeared floating in the air above us. They wrapped around each of us, tightening until I gasped. The two women rose from their thrones and walked down the steps. As they got closer, the air grew chillier. From up close, I noticed their skin looked odd, as if it were coated with frost and seemed to sparkle as if lit from within.

Aunt Gwynna stopped as she stood in front of me. She reached out and plucked the radish from my hands. I felt completely helpless to stop her as she took a step away from me, the radish cradled in her palm.

"You can't do that!"

"Why not?"

"Because—"

She flicked her wrist, and the ropes creeped around my neck, choking me.

"Stop!" Raj said.

Aunt Gwynna paced to Raj, her heeled shoes ringing out. "It seems we have a prince in our midst, sister."

"Aye, we do."

"Shall we kill him?"

"Oh, yes! What a splendid idea. Behead him, I say. That's the best way to do it."

"Yes, it would be so lovely."

Gasping, I wanted to scream for them to stop, but only managed to choke.

"I shall draw my sword this instant and behead you both if you do not release Gothel," Raj shouted.

The sisters laughed. Gwynna snapped her fingers and the rope loosened around my neck. I breathed deeply, not sure I'd ever felt so grateful for air.

"Don't... touch him," I gasped.

"Demanding, isn't she?" Aunt Neleia said.

"Yes, perhaps if they spend the next year in the dungeons, it will help to break their spirits."

Drekken cleared his throat. "Madams, if I may, I do not wish to cause any trouble, but—"

"Hush, you." Aunt Gwynna said, waving her hand. His voice stopped working. His eyes widened, and he grabbed his neck, though no sounds escaped his lips.

"What did you do to him?"

"Silenced him, of course. A voice like his carries too much magic in it. He's a dangerous traveling companion, niece Gothel. I wonder why you decided to choose such a vile elf to join you on this quest."

"And what of this one?" Aunt Neleia chimed in, pointing at the wolf. "A mongrel shapeshifter? Dear niece, perhaps our sister never trained you as a proper witch. Traveling companions like these are hardly worth your time."

I expected the wolf to growl or react. I prayed he didn't change, or we'd all be dead in two seconds.

Please. Do not change.

He remained politely seated, his wagging tail thumping the floor, and I breathed a sigh of relief.

"Who I choose as my traveling companions is my decision. Could we please discuss the shears? If you give them to me—"

"Give?" Aunt Gwynna laughed, a cackling sound that made my skin crawl. "We give nothing. Ever."

"But for the radish?"

"Yes, a gift that will keep us from killing you where you stand. We shall discuss your plight while you wait in the dungeons where you'll be guarded by our dragon."

"No, wait, if we could just talk—"

Aunt Neleia waved her hand. The world around us disappeared, and a cavernous dungeon appeared around us. I fell on the ground, my back taking the brunt of the impact, and my teeth rattling in my skull. I rubbed my sore backside as I stood. As I inspected our new surroundings, I cursed my luck. I knew this wouldn't be easy, but I'd at least hoped to talk to them for a little longer.

"Where are we?" Drekken asked, his voice echoing.

"In the dungeons, I think."

"These don't look like dungeons," Raj said.

I glanced from the stone floor, up to the rock dome soaring above us, to the rough stone pillars. Only a little light illuminated the room, though I wasn't sure where its source came from.

"This is probably a cavern in the ice mountain. There's most likely an entrance to the castle somewhere."

"Could we use it to escape?" Raj asked.

"I doubt it," I said. "I don't mean to sound grim but I'm not sure it's possible to escape. Plus, we need to be wary. They mentioned something about a dragon."

"You think there's a dragon down here?" Raj asked.

"Yes, I don't think they would lie about that."

Raj sighed, looking up at the towering stone above us. "Let's at least have a look around." He unsheathed his father's dagger, and I also removed the knife from my boot. Our footsteps sounded loud as we walked over the uneven floor. Water dripped somewhere, a rhythmic sound that echoed through the cavern.

We approached a large mound that glinted in the faint light. As we narrowed the distance, the golden pile of coins, goblets, and crowns towered over us. A bleached white, human skull peeked from the mix, staring at us through empty sockets.

"I'm beginning to agree with Gothel," Raj said. "It seems there must be a dragon down here."

"What's to keep it from eating us?" Drekken asked.

"I don't know," Raj answered.

Beside us, the wolf glowed, then changed shape. The dwarf sat on the floor, his face pale as he breathed heavily staring up at the enormous pile.

"Dragon's teeth! I've never seen so much gold." He reached for a coin.

"Stop!" we all shouted as he grabbed it.

"Now you've done it," Drekken said.

"What?" he asked.

"Dwarves and their filthy coins. What if it's cursed? Did you think about that?" Drekken asked.

"Nonsense." The dwarf stuffed his pockets with coins.

"You're really going to steal from a dragon's hoard?" I asked.

"I see nothing wrong with it. I don't know why you're all being so judgmental. This gold is going to waste just sitting here. I don't see any reason not to take it."

"Because you'll attract the dragon's attention, and it will eat us alive in a horrific and gruesome fashion. Is that a good reason not to take it?" Drekken asked.

"I've seen no dragon here. I don't think there is one."

I rubbed my forehead, feeling a headache forming. He was more frustrating than Rapunzel.

"But on the off chance there did happen to be a dragon, wouldn't it be a good idea not to take its gold, so it won't have a reason to kill us?" I asked.

"Nay, you're all worrying too much." He looped a golden necklace around his neck. The ground rumbled beneath our feet.

The sound of grinding stone came from behind us. We rounded to find the wall splitting apart.

"What's happening?" I called.

"I don't know!" Raj called back.

The rumbling ground shook harder, nearly throwing me off my feet. The fissure in the wall grew wider. Sunlight blinded our eyes, and I had to shield my face. Icy wind blew inside from the opening. Whooshing wings accompanied the clatter of moving stones. The silhouette of a flying dragon appeared on the horizon. As it drew closer, its long, outstretched wings blocked out the sunlight.

"Ready your weapons!" Raj called.

A fireball erupted through the cavern.

SEVENTEEN

WE DUCKED AS THE FIRE engulfed the room. Heat singed my skin as I rolled behind a pillar. The dragon's enraged roar pierced the air. I glanced around the pillar to find the dragon had landed on a platform just outside the cavern. Sleek white scales covered its head and neck, though white feathers covered its large, lithe body.

Another burst of fire streamed from the dragon's mouth. The dwarf cried out, then changed his form to a wolf, loping away as a trail of fire followed. I gripped my dagger, but what good could my blade be against a dragon of that size? Raj crouched near me, his sword held at the ready in one hand, his father's dagger gripped in the other.

"Can you distract it while I attack?" he yelled over the noise.

"Yes, I think so." I slung my bag off my shoulder and rifled through the contents, frantically searching for anything that would distract a dragon. I grabbed a vial of crushed Chimera scales and held it at the ready.

"Go when I tell you," I said.

Raj nodded. The barrage of flames let up for a moment.

"Now," I yelled.

He jumped from behind the pillar and raced toward the dragon. I did the same, unstopping the cork and flinging the powder in the dragon's face. The dragon reared back, and Raj rushed at it with his sword, but the dragon whipped around and knocked him back with its tail.

Raj fell back, and I hurried to his side. Blood seeped from a gash in his head. Behind us, the dragon roared. Raj got to his feet, and we rushed behind another pillar as the fire trailed behind us.

Drekken also crouched behind the pillar, cradling his lute, his face pale.

"Drekken," I yelled. "What are you doing? Play!"

"I-I can't…"

"Play! Play now!"

"I can hardly move my fingers…"

"Buck up, man!" Raj yelled. "If you don't play then we all die. Play!"

Drekken nodded, his fingers shaking as he strummed an ill-tuned chord. He played another, then softly picked a tune on the strings. The dragon roared again, though its voice grew more subdued as Drekken's song continued.

I peeked around the pillar. The dragon shook its head as the music grew louder. Raj crept up on the creature, ready to impale its chest when bright light surrounded it. He fell back as the light blinded him.

I stood beside Raj as the dragon transformed from a beast to the form of a beautiful woman who collapsed to the ground. Breathing heavily, her gown of shimmering white fabric and feathers rose and fell with her inhalations.

Taking a guarded step forward, I tried to make sense of what I saw. The dragon was a shape changer?

Her light blonde hair looked silvery in the faint light

as it fanned out around her shoulders and cascaded down her back.

"Ouch," she said, rubbing her head.

Drekken still played his lute as he walked behind me and Raj. The wolf appeared from behind the pile of coins, his tail singed, but otherwise healthy.

"Who are you?" Raj demanded as he approached, his sword still held at the ready.

She sat up, and I was struck by her flawless skin and almond-shaped eyes. She looked ethereal—a true creature of magic. She narrowed her eyes at us, anger burning in her expression.

"Who am I? Who are *you*? Intruders? With that horrible music..." She rubbed her head again.

"Horrible?" Drekken said.

"Worse than horrible. Dreadful. Awful."

Drekken continued playing. "I'll have you know I've outplayed all the minstrels in every tavern of the western lands."

"Ha! Is that something to brag about? In taverns. Were the others drunk?"

Raj took another step forward. "Who are you?" he repeated.

"No one of your concern," she snapped back, then glanced at Drekken's lute. "Though I might be persuaded to speak if he stops with that noise."

"Will you try to kill us again if he stops?" I asked.

"I promise nothing." After a pause, she added, "But I couldn't transform into a dragon again anyway. I'm cursed to stay in this form until morning, so you might as well stop."

"If you try to kill us again, he will play."

196

"I won't try to kill you again." She crossed her arms. "I'm useless at slaughtering anyone in this form anyway."

I looked at Drekken and nodded. He stopped playing, then took a step toward the woman on the ground.

"You're a dark elf," he said.

"Am I?" she asked sarcastically. "What gave it away?"

"I thought the shape changers were extinct."

"They are. All except for me and one other."

"How did you come to be here?" I asked.

"As I've said, that's none of your business." She got to her feet and straightened, facing us. An aura of magic radiated around her, persuading me to step away, but I stood tall. "My name is Odette Von Alarissa, reluctant protector of the caverns of Ice Crystal Mountains. You are intruders."

"We thought we were prisoners. Although…" Drekken looked her up and down, his eyes lingering on her shapely frame, then he slung his lute over his shoulder and plastered on his charming smile. "To be honest, I think I could learn to live with being your prisoner. You'll get no complaints from me so long as you stay in that form and not the other."

She rolled her eyes, ignoring him. "You're prisoners?"

"My aunts' prisoners," I clarified. "They sent us here."

Her eyebrows rose. "Your aunts?"

"Gwynna and Neleia."

"I see," she said. "That's a pity. I couldn't imagine having them as relatives."

"I deal with it."

She walked around us, her bare feet quiet on the stone floor. "You should know I'm also their prisoner. It's not a situation I'm fond of, especially since I despise the cold. I plan to escape as soon as I can."

"Why did they imprison you?" Raj asked.

She smirked, and her eyes glittered as if she knew a secret. "That's a long tale. I'll have to save it for another time."

"How long have you been here?" I asked.

"Too long. Many years. But the question is, why are you here?"

I filled her in on the story of Rapunzel and the shears—how High Sorcerer Varlocke would continue to ravage our world unless we got them and freed Rapunzel and saved Prince Merek.

"The witches would never give you the shears," she stated matter-of-factly. "Even with the radish to trade. You've failed."

"We haven't failed yet," I said.

She turned her sharp gaze on me. "Maybe. They allowed you to live, which they don't do for anyone—especially for fools like you who choose to come to this gods-forsaken palace."

"Can you help us?" Raj asked.

She eyed him. "Help you? I help no one. But perhaps we may come to an arrangement. I could aid you, but I have my price."

"What's your price?" I asked.

"I want you to help me escape."

"If we do that, my aunts will kill us," I said.

"They'll also kill you for taking their precious shears. Either way, you're doomed."

She had a point.

"Do we have an agreement?" she asked.

I glanced at Raj. I half expected him to object, since

we'd already helped two pitiful creatures already, but he didn't speak up, so I took that as his answer.

"Very well," I said. "We'll do what we can, but only if you help us find the shears first."

Her eyes glittered, and I didn't like the look she gave us. "I give you my promise," she said.

Could I trust her? I had a feeling she would help us if it meant she was freed of this place, but what if that didn't happen?

"Well," she clapped her hands together, all smiles now that we'd promised to help her escape. "Are you hungry? Let me prepare a meal."

"We're starving," Drekken said. "And terribly thirsty, too. Do you have any elven ale by chance?"

"Elven ale?"

"Yes."

"Perhaps," she answered hesitantly. "As long as it doesn't loosen your tongue and cause you to play that ridiculous lute again. Follow me this way."

"Ridiculous?" Drekken muttered as we followed her around the pile of coins to the far side of the dungeon. An arched stone alcove overshadowed us, and colorful blue tiles decorated this section. A sheepskin rug covered the floor. She sat on it and motioned for us to sit in a circle around her. We sat, though I wasn't sure what was happening. I didn't want to be rude, but where was the food?

She cupped her hands, and blue light glowed, growing brighter, illuminating the white feathers lining the outer edges of her gown. As the light warmed us, a spread of assorted meats, cheeses, breads, exotic fruits, and tankards of ale appeared before us. The smell of seared meat made my stomach growl.

"Eat," she said, motioning to the food. No one argued as we placed food on our platters. Drekken grabbed the tankard, of course. I savored the sweet tastes of honeyed fruit, fresh bread, and tender meat. Somewhere in the back of my mind, I worried the food might've been poisoned or tainted with magical spells, but I was too tired and too hungry to argue. Besides, if Odette wanted to kill us, there were easier ways to do it.

"We need to leave soon," Odette said. "When the sun rises, I'll be transformed into a dragon. I'll have to leave the caves again, which means we only have until morning to find the shears and set me free."

"Where are the shears?" I asked.

"In the palace vaults. Escaping the dungeons will be dangerous. We've got to get past the ophiotaurus."

"Ophio-taurus?"

"Part bull, part serpent. A deadly creature. But..." she glanced at Drekken. "With the help of your lute, no matter how dreadful it may be, we should be able to escape."

"Dreadful? I beg to differ."

"Beg away," she said demurely, then stood, ignoring his glare.

We stood and walked toward a narrow stone-lined hallway. Raj walked beside me, and I felt grateful for his presence.

"It seems like we're finally getting somewhere," he said.

"I agree. We're so close to the shears now. I can hardly believe we've made it this far."

He took my hand in his and gave it a gentle squeeze. "I'm glad we made this journey together. I couldn't imagine doing it with anyone else."

I almost had to pinch myself to make sure this was

real. I'd never imagined a person making me feel so happy and loved—almost as if he were a missing part of myself that I'd finally found. But what did our future hold?

"Raj, after this is over with, assuming things turn out the way we hope…" I couldn't finish. I hardly knew what to say anyway.

"Assuming things turn out the way we hope, will we still be together?"

"Yes," I answered hesitantly, afraid of what the answer would be.

"If we get separated, I will make it a point to find you. I give you my word."

He smiled, making my heart flutter. I supposed I wanted him to say more—that he would do more than just find me, but even those words gave me more hope than I'd had before.

We walked through a narrow corridor and stopped as it opened into a larger chamber.

"The ophiotaurus is in here," Odette whispered. "This is the only way into the castle. Elf, get your lute ready."

He frowned. "My name is Drekken Von Fiddlestrum—not elf."

"Von Fiddlestrum? You're from the Malestasian Isles?"

"*Was* from."

"You left your tribe?"

"Not exactly. I was banished."

"Banished?" she asked, eyeing him. "How?"

"That's a story for another time, isn't it?"

"Hmm." She studied him. "I suppose we both have our stories."

"Yes, that we do."

They shared a look. Drekken cleared his throat, then

slung his lute off his shoulder. He cradled the lute's bowl, the painting of the flaming skull shining in the firelight as he played a simple tune.

We walked into the chamber. A giant of a beast rested in the room's center. The muscular torso of a bull took up its front half, and the tail of a rough-scaled serpent comprised its back portion. As we entered, it sat up and snorted loudly. Its eyes widened as it focused on our group. Behind it I spotted a small wooden door.

It shook its massive head, making the ring in its nose jangle. It stood, and its tail slithered around it, coiling. The bull roared, the sound nearly knocking me from my feet.

Drekken continued to play, and I prayed the song lulled the bull. I stepped along the edge of the room, the serpent's thick body only inches from my feet.

The bull roared again and stamped its feet.

"Drekken, keep playing," I muttered. I reached the door first and grabbed the handle, but before I could lift the latch, the sound of a string breaking echoed with a sour clang, and the bull roared so loud I was certain to go deaf.

The snake's body hit my back, sending me sprawling across the floor. My companions screamed as the bull charged them. Raj had his sword out with swift accuracy, and the wolf charged the bull, snapping its jaws around one of the beast's legs.

My head spinning, I did my best to catch my breath as I sat up, yanked my pack open, and pulled out the first vial I found. I read the label. Siren-song. It would have to do. As I opened the lid, its scream shrieked through the room, catching the bull off guard, and allowing my friends time to run to the door.

The snake's loops tripped Odette, grabbing her. They dragged her toward the bull's body. Drekken sprinted to the woman as the bull charged, but the beast knocked him back as it raced toward the woman.

Raj leapt at the bull, stabbing his sword into its hide. The creature bellowed, lashing out and hitting Raj to the ground. Raj got back to his feet in an instant. He unsheathed his knife and jumped at the bull, but the beast charged, nearly impaling Raj with its horns.

The bull reared up and attempted to trample Odette, but Drekken wacked the beast with his lute. The snake's coils relaxed for an instant, and Odette climbed free. I yanked the door open.

"Run," I screamed at the others. They raced through the door. I followed behind. As soon as everyone got into the corridor, I slammed the door behind us. We ran through the dimly lit hallway. My heart pounded as my feet hit the paving stones.

We stopped when we reached an open chamber. Breathing heavily, I tried to get my bearings. We stood in a circular chamber with a tall ceiling. Above us, moonlight shone through the blue glass of a skylight.

"Is anyone injured?" I asked, scanning our group.

"Nothing that will kill us," Raj said.

"My lute's broken," Drekken said, holding up two halves of his wrecked instrument.

"I'm sorry," I said. "Can it be fixed?"

"Maybe. But it won't be easy. If it's even possible." He sighed, looking with sadness at the broken wood. "Maybe I should've never left the dark lands."

"Nonsense," Odette said. "Not enough of our kind leaves the dark lands. You did a brave thing."

"Brave?" he asked, quirking his lips in a curious expression.

"Yes. Don't let it go to your head."

"Where do we go from here?" Raj asked.

Several hallways branched from the room where we stood.

"Yes, where do we go?" I asked, my voice quiet, though still echoing. It hit me then that we'd made it back inside the castle, and we were in danger of being discovered by my aunts—who would most likely kill us as soon as they found us. But we had no choice but to get the shears, escape, and do it before they discovered we'd left their dungeon.

"The shears will be in the archives in the topmost tower," Odette said. "We'll have to keep quiet. Although the sisters will be sleeping, there's a small chance they'll discover us if they're awoken."

"How do we get to the topmost tower?" Raj asked.

"Upstairs. We'll have to find the stairwell. I've been allowed inside the castle a few times. We'll find the stairs through this corridor. Follow me." She walked to the hallway straight ahead. We followed, walking on quiet feet. The castle remained eerily quiet except for the sounds of our footsteps. The only light came from the windows. Milky white moonlight shone over the crystal cold walls and floors.

We got to another room where a staircase spiraled upward.

"This way," the dragon lady said, leading us to the stairs. The steps were made of ice and sparkled faintly in the light. I held tightly to the banister—also formed of ice—though the steps weren't as slippery as I expected.

The ice shone faintly blue, as if lit inside by magic. After climbing past several floors, we reached the topmost point, and stepped onto an open floor with windows ringing the walls. Outside, the snowy mountains surrounded the castle, looking ghostly in the moonlight in front of a backdrop of stars.

Odette led us to a set of large bronze doors carved with images of nymphs and mermaids.

"The archive is through these doors," she whispered. "Keep quiet."

She pushed the doors open and we entered. My mouth gaped, and I wondered if I were dreaming.

I'd never been inside such a magnificent place. Rows of ice-carved shelves lined the mosaic-tiled floors. Ice sculptures made to appear as trees stood among the rows, their gently curving limbs glowing soft blue and stretching across the ceiling.

Long rows of talismans sat on the shelves, and the overwhelming number of objects made me lose hope. How would we ever find the shears?

"Where are they?" I asked Odette, who stood looking over the shelves.

"I don't know. Let's split up and search."

"Is that wise? What if we are attacked?"

"We'll have to risk it. We don't have much time before morning. Stay quiet."

We spread out across the immense library. I walked near the windows through the rows of objects, looking hastily from one talisman to the next. Some of the objects glowed faintly with magic, others held a taint that sent a shiver down my spine. As I wandered the stacks, I lost track of where I was walking, until I wandered into an unfamiliar part of the room.

Stopping, I looked at the open floor, the mirrored, mosaic tiles forming a whirlpool of silver and blue, the walls also made of mirrors.

I caught my breath as I looked at the person standing at the center of the floor.

No, it can't be.

Blinking, I wondered if I'd lost my mind. The woman's deep hazel eyes bored into mine. Her blonde hair fell in soft curls down her shoulders, and her silvery blue gown matched the tiles.

"Mother?" I asked hesitantly. I was certain I must've been looking at a ghost—or perhaps a shape shifter.

"Yes, daughter. You've found me."

EIGHTEEN

"Is it really you?" I asked the woman standing in front of me—the woman who appeared to be my mother.

"Yes, it's me."

"How? You died!"

"Yes." She took a step forward. "But someone like me can't really die. We are creatures of magic, my sisters and me. I came here after my death, and I can never leave. Come to me." She stretched out her hand, her skin white and pearlescent. "It's been so long. I've missed you, Gothel."

"No. I can't believe it. If you are who you appear, then why didn't you contact me? I've been alone for so long."

"I wanted to, but as I said, I am bound to this place."

"You couldn't have sent a message?" I asked.

"No."

"Why not?" She took another step toward me, but I backed away. I'd hated her for so long—hated what she'd done to my life, but this wasn't her. It couldn't be.

"This has to be a trick."

"It's no trick." Her voice sounded harsh, reminding me of the way she'd spoken when I was younger, bringing back memories I thought were forgotten. I flinched when she reached for me.

"Do you fear me?" she asked.

"I don't know who you are."

"Yes, you do. You know it's me."

"No."

"Gothel, take my hand." She outstretched her hand, palm up.

"I don't want to." In truth, I didn't want her back. She'd shattered my world. But then again, I desperately missed her. We'd shared happy times among the chaos.

"You can do this. Just take my hand."

Hesitantly, I reached out and grasped her fingers. They felt warm, her skin soft, just as I remembered.

"Mother?" I whispered. "It's really you?"

"Yes, of course it is." She pulled me to her chest and we embraced. The scent of cloves and clean linen enveloped me.

It's really her.

I'd spent so many years feeling sad and angry, but as she hugged me, those feelings seemed so distant. When she pulled away, she brushed a tear from her cheek.

"My goodness, you've grown into a woman."

"I'm hardly a woman."

"Yes, you are. Look at you. You're not a little girl anymore." She lifted strands of my hair. "Still blue, I see."

"Yes."

"Why did we never think to use a spell to change it?"

"I've tried. Many times."

"Well, it's still a nice color all the same."

"I suppose." I glanced around the silent library. My friends were there somewhere. "Mother, I need your help. We're here to find the magical shears and cut Rapunzel's hair. You have to help—"

She held up her hand. "I know why you're here."

"You do?"

She nodded.

"How?"

"You forget. Your aunts and I know many things. Come, I will show you."

She took my hand and tried to guide me away from where we stood, but I resisted. "You won't take me to them, will you?"

"Of course not. I may know what they know, but I haven't become like them. Not yet." She sighed. "Now, let me show you what I have seen. It concerns Rapunzel."

"Rapunzel?"

"Yes, and I am afraid it's grave news."

If it concerned Rapunzel, then maybe it was best that I follow her. We walked out of the open area and back into the stacks until we reached a stairwell. The glass-like walls reflected our images as we stepped down. Glancing up, I hoped I didn't lose my friends as we paced down to the bottom floor.

We entered a small, circular room where a large crystal orb hung suspended in the air.

"What is that?" I asked.

"A scrying orb. I can look anywhere I please—even at your tower."

She waved her hand. The cloudy glass cleared, revealing an image of the tower standing tall against the night sky. Fires burned around it, and in the light cast from the flames, I saw the silhouettes of hundreds of soldiers as they burned and hacked down the forest.

I gasped as I watched them work. My heart sank.

"They're burning the forest!"

"Yes. These are Varlocke's men."

"But... why?"

"Because they cannot enter the tower, so they're attempting to destroy it instead. Varlocke no longer cares for the life of his daughter, but because of the spell, he cannot enter the tower. The tower's magic keeps it safe from the fire for now, but it cannot last much longer."

"How is that possible? He never had any trouble entering the tower before."

"No, but you cast a spell on Rapunzel, did you not?"

"It was only a sleeping spell."

"It was more than that. It was the spell given from one kindred spirit to another. Plus, you used your own life's blood in the potion, didn't you?"

I nodded.

"That spell was more powerful than you realized. It not only affected Rapunzel, but the tower itself, and the forest surrounding it. Even the plants and stones will protect Rapunzel now. The high sorcerer knows this, which is why he's burning the forest to get to her. He believes he can no longer let her live. If she were to marry, her husband would be able to take his place as ruler. He will kill his only offspring to make sure that never happens."

"We have to do something."

"Yes, you must get to the tower as soon as possible, use the shears to cut the princess's hair, and free her from the tower before it's destroyed."

"But what about the foretelling of the prince saving the princess and killing the witch. That's me, isn't it?"

"True, it is you. Don't worry. Avoiding a foretelling is easier than you think. You only need to alter the people it speaks of. You must simply kill the prince before he kills you."

I choked. "Kill him? I could never do that."

"Why not?"

"Because he's a good person."

Her eyes darkened. "There is no such thing as a good person. Everyone has darkness inside. You'd do well to learn that. Once he frees Rapunzel, you must kill him without hesitation or he will kill you."

"I refuse to do that."

She eyed me, her gaze calculating. "Have you grown fond of this prince?"

"I…" My cheeks grew red.

"You have, haven't you?"

I took a deep breath. "I suppose there's no point in denying it, though to be truthful, I don't know what love is. I'm sure I don't love him, not the way you loved Father."

"Well, this does complicate matters, doesn't it? Do not worry over foretellings, child. I may not be a believer in the goodness of our kind, but I do believe in kindness and love. If you are meant to be with him, old soothsayings will never stand in your way. Be brave. You will survive if the goddess wills it."

"Thank you."

"Now, about the business of these shears. I will do what I can to help, although not all will turn out as you like."

"Why?"

She shook her head. "I can tell you no more than that." Voices came from overhead. "We must hurry," she said.

I followed her back up the stairs. My friends waited at the top, and their eyes widened as they spotted my mother walking along with me.

"Who is this?" Raj demanded.

"This is Aethel. My mother," I answered.

"You said she was dead."

"Yes, she died but was reborn."

"How does such a thing happen?" Drekken asked.

"Because I am a fey creature of magic," Mother said. "My body indeed died in Varlocke's castle, but I was restored in this place. Unfortunately, I can never leave. But I can help you."

"What reason do you have for helping us?" Raj asked.

Her eyes narrowed. "Because I hate Varlocke. I will do whatever it takes to see him dead."

Yes, this was my mother. There was no denying it now.

"How will you help us?" Raj asked.

"For starters, I will give you these." She held her hands out, palms up. A white glow encompassed her skin, and a narrow object formed, sparkling with golden light. When the brilliance faded, I stared in awe at a pair of golden shears sitting atop my mother's outstretched hands.

"I can't believe it," I gasped. "Are these really the magical shears?"

"Yes, the very ones. But I will warn you—my sisters will know as soon you remove these from this archive. Escaping with this talisman will not be easy."

"Can't you help us?"

"I will do what I can, though my powers are not as strong as my sisters'."

I stepped closer to my mom and ran my hands over the magic-crafted metal. They looked no different than an ordinary pair of shears, and even had a bit of rust around the tips of the blades, but a faint golden glow warmed my hands as I touched the metal.

"This is an ancient object—created at the time of our world's birth, an object used by the gods themselves."

"As long as they cut Rapunzel's hair, I don't care who made them," I muttered.

Mother raised an eyebrow but didn't reply as she handed the shears to me. "Treat them with care."

I took them from her. They felt surprisingly light in my hands, and the metal warmed my skin. Quickly, I stuffed them into my bag.

"Now we've got to escape," Odette said. "And we'll have to do it quickly."

"I understand," Mother said. "I can show you a secret passageway, but there is no guarantee we'll make it out unscathed."

We followed my mother through the archive room and to a small wooden door. She turned the latch and opened the door, and we followed her into a narrow hallway.

We stopped inside a large, open tower that led us to a crystal staircase. Our footsteps reverberated as we paced down the stairs. On the bottom floor, we entered a domed room with ice sculptures crowding the floor. All kinds of beasts had been carved from the ice, and I worried walking so near them would make them wake. But perhaps I'd been reading too many of my mother's fairy stories.

It amazed me that she was here—alive. I had trouble realizing it was really her. Perhaps I should have been more excited, but her presence reawakened emotions that I wasn't ready to face. For so long, I'd felt anger at her decision to curse Rapunzel. It had been a selfish act, one that I still paid the price for. I'd thought I'd forgiven her. But the truth was more complicated.

Raj walked beside me, his eyes guarded as he stared toward my mother who led the group.

"It's hard to believe she's alive." He spoke quietly, out of earshot of my mother who walked several paces ahead, with the others between us.

"Yes."

"She never contacted you, though?"

"No. She said she couldn't."

"I see," Raj said.

"Does that seem odd to you?"

"Yes," Raj said. "If I'd lost someone close and returned again, I think I wouldn't stop until I contacted them."

I swallowed the lump in my throat. "She's not like most people. Greed and hatred have always driven her actions. She loves me, but she hates others more."

"Can we trust her?"

I hesitated before answering. "I believe so, but only because we're going after Varlocke. If we weren't, then I might answer differently."

He nodded. "I'm sorry."

"For what?"

"Sorry you had to be brought up by someone like her. That isn't right."

"She wasn't a monster all the time. She was kind to me, and I knew she loved me. But she had different motivations than most people."

The looming shape of a dragon overshadowed me, and as I glanced up, I almost thought the creature was real. The ice sparkled in the dimly lit chamber, making its scales shimmer. We made it through the chamber and into another hallway, then another chamber and series of hallways, making me realize how enormous this place was.

Up ahead, the roaring of water echoed. We stepped out onto a balcony overlooking a waterfall. A gray sky loomed beyond the snow-covered mountains.

"Morning is coming," Odette said. "Hurry."

"Are we supposed to climb down there?" Drekken asked, looking down at the thundering waterfall.

"This is the only way out," my mother said. "Odette, you must take them back to the tower."

"Me?"

"Yes, you must transform when the sun rises."

"What about the curse? I'll have no choice but to return here when the sun sets. I'll never be able to fly to the tower and make it back before the day ends."

"Then how do we break her curse?" I asked my mother.

"There's only one way. Someone else will have to take her place."

"Take her place? Surely there's another way."

"Unfortunately, no, and once the sun rises, my sisters will know of what has happened here. You will have to leave quickly, but one of you must remain behind."

"Why didn't you tell us this sooner?" I asked.

"It would have done you no good, nor would it have made any difference."

I glanced at the wolf, knowing who I would choose. Maybe it was wrong of me to think that way. I almost felt guilty.

Almost.

"This person must stay willingly," Mother said.

"Of course," I mumbled. No throwing the wolf to the witches.

The sky grew lighter, and morning was only minutes

away. My heart raced as I stared out over the landscape. We were so close. We'd gotten the shears, and the dragon would take us back to Rapunzel's tower, but that would only happen if someone stayed behind.

"I will do it," Raj said.

"No," I answered. "I'll need your help once we get to the tower."

I glanced at the wolf. Was there a chance? "You've been awfully quiet. What about you?"

He yelped as he sat by my feet, his tail thumping the floor, though he didn't transform, nor did he volunteer—unless one counted the yelp, which I was tempted to do.

"I will do it," Drekken said.

"What? Drekken, no!" I said.

"Yes, it must be this way."

"But what of your music? You wanted to see the world and play for people you met. You won't get to do that here."

"No," Raj said. "None of us will stay. Drekken, I appreciate your bravery, but we will not allow anyone to become a prisoner. There has to be another way."

"There is none," Mother said, her voice sharp. "If you want to escape, one of you must stay behind."

"No. We go together or not at all."

My mother laughed—a sound that caught me off guard. Her body glowed white, then she transformed. My aunts stood where she had been. My heart dropped. I should've known they'd do something like this. Anger formed in the place where my shock had been.

"You pretended to be my mother?" I asked.

"You wouldn't have trusted us as us, would you?" Aunt Gwynna said.

"Yes, you know we get no visitors here. Is it so wrong

to have a little fun?" Aunt Neleia chimed in.

"But you pretended to be my dead mother!"

"Dead? No." They stepped aside, and I saw my mother standing behind them.

"We three are one part," Mother said. "We live and die with one another."

"So, you were aiding them this whole time. Are the shears even the real thing? Or was that a trick, too?"

"They're real," Aunt Gwynna said. "Your mother convinced us to give them to you. We had to agree that it would be greatly entertaining to watch you kill the high sorcerer. As we said, we bore easily."

"Then you'll let us leave?" the dragon woman asked. "All of us?"

They laughed, though it was a mirthless sound filled with no cheer. "Not you, of course. You are our prisoner."

Odette ground her teeth. "I've been here for so long. You have to set me free!"

"Absolutely not. You are our prisoner, and you shall always be. However, we might be willing to come to an understanding."

"An understanding?"

"We want to see Varlocke dead, and since he is attempting to burn down the tower and kill his own daughter to gain ultimate control of our lands, we have little time to waste. We will remove your curse for a time so you will be able to fly Gothel and two others to the tower during nightfall, but one must remain here and take your place until you return. After that, you must become our prisoner once again."

She balled her fists. "This isn't fair."

"Fair?" Aunt Gwynna said. "This is the law of magic.

Fair or not, this is our kingdom, and you will live under our rule."

"Let me do it," Drekken said, standing tall, what remained of his lute clutched in his hands. "I will remain here."

"Very well," the witches said. "He will take the dragon's place until she returns—and she had better return."

"No, you can't make him do this," the dragon lady said.

"Will you challenge us?" they asked. Blue flames danced around their bodies and shone in their eyes. The heat scorched my skin. Aunt Neleia raised her hand, and the flames wrapped around the woman. She cried out. Flames licked at the exposed skin of her face and arms. Its crackling heat smelled of burned flesh.

"Stop this!" An overpowering heat coiled painfully tight in my chest. A blue glow radiated from my skin, then blasted outward. Magic flew from my fingers, striking Aunt Gwynna in the chest. Buzzing filled my ears as the air went quiet, and my aunt's magic no longer surrounded Odette.

Drekken caught the dragon woman as she fell.

"You," Aunt Gwynna said, looking murderous as she stared me down. "How dare you strike one of us!"

"I-I'm sorry. I didn't know that would happen."

"She's using her magic?" Mother asked, stepping forward. "I can't believe it."

"Gothel, your hair," Raj said, stepping beside me. A strand fell over my eyes. It glowed blue.

"I should have known," Mother said.

"Known what?" Raj asked.

I shook my head, not wanting Mother to say anything else.

"Leave her be, Aethel," Aunt Neleia said. "She's to be punished."

"No, she's my daughter, and you know as well as I who she is." She smiled, stepping close to me. "Oh, Gothel, I always knew you were special."

"Special? What do you mean?" Raj asked.

"Why, my dear boy, don't you know? Only the offspring of two magic users can produce a person with natural powers—powers that she just demonstrated."

I stood stunned, rooted to the floor, not wanting to move.

"Oh, Gothel," Mother said. "I'm so pleased. This is such wonderful news."

I couldn't speak. My lungs squeezed tight, and I couldn't draw in a deep breath.

"Does this mean her father isn't who she thought?" Raj asked.

"That's exactly what it means," Mother said. "Her father is Varlocke."

Varlocke? No. I couldn't speak, didn't know what to say in the first place.

"Is it true?" Raj asked.

"Yes," Mother answered. "There's no other explanation."

"It can't be true," I whispered, my hands trembling.

"It is true."

"No," I said, my voice barely audible. "If it's true, then why didn't you tell me sooner?"

"Because I never believed it was him, although I always knew there was a possibility. Since you didn't possess natural magic, I assumed you weren't his child."

"She's a late bloomer," Aunt Neleia said.

"Yes, very late," Aunt Gwynna added.

He's my father. High Sorcerer Varlocke is my father. I couldn't believe it. It had to be a lie.

"This is such wonderful news," Aunt Gwynna said. "Gothel, you remember what we told you all those years ago, don't you?"

I couldn't find the words to answer.

"Yes, of course she remembers," Aunt Neleia said. "She'll become a great sorceress. And she'll do it by killing someone close to her."

"That's not true. It can't be," I said.

"My dear, it is true," Aunt Gwynna said. "We're so happy for you. You're more like us than you know."

Mother ran her fingers through my hair. "I always wondered why it was blue. Do you suppose she's had magic in her hair all along?"

"Yes, it must've been," Aunt Neleia said. She smiled when she looked at me, but it didn't put me at ease. "You, Gothel, will use your magic to kill your father."

Nineteen

"My father is dead," I said to my aunts, who stood smiling as if they'd just given me the best news—that my father was a maniacal killer and I would be the one to kill him. But I didn't believe them. How could it possibly be true? "Varlocke is an evil monster. It can't be possible."

"He wasn't always a monster," Mother said. "There was a time when I loved him, and when I believed he loved me."

As the truth sank in, the truth of who I was and the truth of my mother's past, bitter bile rose into my throat. "You were unfaithful to Father. With *him*?"

"Sadly, yes. When my husband was away, traveling for months at a time, I became lonely, and I allowed Varlocke to get too close to me. I believed he loved me. There were times he wasn't so bad, when he pretended to be kind. But I should have realized who he was. I was wrong to trust him.

"When you were born, I knew there was a chance Varlocke was your father, but I put it out of my mind after I discovered you possessed no natural magic. It seems I was wrong. You do possess magic, and Varlocke is your father."

I glanced at Raj, tears forming in my eyes. Would he

221

hate me now that he knew who my father was—the man who had butchered his people and burned his city?

My aunts had warned me of my heritage. They'd come to visit the castle when I was younger, and I'd always feared them because of it. But I still couldn't accept it.

"No," I said. "You're tricking me. It isn't true."

"It is true," Aunt Gwynna said, her voice surprisingly calm. "You are his daughter, and you will be the one to stop him. Go now, before he kills Rapunzel. Stop him from claiming King Duc'Line's kingdom and taking our land."

The world spinning around me, I closed my eyes, wishing I'd never come on this quest.

Raj placed his hand on my shoulder, as if reassuring me, yet I didn't know how he could stand to be near me. This was all wrong.

"We can still do this," Raj said. "This doesn't change anything."

"Except that I'll have to kill my own father."

"He isn't your father. Perhaps by birth—but he didn't raise you, so you're not his."

I took a deep breath. Raj was right. This changed nothing. We'd come this far, and we had the shears. We only had to return to the tower and save Rapunzel and the prince. Squaring my shoulders, I faced Raj, my only friend through all of this.

"All right," I said. "Let's finish this."

"Very well," Aunt Gwynna said. "Leave now, but one of you stays behind."

I looked at my companions, frustrated that we couldn't all leave together.

"It will be me," Drekken said.

"Someone else can do it. It doesn't have to be you," I said.

"Yes, it does. I'm a lost soul from a foreign land. No one will miss me if I'm gone. But you—all of you—have a greater purpose than me. I only ask that you remember me."

Odette stepped forward. Behind her, the sun rose, catching the coloring on her gown, which I now realized was covered with tiny shimmering scales.

"Your heroism won't be forgotten."

"I appreciate your words, but the question is, will you come back for me?"

She hesitated, as if debating whether to choose freedom or bondage, her life for his. "I will," she finally answered." "I'll come back, but don't think you won't owe me."

He nodded. "I won't forget, my lady."

"Call me Odette."

She moved away from him, then stood before the witches.

"The curse," she said. "You promised to remove it so I can fly during nightfall."

"Only for a short time, child. Then you must return to us." Aunt Gwynna waved her hands. Magic formed, coalescing into a glowing orb that formed in her cupped hands. The light grew to encompass Odette in shimmering waves. As the magic lifted, Odette breathed deeply, then she took a step back. Her eyes caught my attention—dragon-like—with long, slitted pupils. She looked at her hands, then scanned her arms and body.

"The curse is lifted?"

"For now," Aunt Neleia said, a warning edge to her

voice. "You'd best return quickly."

"Very well," Odette snapped, then backed away. We followed her to the ledge where the waterfall thundered. Odette stood on the edge, water droplets splashing her skin, then raised her arms. As the woman dove off the ledge, her body morphed, an elegant neck forming, and her long gown lengthening to create wings. With powerful thrusts, she beat her wings and gained altitude until she flew level with the platform where we stood.

Raj and the wolf both leapt atop the dragon's back, but I hesitated, looking back at my mother.

Despite the hurtful feelings I harbored toward her, I had trouble leaving. We'd only just reunited, and my heart ached at the thought of leaving her—and of being alone once again.

"Mother, I'll miss you," I said.

She came to me, hugging me to her chest. Tears sparkled in her eyes. "I love you, daughter. I know I'm not a perfect person. I've done many things I regret, but I will never regret being your mother. I am so proud of you. You're a better person than I am. You'll do great things."

I nodded. "Will I see you again?"

"You may visit me in my palace any time you wish. But I can never come to you. I'm sorry." She brushed the hair from my face. "You're such a beautiful, brave girl. There's much you have to learn about yourself and about your own powers. Don't forget who you are. You're stronger than you think."

I couldn't speak past the lump in my throat. I only hugged her, wishing I could've stayed longer, feeling cheated at losing her too early.

But I wouldn't let this moment go to waste. For one

thing, she was alive, and I had a chance to prove myself and make her proud. Even if she wasn't perfect, she was my mother, and despite her faults, I knew she loved me.

I pulled away from her, standing tall, realizing that I stood a few inches taller than her now.

"I will be watching over you," she said. I nodded, stepping back toward the dragon. I gave one last look at Drekken.

"We'll return for you," I said.

He gave me a small smile, held up his flask, and nodded. "I'll be waiting."

I turned toward the dragon. Air whooshed as the massive beast flapped its wings. It was then I realized how enormous this creature was. Raj reached out his hand. I grabbed it and leapt behind him. Smooth silver scales spread out before me. In front of Raj, the wolf crouched, and Raj held him tight to his chest.

With a flutter of beating wings, the dragon soared away from the tower. A landscape of ice and snow spanned beneath us. Jagged mountains loomed in the distance. I caught my breath as gusts of cold air rushed past my face, though I barely noticed the chill, and had to laugh at how free I felt sitting atop the dragon, watching the world unfold beneath me, realizing we'd escaped my aunts' palace with the shears.

We climbed higher, and mountains turned to sloping hills, then to plains. As we flew south, the snow disappeared, replaced with forests of red and orange that looked like flames from this perspective.

Clouds passed us by, their dampness cool on my exposed skin. As we flew, it gave me time to ponder what I'd learned at my aunts' castle. I still had trouble believing I was the daughter of the evilest person in the land.

In truth, I had to admit I'd suspected it. Mother had spent a great deal of time with the high sorcerer—too much time, really. I remembered their quiet conversations, the times Varlocke had shown up at our cottage for no good reason, and the looks they'd shared. Now that I thought about it, it made too much sense.

How would I ever be able to confront him now that I knew the truth? Would I really be able to defeat my own father?

Sighing, I leaned forward, resting my head on Raj's back. His clothing had the spicy, male scent I'd become used to, and having him near made my fears grow distant. How much longer did I have with him? I didn't want to think about it. The reality was that after this quest was over, he would go his way and I would go mine. He had important things to do, and I wasn't sure if there was a place for me. I could only hope there was. Otherwise, I would continue how I'd always been—alone. Except now, assuming everything went the way it was supposed to go, Rapunzel would be freed from the tower, hopefully married to Prince Merek, and I would be even lonelier than I'd been before.

I supposed I could go back and stay with my mother and aunts, but they hardly seemed like the sort of company I wanted to keep.

It did me no good to worry about any of this. Right now, I had to focus on one thing: Rapunzel. My sister. I had to set her free. Nothing else mattered.

The air warmed as we flew south, and the sun broke free from the clouds. I took in the scenery. Small villages dotted the winding roads. Lakes and large, dark forests appeared in patches as we flew. Seeing the world from this angle made everything look so small—like our entire journey to my aunts' palace had gone by in a blink.

We stopped only a few times for a brief meal and sips of water, and then we continued once again. Raj and I didn't speak much. We only made a few brief comments to each other. The wind made it hard to hear him, so I remained content with being near him, thankful I had a day to spend in peace before we arrived at the tower.

When the sun descended toward the horizon, a cloud of smoke darkened the sky. Its sharp scent burned my nostrils. Night was approaching when I spotted the spire of the tower peeking above the trees. The evening light made it look blood red. Fires burned the forest surrounding it. At the sight of the flames, my heart grew heavy. The tower and the forest surrounding it had been my home. They were part of me. I'd given my life's blood to protect them. To see the trees engulfed in flames came as a shock.

"King Duc'Line's army is down there," Raj shouted over the wind.

"Are you sure?"

"Yes! He must be defending the tower. This is good news."

"I hope so!"

The dragon circled the tower. Fires raged beneath us, some of them so tall, I could feel their heat from up here. When we spotted a clearing, the dragon began her descent. The wolf shifted nervously in Raj's arms, growling as we neared the ground.

Shouts echoed beneath us. I searched the silhouettes of the soldiers against the firelight, hoping to find my father, but had no luck. Maybe it was better that I didn't find him. I was hopeful I would be able to sneak inside the tower, cut Rapunzel's hair and free her from the spell, and escape without having to confront him. Prince Merek could marry the princess, take the power away from the high sorcerer, and all would be well.

But perhaps that was wishful thinking.

A flash of light blinded me, catching me off guard. A fireball whizzed past, then volleys of more. One of them caught Odette's wing. She shrieked, beating her wings frantically before she hit the ground hard.

I tumbled from her back, rolling over sticks that poked my flesh, though I managed to hang onto my pack. As I sat up, my heart pounded as I searched for my friends. The soldiers' shouts came from the forest. Through the trees, the tower loomed.

Getting to my feet, I held my pack close and stumbled through the woods. The dragon and Raj lay in a clearing. As I walked toward them, the wolf trotted toward me.

"We have to get to the tower," I said as Raj stood. Behind him, the dragon breathed heavily, though I saw no injuries.

"How do we get past the army?" Raj asked.

"I can use a spell," I said.

Odette transformed, and her shimmering robes rustled as she sat up. I went to her. "Are you okay?"

"Yes," she said, rubbing her forehead.

"But they shot you. Are you sure?"

"Yes, my wing. It won't affect me while I'm in this form."

"Good. Go with the wolf into the forest and find somewhere to hide until we return."

"Don't you want my help?"

"I appreciate the offer, but the more people with us, the easier we'll be spotted. They already know we're here and they'll be looking for us. Right now, staying hidden is our only advantage."

She nodded, and Raj and I took off toward the tower. Leaves and twigs crunched beneath my boots, reminding me of the many times I'd hiked through this forest, though it seemed an unfamiliar place now.

"Wait," Raj said, reaching out to stop me. We stood on the edge of the forest. Trees burned around us as we faced the clearing. War raged not far from where we stood, though we had a straight line of sight to the tower.

"If we try to make it across the clearing, they'll spot us for sure," Raj said.

"I can use a spell to cloak us, but it will only last a few minutes."

"That's good enough."

After I took my pack off my shoulder, I searched inside until a small glass bottle brushed my fingertips. I removed it and inspected the label under the glow of the firelight, barely able to read the handwriting. *Rosalind oil.* When I uncorked it, the scent of roses filled the air.

"Hold out your hand," I said.

He did as I said, and I rubbed a small amount of the oil into his palm. As I did, his image blurred, blending with the trees. I did the same to my own hand until I felt its tingling seep into my skin, making me camouflaged.

"That's impressive," Raj said, holding up his hand and inspecting it. I could only see an outline of his form, as if he were a shadow.

"It won't last long," I said. "We need to get to the tower quickly."

"I agree. But we can't go just yet. I need to make sure it hasn't been infiltrated." He pulled his dagger from its sheath. Its rubies glinted deep red in the firelight. He took off through the trees, dodging the fires, until he disappeared completely.

I stood waiting, holding my breath, counting the seconds as they ticked by. It was hard not to let my mind go to that place it went, where I imagined the worst.

Raj would be okay.

He was a good fighter. Plus, he had my spell to help him. Tree branches creaked, and I rounded, startled, to find the blurred image of Raj behind me. If I hadn't known it was him behind that shadowy spell, I would have been frightened out of my wits.

"It's me," Raj said.

"Good. What did you find?"

"The high sorcerer's army hasn't breached the tower yet. Duc'Line's men are holding them back for now, but I don't know how much longer that will last. We've got to get inside now and escape with the prince and princess. You have the shears ready?"

"Yes, in my pack."

"Good, let's go."

We neared the edge of the forest and stared out over the clearing. Milky moonlight turned the grass to blades of silver. A gentle breeze rushed past, stirring the tree limbs. Swords clanging and men screaming roared through the forest. It was only a matter of time before they spotted us.

We darted across the field. I glanced across the forest only briefly, catching glimpses of fighting warriors, their armor reflecting the raging fires. The tower rose over us, an imposing structure of weathered stones and mortar.

We stopped at the bottom, looking up at the only window. It seemed so much taller than I remembered.

I feared calling out the spell. Magically glowing hair hanging from the tower's only window was sure to draw attention to us, which was something we didn't need.

"If I use the spell, it would alert the army. Should we chance it?"

"No. We'll have to find another way. Can you use some other spell that would be less noticeable?"

"Possibly. I have some enchanted seeds in my bag. I could use them to grow into vines."

"Would they glow?"

"No. I won't use any natural magic. They won't glow."

"Then let's try it."

I reached into my bag, searching for the bottle of seeds. My fingers snagged a small, cylindrical bottle. I pulled it out, then knelt on the ground and dumped the seeds on the grass. Placing my hand atop the seeds, they grew warm, and I stepped away.

Small shoots, barely visible, peeked from the ground, then grew into vines that snaked up the tower until they reached the window. Raj grabbed one of the vines and I grasped another. My hands burned as I climbed up, but all the traveling on horseback had toughened my legs, and I used that to my advantage. As I climbed, sweat slicked my palms, making it difficult to get a good grip. I held on as best as I could, my breathing labored, picturing Rapunzel's face, wondering how she would react once I told her we were sisters—thinking of how close she was to being set free. Those thoughts kept me moving until I finally reached the window and grabbed the ledge.

Raj climbed beside me. We both breathed heavily as

we collapsed inside the tower.

"We made it," I whispered.

"Yes, I just hope we're not too late."

Darkness shrouded the room, and only a few objects stood out in the moonlight. I spotted the white coverlet on Rapunzel's bed and crept toward it. As I moved through the tower, I walked without stumbling over the piles of hair.

Seeing anything was hard to do, but as I searched, I didn't spot any hair anywhere.

My heart raced. Had someone taken her already?

When I got to the bed, my fears were confirmed. I pressed my hand to the empty bed sheets, shocked.

I turned to Raj who stood behind me.

"She's gone," I whispered frantically.

"How is that possible? I thought she couldn't leave the tower."

"I thought so, too, but my father must've found a way around the spell. He must've taken her already."

"If that's so, then why are they still fighting outside?"

"I don't know. It doesn't make sense."

"Let's search the tower. Maybe she's still here."

Something rubbed against my legs, and I darted back, afraid it was a spider or something worse, when I spotted the sleek black fur of a cat.

"Jester!" I hissed, frightened and relieved at the same time. I knelt and patted his head. "You scared me, you silly beast."

He mewled, and I rubbed his back. "Where is Rapunzel?"

Knocking came from somewhere, echoing with hollow thuds. I stood, pacing the room, searching for the sound.

"Over here," Raj said, walking to the well.

Jester followed me as I crept toward the raised ring of stones. The knocking came again, louder this time.

A wooden lid sat atop the opening, and Raj pried it off. Tangled loops of hair spilled out, smelling of dampness, and the bone white visage of Rapunzel's face smiled up at us.

"You found me," she said, her voice hoarse and cracking.

"Rapunzel, what are you doing in the well?"

"I had to hide somewhere. The troops were coming."

"But how did you break my sleeping spell?"

She smiled but didn't answer.

"Where's the prince?" Raj asked.

"He's in here, too, and he's very uncomfortable to sit upon."

"How did you even get in there?" I asked, reaching for one arm as Raj grabbed the other. We pulled her free, though removing the long ropy hair took another five minutes. When we pulled the last of her hair from the well, the strands uncoiled to reveal the prince.

His body thumped limply to the floor.

"Is he dead?" Raj asked, his voice panicked.

I knelt by the prince, hearing the faint sounds of breathing exhaling from his mouth. "No, he's alive. If we cut Rapunzel's hair and remove the spell now, he'll make it."

I turned to Rapunzel, who lay in a heap haphazardly on the ground, her legs bent awkwardly beneath her, revealing her bony knees, both scraped and bleeding.

She smiled as I knelt by her.

"I got the shears." I patted her shoulder. "Everything's going to be made right now. You'll see." I opened my bag. When the cool metal met my hands, I grabbed the handles and pulled them out. The golden glow radiated around the room.

She shied away. "No."

"What's the matter?"

She breathed shallowly, her eyes fixated on the shears. "What if it hurts like the other times?"

"It won't. These aren't like the other shears. They're magic. They're the only ones ever created that can't hurt you."

"I don't know."

"Gothel," Raj interrupted. "Listen."

Outside, shouts grew closer. The sound of rustling vines came from the window. Raj unsheathed his dagger and crept toward the window.

"I'll cut the vines," he said.

I turned back to Rapunzel. "We don't have time. I'm going to cut your hair now, okay?"

"You're sure about this?" Her eyes were wide and dark, and they glimmered in the moonlight. The protruding bones in her cheeks made her face look skeletal.

"I'm sure," I said.

"But what about the magic?"

"What do you mean?"

"The magic in my hair. Will that be gone, too?"

"I don't understand. There isn't any magic in your hair. There's only the spell my mother put on you, and once we cut your hair, the spell will be gone."

"You're wrong. There is magic inside my hair. I can feel it inside!" Her voice rose, and I knew I couldn't sit

234

here talking to her when everyone's lives were at stake.

"Rapunzel, I'm sorry, but I have to do this. Please, you know I wouldn't hurt you. Let me do this."

She nodded, tears brimming in her eyes. She didn't resist as I opened the shears and attempted to cut the hair, but the tangled masses were too thick, and I had no choice but to separate the strands and cut them in small sections. Rapunzel didn't flinch as I cut the first sections, and then more.

Behind us, a soldier leapt into the room. He screamed as Raj fought him back. I wished I could cut her hair faster, but I could only cut small chunks at a time. As the hair fell away, a glow emanated around her head in a golden halo.

Was it possible? Did Rapunzel have her own natural magic the same as me?

The glow increased as I cut the last strand. Rapunzel turned toward me. Tears flowed down her face.

"Did I hurt you?" I asked.

"No."

"What's the matter?"

"Nothing. I feel like myself again."

"You do?"

"Yes." She smiled up at me—a genuine expression of joy. One I hadn't seen in a very long time. "Gothel, you saved me."

She hugged me, her bony frame embracing me with more strength than I thought possible. When she pulled away, I grabbed her hand. I knew we didn't have much time, but I had to tell her the truth.

"Rapunzel, there's something I need you to know about me. My father isn't who I thought. He's the high sorcerer—which makes us half-sisters."

"Sisters?"

I nodded.

"Is it really true?"

"Yes. My mother told me after I used my magic."

"You used magic?"

I nodded. "My aunts were hurting someone, and my magic reacted. That's never happened to me before. I didn't understand it. But then my mother told me that someone with that kind of magic has to have two magical parents."

"Yes. I know. I have it, too."

"You do?"

"Yes. My mother was a sorceress, but she never told anyone. I only recently learned to use my magic. That's how I was able to break your spell and hide in the well."

Beside us, the prince stirred. Rubbing his forehead, he moaned as he sat up.

"Where am I?" he asked.

"In my tower," Rapunzel said. "Don't you remember? We've been sitting in that dreadful well for the last day and a half."

"A tower—and a well? What?"

"You were under a spell," I said.

A choked scream came from near the window as Raj defeated the soldier. The limp body of the soldier slumped as Raj turned to face us. His heavy breathing made his broad chest rise and fall as he neared us.

"Prince Merek?" Raj asked.

"Raj?"

"It's good to see you awake," Raj said, kneeling beside the prince. They clapped one another's shoulders.

"Raj, what's happening? Where am I? The last thing I

remember, I was climbing into the tower, and then… oh yes. You." He looked at Rapunzel. "You're the princess, aren't you?"

She nodded, biting her lip. Her hair fell loosely to her shoulders, glowing faintly with a golden light as the shears had done. She looked like a grown woman now—no longer the child she had once been.

Prince Merek got to his feet, holding to the edge of the well as he straightened. "I came to rescue you. Am I too late for that?"

"No," she said shyly. "You're not too late."

Their gazes met, and Rapunzel's cheeks turned pink. Prince Merek took a step toward her, walking on shaky feet until he got to her side and held out his hand. "Will you allow me to free you from this tower?"

"Yes, of course." She took his hand.

Prince Merek flashed us a smile. "Well, it seems rescuing the princess from the tower wasn't nearly as hard as you thought, Raj."

"That's because you slept through it," Raj mumbled.

A roar erupted behind us. I turned around as heat blasted my face. A raging fireball knocked me from my feet. The others screamed as they landed beside me.

A cloaked figure coalesced in front of the window. As his form took shape, I gasped, peering into the familiar blue eyes that conjured memories from my childhood—eyes that looked a lot like my own now that I thought about it.

The high sorcerer. My father.

TWENTY

WE GOT TO OUR FEET as the high sorcerer approached us. His bootsteps echoed through the tower. A breeze came from the window, making his cloak billow around his muscled frame sheathed in black armor. Like his soldiers, the red emblem of the coiled basilisk had been etched into his breastplate. His silvery white hair appeared blue in the moonlight, and his staff carved with a snake's head thumped the floor as he walked toward us.

Several soldiers entered the room behind him. My blood turned cold as I recognized the bald head and beefy frame of the guardsman who'd stabbed me. My abdomen throbbed with phantom pain as his eyes glittered with madness and rage.

An uncontrolled shiver ran down my spine.

"That one," the soldier said, pointing to Raj. "He took the witch from the tower and nearly killed me."

"An Outlander?" the high sorcerer said, his voice deep and smooth, those two words bringing back a host of memories I wanted to forget.

"Yes, that's him."

"I wondered how it happened," the high sorcerer said. "When my squadron reported that my daughter had been

238

left unguarded, and Gothel was missing, I thought there must have been a mistake. Gothel would never leave the tower willingly. She knew the consequences. She knew the punishment." His sharp eyes flashed with hate as he focused on me. "But then I learned someone had aided her in her escape. A squire in King Duc'Line's army. An Outlander boy. An Outlander!" His raised voice made me jump. My heart raced, remembering that same voice before he hit my mother. Over and over again until she was too weak to scream.

The blood.

Sweat beaded on my skin, and the palpable fear froze my joints. The memories came back in a rush. He'd beaten her. He would do the same to me.

He paced toward Raj. "I wanted to kill her and this Outlander, but look, my daughter Rapunzel has revived from the spell—and what else do I find? Prince Merek's son ready to steal her away from me. How can this be? How can so many betray me? There will be so much bloodshed on this night, but it will not be undeserved. You—all of you—will be executed. Your bodies will be torn to pieces and hung to rot in the four corners of my kingdom as a warning to all."

"No," Rapunzel cried. "You can't! I'm your daughter—and so is Gothel. You can't kill your own children. Please, Father. Don't do this!"

"Gothel." His eyebrows rose as he looked at me. "Is this true?"

I stood tall. "It's true. Mother isn't dead. She lives with her sisters in the northern lands. She told me. You are my father. I possess magic, just like you, and I will use it if I have to." Granted, I'd only ever used it once, and wasn't sure how to control it, but he didn't need to know that.

"No," he snapped. "It makes no difference if you are my flesh and blood. You have defied me. You all have defied me. You all will die."

"Not if I've got anything to do with it," Raj said, his voice deep and full of warning. The intensity of his words made me pause. I'd never heard him speak with such fervor. If I had been anyone else, I would've been frightened. He stepped in front of us, blocking us from the high sorcerer as he grasped his sword. "You won't harm anyone."

High Sorcerer Varlocke laughed. "I'll kill you all, and you'll suffer the most, Outlander. You and your people are a plague. After I kill you, I'll take your body to what remains of the Outlander people. I'll burn it for all to see, and then I'll slaughter every last one of your kind until no one remains."

If Varlocke's words bothered him, Raj didn't let it show. "Not if you're dead."

Raj lunged at him, striking with a fierce attack aimed for the high sorcerer's heart. The high sorcerer struck out with his staff. Lightning exploded from its tip. Raj dodged aside, but the bolt caught his hand. He screamed, losing his grip on the sword. It clattered to the ground. The high sorcerer grabbed up the weapon and tossed it out the window. Raj unsheathed his father's blade using his uninjured hand, then leapt at the high sorcerer and stabbed his shoulder.

The emperor screamed. "Kill them all!" he bellowed.

Chaos erupted as the high sorcerer's guards attacked us. I grabbed the dagger from my boot, leaping in front of Rapunzel as one of the guards rushed at me. I deflected the blow from his sword, rounded, and kicked the back of his knees. He pitched forward, and Rapunzel pushed him into the well. With lightning fast speed, she grabbed the rope holding the bucket and untied it. Screaming echoed as the bucket plunged, leaving the soldier to fall into the water dozens of feet below.

Rapunzel gave me a sly grin, and I wanted to congratulate her, but more soldiers came at us. Prince Merek leapt into the action, cutting and hacking with his sword, deflecting blows from every direction.

The soldier who'd nearly killed me in the stable leapt in front of me. His beefy frame flexed as he held a heavy broadsword. His eyes glittered with madness. Long scabs crisscrossed his face, one bisecting his eye. They must've been wounds from when he'd fought Raj.

He laughed as he focused on my flimsy knife. "It's time to die now."

"I don't think so."

He lifted his sword over his head and screamed as he charged at me. I lunged aside, though the blade caught my calf. Screaming, I fell, holding my leg. Warm blood seeped from the puncture, coating my fingers, though the wound didn't feel deep.

He came at me again, and I rolled to the side. His blade slammed into a wooden support post, nearly cleaving it in two. His enraged yells echoed through the tower as he yanked his sword from the beam.

He spun on me, fire in his eyes as he stabbed for my chest. I dodged again but wasn't sure how long I could keep it up. I had to find a way to stop him or else one of those blows would kill me. But what options did I have? My blade was so small. I'd lost my pack somewhere in the commotion. Frantically, I searched the tower, looking for weapons or anything that would stop him. Having natural magic should've been helpful, though I had no idea how to use it or control it.

I caught glimpses of my friends battling the soldiers. Rapunzel and Prince Merek fought fiercely, though they had just woken and could barely stay upright as it was. If we didn't stop my father and his soldiers soon, we'd all be dead.

A whack hit the side of my face as the cold metal of a broadsword made my teeth rattle in my skull. Pain exploded through my jawbone and into my head. I tried to sit up but collapsed.

The guard loomed over me. He placed the blade's tip under my chin. Cold metal pierced my flesh.

"High Sorcerer Varlocke wanted to execute you, but I don't think he'll mind if I dispatch you myself. You've been nothing but a pain. I'll enjoy killing you." His leering smile sent fear shooting through my spine.

I tightened my sweaty palms into fists. How could I die this way? It couldn't happen like this. But what chance did I have of stopping him? Fear raced through my heart. I wouldn't die this way. I refused.

A mewl caught my attention. Jester sat atop the shelf beside my row of glass bottles. Greenish poison glittered in the jug beside him. Liquid morrid bane.

The guard lowered his sword, and I only had a moment to react. I kicked his midsection. He fell back with a grunt, and I lunged toward the bottles, grabbing the morrid bane. The guard loomed behind me. I rounded, smashing the jar against his head. It shattered, spilling its contents over the scabs covering his face.

Screaming, he fell back, dropping his sword, his hands clutching his face. He stumbled back, his cries mingling with the other soldiers' as Rapunzel and Prince Merek fought them off.

Prince Merek fought like a demon, his sword impaling one soldier after another. Rapunzel also held her own, her fists alight with a golden glow as she slammed them into their faces.

I stumbled toward the window where Raj fought with the high sorcerer. My leg stung where the guard had injured me, but with my blood buzzing with added energy, I hardly felt it. The sound of clashing swords resounded. They fought with frenzy. Blood seeped from cuts on both their bodies.

As I approached them, Raj swung his sword, but the high sorcerer lashed out with his staff, hitting Raj with a blast of magic in his face. Raj flew backward and hit the floor, his body landing with a loud thump.

"Raj," I screamed. I sprinted to him and knelt at his side. His eyelids fluttered, and he breathed heavily.

"Are you okay?" I asked.

"Yes," he said with a weak smile. "As long as you are alive, I am well. I swore to protect you. I always will."

Behind us, a shadow loomed, and the high sorcerer approached. His face twisted into a grimace as he focused on my fingers intertwined with Raj's.

"You care for this Outlander?" he asked.

"Yes," I answered without hesitation. "I love him." There was no point in denying it. I loved him, and I didn't care who knew. Raj gave me a slight smile, his eyes twinkling with understanding.

"This is heresy," Varlocke spat. "Never did I image a

child of mine mixing with a filthy Outlander. Tainting our blood. There is no chance of redemption for you now. I will slit your throat until your blood runs dry."

Slowly, Raj unlaced his fingers from mine. He stood, facing my father, still gripping his dagger. "You will not touch her."

"No? Then perhaps you'll do it for me. What do you say, Outlander?" He stretched out his arm, his hand forming a claw that transformed, morphing until the nails lengthened and the skin turned to black scales. "I've learned much about the dark arts. I've learned to change my own flesh, and I've learned to control the flesh of others. I won't touch her, that is true. But you will!"

Gray shadowy magic, slimy and cold, radiated from his mutated hand. The fog gripped Raj, surrounding him. Raj choked. The fire in his eyes burned away, replaced with a blank stare.

"What are you doing to him?" I asked.

"Allowing him to fulfill the soothsayings, daughter." He spoke mockingly, an evil smile lighting his face as his hand formed a fist.

Raj's foot slid forward. Sweat beaded on his skin as he took another step. Lightning fast, he grabbed me around my waist and pressed his father's dagger to my throat. Its tip pierced my skin. My heart pounded. I grabbed his arms, trying to pry him away, but he held me in an iron grip.

"Raj, no," I pleaded, knowing there was nothing he could do to stop my father's spell, but hoping my words would get through to him nevertheless.

"Father, stop," I screamed. Tears blurred my vision. I couldn't die this way—killed by the only person I'd ever loved. The knife pressed more deeply, puncturing through my skin. Only a little deeper and it would cut through my life's vein. I pried at Raj's arms, my nails bending as I attempted to break free from his grasp.

The soothsayings were true. I would die at the hand of the prince. But I refused to let it happen this way. I could beat this. I wasn't a slave to magic—I controlled it. And I would control it now.

Closing my eyes, power coiled around me, thick like dense fog. The enchantment brushed my arms, and then blasted out, sending Raj and my father to the floor.

My knees buckled. I breathed deeply to keep from passing out. The room spun around me. I glanced at Raj, his prone figure lying on the floor, wanting to go to him, knowing that I would collapse if I took a step toward him.

My magic was gone. Inside, an empty shell replaced the place my powers had been.

In the corner of my eye, I saw my father rise. He moved toward me fluidly, as if he flew, a black cloud that soon surrounded me.

I tried to move away, but I stumbled, and he seized me. His clawed hand tightened around my neck while his other arm gripped my waist.

"I suppose I'll have to do this myself," he breathed in my ear.

The scales of his claw felt cold and unnatural against my skin as he dragged me toward the window. We stopped at the ledge.

The chill, nighttime breeze washed over me. Crickets chirped from the field far beneath us. My heart pounded in my chest, and I had trouble breathing. Panic gripped me. This man—this murderer—my father, was going to kill me. There was nothing I could do to stop him. Whatever magic I'd used was spent. I had nothing left.

"Please," I pleaded, my voice so panicked I barely recognized it as my own. "Don't do this."

"Don't beg, Gothel. It's unbecoming."

"But I'm your daughter."

"Does that make any difference?" he yelled. I shuddered, the anger in his voice bringing back memories I thought were forgotten. "Your mother was a fool. I'll kill her after I kill you."

"No, you can't!"

"I will. I'll drag her out of that castle and kill her. I've done it once. I'll do it again, but this time, she won't be coming back."

I tried to wriggle free from his grasp, which only made him tighten his grip around my neck, choking me.

Raj slowly got to his feet. Breathing heavily, he limped as he made his way toward us. "Leave her alone," he demanded.

"Never. She's got to be executed. She escaped the tower. Defied my orders. Worse, she fell in love with a cursed Outlander. She must die. There's no other way this ends. I will execute her for all to see. She'll become an example of what happens to someone who defies me."

He took another step back, his magic coalescing around us. Its power tingled on my skin. He would use his powers to transport us away to my execution. If I didn't stop him now, I never would.

As he prepared the spell, his grip around my neck loosened. Breathing deeply, I focused on his magic—powers that felt strangely like my own. He'd learned to morph his own body and control others. Was it possible I could do something similar? Could I make his powers become mine?

I called on his magic, drawing it to me. It resisted at first, but as I prodded, the enchantment gained substance until my father's magic gathered painfully tight in my chest. He gasped as the magic left him.

"What are you doing?" he breathed. "Are you taking my magic?"

"Yes."

"H-How?" he stuttered. "Stop this now!"

"I can't do that. I can't let you hurt anyone else. I'm sorry, Varlocke." I'd used his formal name because I refused to call him father. He never was one to me.

I released his own magic against him. Electric power crackled around me, through my skin, and into the strands of my hair that glowed brightly. A thunderous boom shook the entire tower as the magic blasted outward. The high sorcerer lost his grip around my waist. The force flung him backward. He flew off the ledge, screaming as he tumbled through the air, shrieking with an inhuman wail as his body hit the ground with an echoing thump—and then all became silent.

Gasping for breath, I stood looking over the ledge. Clutching the worn stones, I focused in horror and relief at the broken body lying at the foot of the tower.

The others gathered around me. We stood unspeaking, looking toward the horizon as the sky lightened beyond the forest. Most of the fires had died out, leaving only thin trails of smoke that snaked upward.

The gathered armies had stopped fighting. Perhaps they'd seen the high sorcerer's body fall from the tower.

"Are you okay?" Raj asked.

I lightly touched my neck where he'd stabbed me. The

blood had grown cold and sticky and no longer trickled free. "Yes."

"I am so sorry—"

"No." I pressed my finger to his lips. "You weren't under your own power. Varlocke did this. Not you. Don't apologize. Please."

He smiled—that brilliant expression that stole my breath. "Fine," he said, squeezing my hand. "I won't apologize. How about I congratulate you instead. You did it. You defeated the high sorcerer."

"Yes." I wasn't sure killing my own father was something I could be proud of, yet relief replaced my panic— relief that not only I would live, but that everyone else would live as well.

TWENTY-ONE

WE STOOD IN THE IMMENSE, crowded courtyard of King Duc'Line's castle. A month had passed since we'd killed the high sorcerer. I'd experienced my fair share of guilt for killing him, yet as the weeks wore on, and the kingdom repaired the damage he'd done—and prepared for a special wedding—my guilt faded.

Raj held my hand as he walked beside me. He flashed his charming grin, the one that had made me weak in the knees from the beginning. Curse that smile. It brought nothing but trouble, though I had to admit, I liked it.

Odette and the wolf also walked beside us. The dragon woman chatted as she went, and the wolf walked with a lolling tongue and wagging tail. The sun shone brightly in the cloudless sky beyond the towers. After we'd defeated Varlocke, I'd talked to Odette about going back to the witch's castle to rescue Drekken. She'd agreed but wanted to wait until after the wedding. She had a difficult choice ahead of her: to trade herself for Drekken's freedom, and I didn't envy her. But for now, I only wanted to enjoy the day, and I didn't worry too much about Drekken. He had his flask of ale, after all.

We walked under a wide archway into the palace.

Vines with tiny yellow flowers grew up the impressively tall pillars leading to a ceiling with an elaborate mural of a garden. The scent of honeysuckle filled the air. Fairy homes that resembled birdhouses had been constructed atop poles jutting from pillars. Fairies flitted in and out. The soft light emitted from their bodies lit the room in a pale white glow.

At the front of the room sat a wide dais with two ornate thrones sitting atop it. I could hardly believe I was here at Rapunzel's wedding. Only a month ago, I wasn't even sure if she'd live long enough to be married. I'd also worried that she would hate the prince and be forced into a loveless relationship, but to my surprise, she'd fallen hopelessly in love with him the moment he'd woken in her tower, and nothing in the world could dissuade her from marrying him now.

I wasn't sure I'd ever felt so happy for her. She was finally free from the tower, here in this beautiful place, marrying someone she loved and starting a new life.

At the edge of the crowd, I spotted her, and left my friends to walk to her. She smiled as I approached, and I had to blink to make sure it was indeed Rapunzel. She wore a silky golden gown trimmed in pearls around the neckline. The full skirt fanned out around her and swished as she walked. Her hair fell loosely to her shoulders. No longer impossibly tangled and weighing her down, light, wispy strands fell around her face. She was still thin, but her face had filled out a bit, and her rosy cheeks looked nothing like the gaunt skeleton I was so used to seeing.

"Gothel!" Her face lit up as I approached. She hugged me so tightly, I had trouble breathing.

"Rapunzel," I said as she pulled away. "You look like a

different person. You seem so happy."

She squeezed my hand. "That's because I am. I've never felt happier. To be honest, the past five years spent in the tower seem like a dark blur. I hardly remember any of it."

"That's wonderful."

"Yes, I know. But what about you? What will you do now that you're not guarding me?"

"I don't know yet." I didn't want to let my disappointment show. I certainly didn't have the possibility of a future like hers, where I would attend balls, eat feasts every day, and dress in fine clothes. "I might go back to the village and set up a shop. I could sell herbs, tinctures, and such. It would be a quiet life, which would suit me well after all the commotion I've been through. I'll have Jester with me for company, after all. He's been staying here in the castle temporarily, but he hates being confined. I have to admit—I do as well. Life in the village will work out well, I think."

"Yes, that sounds lovely. I will visit as often as I can."

I smiled. "I would like that." Though in truth, I couldn't imagine she'd have much time to travel to a remote village to chat with a lowly cat lady.

Prince Merek walked toward us, and Rapunzel smiled so brightly, her face transformed. No, this was no longer the sickly, half-sane girl I'd known in the tower. She'd broken free from her cocoon and transformed. She was a princess walking on clouds, and a tiny pang of jealousy pricked me.

He took her hand and kissed it, and I had to admit, with his sandy, wind-swept hair, mesmerizing blue eyes, and finely woven clothing, he was every bit of the prince

I'd read about in fairy tales. Rapunzel was getting her happy ending—and I was returning to the village to live alone once again.

Unless…

Was it wishful thinking for me to hope I might have a different future? One where Raj was a part of it? Since we'd defeated Varlocke, he hadn't said anything about a possible future between us. Granted, he'd been Prince Merek's most trusted confidant, and they'd been busy redrawing borders and making negotiations with outlying kingdoms. We'd barely seen one another, and the idea had struck me that perhaps I had no place in his life now. But now wasn't the time to feel sorry for myself, or to pine over what might have been.

Trumpets blared, announcing the arrival of King Duc'Line and the queen as they walked onto the dais. The room quieted.

"This is a new day," the king said. "No longer will our lands be massacred by a tyrant, for today, we celebrate the union between my son and the heir to High Sorcerer Varlocke's throne, Rapunzel!"

Cheers erupted as Rapunzel and Prince Merek climbed the dais to stand beside the king and queen. The king continued his speech, and my mind wandered. Something about being reunited and destroying evil for the good of all the land. I did pay attention when he described the defeat of the high sorcerer, which relied much more heavily on his son's sword and his unshakable bravery. My name was mentioned in passing, which I supposed I couldn't expect much more than that, as I was the illegitimate daughter of the high sorcerer—a witch who had been a servant to Varlocke.

By the time the ceremony and feasting came to an end, I was thoroughly exhausted, and after a brief goodbye to Rapunzel—which I had to fight through the crowds to give—I headed by myself out of the castle and to a quiet hill overlooking a valley, away from the throngs of people.

I stood under a tree as I looked out over the steep gorge, watching the sun as it made its final descent into night, streaking the sky in shades of purple and lavender. A sense of calmness came over me, and I felt pleased with the way things had turned out. I'd saved Rapunzel from the tower, and there wasn't much more I could ask for than that.

Well, maybe one thing.

Behind me, I heard voices, and turned around to spot the wolf, Odette, and Raj trudging up the hill toward me.

"Here you are," Odette said. "We wondered where you'd gone."

"I suppose I'm not one for parties."

"We thought you'd escaped back to the tower," Raj said.

I laughed. "You couldn't pay me enough to go back there."

"Then where will you go?" Raj asked.

"Back to the village. I'm hoping to support myself selling herbs and tinctures. It's the best plan I've got."

"Sounds boring," Raj said.

"Boring isn't always so bad, not after the quest we've been on."

"True. But it wasn't always bad. We did have some nice moments, didn't we?"

Heat rose to my cheeks, and his words brought back memories I'd rather not think about now.

Odette cleared her throat. "I'm going back to the Ice Mountains," she said. "Unfortunately, I've got a certain drunken yet strangely charming elf to save."

"Would you like me to come with you?" I asked. "I'm no match for my aunts, but I may be able to persuade them to help you go free."

"No, that won't be possible. If you got involved, not even your mother would save you. My people attacked them a long time ago. They've never been able to forgive them, so they keep me as prisoner. As long as they have me, they have their revenge. This is a quest I'll make alone."

The wolf barked, and Odette scratched his head. He wagged his tail, its thumping sounding loud on the grass. "Before I go, I need to tell you something." She knelt beside him and whispered something in his ear. His tail stopped moving, and he held still. "Now," she said, standing straight. "I wish you all farewell. Gothel, Raj, wolf, if our paths cross again, I'll be sure not to slaughter you."

She gave us a sly grin, then she walked to the edge of the cliff. Her body glimmered, and she took a diving leap. Wings spread out from her back as she transformed. The last rays of the sun caught her scales, and they sparkled in a prismatic glow. I watched, transfixed, until her body grew smaller and smaller, and I could no longer spot her against the quickly darkening sky.

Raj placed his hand on the small of my back, and I turned to face him.

"Gothel, I've been meaning to speak to you."

"About what?"

"I'm going back to the Outerlands. I have to go home and rebuild my people's empire. Now that you defeated the high sorcerer, I think it's time."

"Doesn't Prince Merek need you?"

"Not so much anymore. I've done all I can to bring peace between what remains of the high sorcerer's armies and our own. Besides, it was Prince Merek's idea for me to return home."

"I see." I bit my lip, hoping the disappointment didn't show in my eyes. "I guess this is goodbye, then."

"It doesn't have to be." He took my hands in his. "I want you to come with me."

"Me?" His confession caught me off guard.

"I don't think I could leave you even if the king ordered it. I know you wanted to sell potions in the village, but if you'd rather—"

"No," I interrupted him.

"No?" He raised an eyebrow, confusion showing on his face.

"I mean no, I don't want to sell potions. I don't want to be anywhere but with you... as long as you'll let my cat come along."

He smiled, pulling me closer to him. "You mean that?"

"About the cat? Absolutely."

"You know what I meant."

I couldn't hide my smile.

"You really want to come with me to the Outerlands?" he asked.

"Yes. There's no place I'd rather be."

"Then I'll have to warn you before you decide for sure. This won't be an easy task. I have plans to rebuild the city of Al-Maar to its former glory, or perhaps even better. It won't be easy work, but it will be worth it to see my city as it should be—and see my people restored again."

"I would love to. I can't imagine a better life."

"You would?"

"Yes. You shouldn't be so surprised."

"Maybe not." He smiled, and I was glad he was holding my hands, because my knees felt as if they wouldn't hold me up. "I don't think I've ever felt so happy."

"Me either."

He leaned in to give me a kiss, but the sound of someone clearing his throat stopped us. I turned to find the dwarf standing behind us, his one eye glowing with glee.

"Dwarf, you chose now to interrupt us?" I asked, my voice heated.

"Ha! I knew you two would get together. Didn't I know it? It was only a matter of time. But that's not the reason I transformed. Ha! I've got some wonderful news to share that I can't keep inside any longer. Would you like to guess what it is?"

"No, I really wouldn't," Raj said dryly.

"Then I shall tell you anyway. It was what the dragon lady said to me, and you'll never believe it. You'll never guess. Ha!"

"If you keep saying *ha*, I'll transform you to a mute dung beetle," I said.

"Then let me say this instead. She gave me my name!"

"Your name?" Raj asked.

"Yes, yes! Isn't this wonderful? I remember it now, and you'll never believe what it is. Are you ready?"

"Fine, tell me and get it over with. If you don't mind, Raj and I were in the middle of something."

"Well, I can hardly understand why you're so determined to shut me up, so I'll let you know this and be on my way. My name… It's Rumpelstiltskin!"

"Rumple what?" Raj asked.

"Rumpelstiltskin, you imbecile. And now that I know it, I no longer need your assistance, my lady, for I have also remembered the witch who gave me this curse, and she's as good as dead." His eyes glowed with an evil look. "But first, she owes me. She owes me a lot. Now, that is all. I shall be off. Good night to you both. Ha!"

He skipped down the path as best as he could with one leg, laughing as he went.

"That was strange," I said.

"I agree," Raj answered. "What an unusual name. No wonder he couldn't remember it."

Raj turned to me, his eyes, dark and dangerous, stirring strong emotions within me. "Now, where did we leave off?"

"Here," I said, kissing him gently. "We left off right here."

"Yes, I'm starting to remember." He pulled me to him in a tight embrace, our bodies pressed together, and I had to remind myself to breathe. "I'll never let you go."

"I never want you to."

As the sun set, he kissed me. For the first time in my life, I realized I'd found the one thing I'd always been searching for, but I didn't realize I'd been looking for it until this very moment. I'd found someone to spend the rest of my life with.

I'd found true, unconditional love. I'd escaped the tower, and I'd found my home.

Acknowledgements

I WANT TO THANK EVERYONE who supported me while I wrote this book. First, a tremendous thank-you goes to my publisher, Clean Teen, and to the amazing women behind it: Courtney Knight, Rebecca Gober, Marya Heidel, and Melanie Newton. They really are a tremendous team, and I couldn't be more thankful to have them by my side.

To my editor Kelly Risser, a fabulous author and editor who helped make The Witch's Tower shine. Also, thanks goes to my tremendous team of proof readers.

To all my beta readers: you're the best. I don't think any author has had a more supportive group. Jenny Bynum, Donamarie Goldsmith, Leah Alvord, Jennifer Lapachian, Wesley Plummer, Julia Mozingo, and Melissa Lopez.

My street team, the best street team ever. I couldn't do any of this without them. I love being able to share all the info with them first. Thanks goes to Nikki Jeffery for "Twisted Ever After."

Lastly, this goes to my husband, David, whose name really should be included on the cover of all my books, since he's my sounding board for all my ideas, and my trusty "Alpha-reader." (His self-proclaimed title.) I also want to thank my five kids: Phoenix, Sequoia, Bridger,

Gabriel, and Ronan, who have to share their time with Mom so she can write. It's not always easy being an author's kid, but hopefully they're learning some valuable lessons in there somewhere.

As always, I would be ungrateful if I didn't acknowledge my Heavenly Father, who's presence is by my side when I need Him most.

About The Author

TAMARA GRANTHAM IS THE AWARD-WINNING author of more than a dozen books and novellas, including the Olive Kennedy: Fairy World MD series and the Shine novellas. Dreamthief, the first book of her Fairy World MD series, won first place for fantasy in Indiefab's Book of the Year Awards, a Rone award for best New Adult Romance of 2016, and is a #1 bestseller on Amazon with over 200 five-star reviews. She has recently signed with Clean Teen Publishing for a fairytale retelling trilogy.

Tamara holds a bachelor's degree in English. She has been a featured speaker at numerous writing conferences and a panelist at Comic Con Wizard World speaking on the topic of female leads. For her first published project, she collaborated with New York-Times bestselling author, William Bernhardt, in writing the Shine series.

Born and raised in Texas, Tamara now lives with her husband and five children in Wichita, Kansas. She rarely has any free time, but when the stars align, and she gets a moment to relax, she enjoys reading, taking nature walks, and watching every Star Wars or Star Trek movie ever made.

CPSIA information can be obtained
at www.ICGtesting.com
Printed in the USA
LVHW012309080219
606968LV00004B/5/P

9 781634 223348